BLOOD SECRETS

THE VEIN OF TRUTH HAS NEVER BEEN MORE DEADLY

J. LEIGH JACKSON

For The Goring.
Thank you for the
exceptional hospitality.
All my best,
Leigh Jack—
July 10, 2022

Blood Secrets

This book is a work of fiction. Names, characters, places, businesses, and incidents either are the products of the author's imagination or are used in a fictitious manner. Any similarity to events or locales or persons, living or dead, is entirely coincidental.

Published by *thewordverve inc.* (www.thewordverve.com)

First Edition 2021
eBook ISBN: 978-1-956856-00-2
Paperback ISBN: 978-1-956856-01-9
Library of Congress Control No.: 2021920291

Cover design by Robin Krauss
www.bookformatters.com

~ For Erick, Claire, and Grant ~

Tess cursed under her breath while grabbing for a dish towel. Rushing against the clock, she'd spilled coffee on the white marble counter.

"I'll leave in fifteen minutes," she promised herself while blotting the expanding pool of dark liquid. With New York City traffic, she only had a small window before the streets filled with bumper-to-bumper cars.

Persistently, her stomach growled. "Food, need food first."

She put a slice of bread into the toaster and then swung open the fridge door—only to find herself face-to-face with a stash of craft beers belonging to her newly *ex*-boyfriend Todd Burkhardt. The sight momentarily stopped her in her tracks.

"Terrific." Miffed, she pushed the clanking bottles aside. They'd planned to taste test the batch as a mix of fun and research for his downtown bar, Whiskey Tales. She shook her head, mumbling, "not anymore," grabbed the butter, and shut the fridge with a swift kick of her hip.

Alternating between sips of coffee and bites of toast with one hand, she focused on her laptop screen, reviewing her updated curriculum vitae as in-house performance counselor for Ludwell Corporation.

Dr. Tess Andreas (PhD in clinical psychology from Harvard) is the sole business performance counselor for Ludwell Corporation. Her responsibilities include organizational talent management, culture building, and employee performance management at an international level. Over the past five years, Dr. Andreas masterfully crafted a bespoke evaluation process for employees— building a scoring system that pinpoints personality traits deemed vital or toxic for particular positions and opportunities.

"Sounds so grand." She rolled her eyes at the formality of it all. Only she knew this scoring system had come about more as a symptom of her propensity to view the world in terms of black and white, right and wrong. Great for business but not so great for her personal life—an Achilles' heel she was well aware of, especially when she thought someone had committed a grievous wrong.

"Someone like Todd," she mumbled, gritting her teeth. "I just have to think about his actions as I would for an employee evaluation. Be objective." She clicked her tongue a few times.

"I know people. I understand the inner workings of the human mind. I know what can and cannot be changed about an individual." She took a deep breath before continuing her pep talk. "My decisions aren't callous. No. When I advise someone to be let go. Well, it's simply the square peg not fitting the round hole."

Her chest ached a little. Was this how she felt about Todd? She straightened her shoulders, held her head high, and then slumped, knowing that personal decisions were never that cut-and-dried.

Sipping her coffee, she eyed the bent envelope resting haphazardly on the kitchen counter, the same envelope that had been slid anonymously under her office door over a month ago. She'd just about slipped on the blasted thing, which seemed almost comical now.

"Don't," she warned herself.

She didn't listen. An icy prickle crawled over her skin as she jiggled the contents onto the counter and stared at the two photographs for the umpteenth time—Todd and some mystery woman kissing in a hotel lobby. Even through the graininess of the images, she could make out Todd's tall, lean physique and his unmistakable wavy, dark-blond hair.

She cringed, replaying what he'd said when she confronted him: "I can explain."

"Hmph," she fumed.

Tapping her fingers on the top photo, a thought hit her. "Of course! I'll call Roger." She picked up her cell and dialed. Roger Palmer, Ludwell Corporation's off-site computer wiz, had been a loyal colleague and friend for years.

He answered with, "Good morning, sunshine." As usual, his words bounced along the measure of a cheery tone.

"Hey. I need to show you something. In person. And today, if you don't mind." The shakiness in her voice betrayed her.

"Sure. Just name the time and the place."

Her mind filled with images of him in his apartment surrounded by a bunch of big screens, curtains drawn, the usual wireless headpiece buried in the thick curls of his dark hair. He'd be wearing a wrinkled Hawaiian shirt, too short so that he'd constantly have to stuff it back into the waistband of his cargo shorts. She fought off the urge to snicker.

"Let's meet at the MET in the Greek art hall in, uh ... twenty minutes." She grimaced at the time, but what did it matter, really? She was already late for the office.

"I'm there." He spoke over background sounds of what Tess assumed to be empty potato chip bags and soda cans being shuffled around. "Let me just ... Ah-ha, here are my keys."

"Oh, and Roger ...?" She paused. "This one's personal."

"No problem. My lips are sealed. Whatever you need. I'm up for the challenge."

She laughed despite her sour mood about all things Todd. "You sound like a local superhero with that response."

"I can live with that."

As soon as they hung up, she texted her driver that she'd be down in five, then took her coffee mug over to the window, where she took in the city view. Tried to regain her emotional equilibrium.

"Enough of this," she said, and gathered her things before heading toward the elevator door in her apartment. Down she went.

"Morning, Dr. Andreas." The fifty-something, short, balding doorman, Miles Green, greeted her with beaming blue eyes as she approached the lobby door. Hearing his crisp British accent in the Upper East Side of Manhattan always made her happy, even today.

"Morning, Miles." She mustered an upbeat intonation that evolved into a subtle bounce in her step. Her shoulder-length, dark-blond hair swayed to the clicking of her heels on the marble floor as she walked, and she almost believed that she'd escaped her anxious mood.

As Miles held the door, she said, "Hey, thanks again for last week. You know—" she waved her hand around "—for being cool about everything."

Miles bobbed his head. "Of course."

He'd outdone himself in regard to discretion when Todd had officially moved out—at her insistence. As far as she could see, no one in the building had even caught wind of the split. Appreciative of the privacy, she had gifted Miles the latest wireless earbuds only yesterday. Regularly, he wore one discreetly in his left ear, the cords meticulously tucked into his jacket. Today, she saw no cords, which brought a smile to her lips as she left the building.

~ 2 ~

WEDNESDAY, SEPTEMBER 5

Roger hacked into the hotel security feed, the one from Tess's photos. "Step one. Easy-peasy," he gloated.

Unfortunately, step two, finding the source of the photos, still stumped him. The security cameras in the building where Tess worked had been undergoing an upgrade at the time, which meant no footage existed to show the photo drop. He'd focus on that later.

"There's more than one way to skin this cat." He swigged his soda. Thumped the keys. Fast-forwarded, zoomed in, reversed footage, taking it all in, logging important areas. He checked the clock: 7:30 p.m. *Not too late*. He telephoned Tess.

She answered with a question straight out of the gate: "Whatcha got?"

"Well, I've got, uh ... *something*. That's for sure." He tried to put some of his usual cheeriness into the statement, but he knew it had fallen flat.

More guarded now, Tess said, "Okayyy. Should we meet?"

"Yes, definitely. Somewhere private."

"Come to my apartment, now if you can."

"On my way."

Roger disconnected, grabbed his coat, and packed up his laptop.

Torn between wanting to show Tess what he'd discovered and not
wanting her to know at all, dread filled his every step.

"She's not gonna like this. At all."

The doorman buzzed Tess's penthouse. "You have a visitor, a Mr.
Palmer."

"Yes. I'm expecting him. Send him up, please. Thanks, Miles."
Clasping her hands, she waited by the elevator door that opened
directly into her foyer until a Hawaiian shirt-clad Roger, wearing a
backpack and earbuds, appeared. He fumbled to remove the bobbles
from his ears, dropping them quickly into his shirt pocket.

"Come in." She led the way to the dining table. "Can I get you a
drink?"

"No thanks." He gripped the straps of his backpack tightly.

"Should I have one?" She raised her eyebrows.

He looked down shifting his feet. "Maybe."

"Well then, I prefer not to drink alone, so would you indulge me?"
She took the liberty of pouring two small scotches.

He obliged.

They sat, and Tess took a sip, the amber liquid warming her lips as
he opened his laptop.

"There's no sound, but the footage is pretty clear." He shimmied the
screen so she could see.

Clutching her glass with both hands, she leaned in and focused as
the mystery woman from the photographs appeared on the screen.
"She arrived at the hotel in a private car with a driver?" The words
unintentionally formed a question.

Roger said, "Yep. Looks like it. I tried to read the license plate, but
there's some sort of shielding, so I couldn't make out anything."

Unblinking, she continued to watch. Tall with broad shoulders
dusted by long, sandy-blond hair, the mystery woman exuded an
overall disheveled look. The two continued to observe as the woman
took what appeared to be a photograph out of her purse and

examined it carefully. Just before entering the hotel, she tucked it away.

"I tried to zoom in on the photo, but the graininess won out," he explained while flipping camera angles like a pro. Then, the footage played again as the woman scanned the hotel's bar, obviously searching for someone.

"Is that ...?" Tess's words trailed off into silence.

"Just watch."

The woman then fixated on a male figure sitting at the bar. She tugged at her too-tight dress, fluffed her hair, and slicked on some lip gloss.

"Yes. That's Todd. Sitting duck," Tess muttered as she pointed at the screen.

The woman said something to Todd, to which he casually nodded.

Tess bit her lip.

Roger fast-forwarded as the woman slipped onto a stool near Todd. She ordered a drink and chatted with the bartender for a minute or so. Todd focused on the papers in front of him, seemingly disinterested at the adjacent chatter. When the bartender stepped away, the woman hunched over her drink. Her shoulders began to shake.

"Is she crying?" Tess asked in astonishment.

Roger shrugged but said, "I think so."

Todd glanced the woman's way a couple of times, then gently handed her a napkin. Roger fast-forwarded again.

Apparently seeing an opening, the woman fumbled off the barstool, stumbled slightly, and moved closer. Todd jumped up to stabilize her.

"She's good," Tess narrowed her eyes.

Roger didn't respond.

Todd and the woman made their way to the elevators, and that's when it happened. The woman kissed Todd.

"Okay. Not great, but not really his fault," Tess said, more for her benefit than Roger's. "Maybe he wasn't lying after all." Her voice barely reached that of a whisper.

Roger said nothing.

The kiss lasted a little too long.

On the screen, the elevator opened. Tess's heart raced as she waited for his reaction.

Todd pulled away.

"Oh, thank God." Tess took a sip of her scotch and focused once again on the screen.

Not giving up so easily it seemed, the woman grabbed his hand, tempting him to follow her. He moved a small step closer.

Tess put her hand to her pounding heart and leaned in closer to the screen.

"You know … I didn't see her check in, so why would she have a room?" The words flew from her mouth before she could shut them down.

Roger cut a side-glance toward her. "I thought maybe she could have checked in earlier. But I went through the footage. She didn't."

Tess held her breath, waiting.

Finally, the moment of truth came. Todd clearly rejected the woman's overture—shaking his head, his hands up in a defensive posture.

But it had taken a few minutes for him to get there.

Downing the rest of the scotch, Tess's shoulders relaxed. He'd rejected the woman.

On the video, Todd padded back to the bar, head hanging. The mystery woman stood abandoned in front of the closing elevator, staring after him in a manner resembling disbelief.

Then the woman turned slightly so her hands were not visible, but she was doing something …

"What's she doing?" Tess squinted at the screen.

"Texting, I think."

Then the woman stormed out of the hotel.

Roger switched camera views.

"Look, isn't that the same car that dropped her off?" Tess pointed at the image as the woman disappeared into the back seat.

"Still can't get a clear image of the plate. See?" Roger took a screenshot, zoomed in. Nada.

"So he's an idiot, but not a liar." Tess made a *tsk*ing sound. "This reeks of some sort of setup. It's undeniable, really." She slumped a little in her chair.

Roger shifted awkwardly in his. "I'm sorry. That's what I think too."

Blinking, she battled the sting in her eyes.

"Hey, I'll do whatever you need. Just say the word," Roger said.

"I know. And thank you. You are a true friend." She patted his arm. "I'm sorry I dragged you into this. But I could use your help figuring out the *why*." She stared across the room. "And the *who*. It just doesn't make sense. What could be the reason for someone to set up Todd?"

~ 3 ~

An hour later, Todd stood stiffly in the doorway of the elevator to Tess's apartment looking uncomfortable.

Scrutinizing him up and down, her lips twisted in anger until she blurted, "Speak of the devil."

"Okayyy. Nice to see you too." He winced before continuing. "I just came by to pick up the beers from the fridge." He pointed in the direction of the kitchen.

"Well, I have some news." Tess stomped behind him to the fridge, where she wasted no time in sharing Roger's findings.

Todd just shook his head as he leaned on the edge of the counter. "I'm not sure which is more disturbing: what happened with that floosy or the fact that you spied on me." His eyes blinked owlishly. "Look, Tess, this doesn't have to be a big deal between us. We can navigate this storm together. Just give me a little credit—you know I'm not a bad guy."

"Maybe not, but you should have told me *before* I got those photographs. End of story." Her words were stern; her body language imitating that tone, arms crossed, chin raised.

"But nothing happened. There was nothing to tell. I don't even think I remembered it by the time I got home. Please ..." He reached out for her hand, but she stepped back out of his reach.

"Todd. You're missing the point ... again. You should have told me because we could have gotten ahead of this. It's obviously a setup."

"I'm not a fortune teller. I. DID. NOT. KNOW that at the time. Why can't you seem to understand that?" He tilted his head and in a softer tone said, "Come on."

"It's not that easy. I am not okay with you withholding information like that—something that could affect our lives. How could you not think that was totally weird?"

"And I'm not okay with you thinking I would lie to you." His cheeks flushed.

"Yet, I'm not unfounded, am I?" She quirked her eyebrows.

He knew exactly what she was referencing. The *other* other woman. He shook his head and let out a slow breath. "That was before we were officially a couple. And you were still semi-involved too."

He was referring to Tess's on-again, off-again relationship with Vail Stuart.

"Yes, but I told you all about my situation. And you ..." She paused and almost whispered, "... didn't." Innuendo shrouded her voice.

"You know it wasn't that simple. You're rewriting history now, Tess. The truth is our relationship started with baggage, mostly yours. And you know it."

Her eyes flashed in anger.

His head dropped, and his voice softened. "And, yes, I didn't commit to you right away, but at no point have I lied to you ... since her." He raised his head to slowly meet her gaze.

She leered at him with folded arms. "No, withholding is more your style."

"You're seeing this all wrong." He shoved his hands through his hair, obviously frustrated, ultimately claiming that his omission then and now had been to protect her from herself.

"From what, Todd? From reality?"

"From this. From your all-or-nothing, do-or-die way of seeing everything. Life has nuances." He accentuated his rising voice with a *voila* motion of his hands.

"You know what? I happen to know very well why people hide things behind nuances—handy little smoke screens to keep from dealing with the truth. I'm going to take a bet that your nuances numbed your guilt."

"Guilt? For not doing anything? You should check that psycho mumbo-jumbo degree of yours."

"Real mature. Guilt because maybe you wanted to follow that woman, huh? Or maybe because you almost did."

"How convenient. Punish me for something I *could have* done but *didn't*."

"This time," she muttered.

"Come to think of it, maybe I should be asking you where your guilt is for spying on me. Hmm?"

Tess stared coldly, allowing an awkward silence to build before she spoke. "It wasn't technically spying. You know that."

"And it wasn't technically lying. You know that."

She bit her cheeks, staying silent and thinking it didn't really matter at this point.

Frustrated, his knuckles whitened as his palms pressed the countertop. "We have a much bigger problem, don't you think? Let's focus on that for a minute!" Shouting now, he seemed to have lost control of his emotions completely.

Tess on the other hand remained outwardly cool, calm, even though her heartbeat thumped in her ears.

He turned away, breathed. "I'm going to work. It's almost nine. Let's cool down. We can talk tomorrow."

"Or not." Her eyes lit with a challenge to continue the row.

He shook his head, regret showing on his chiseled features. "This does not have to be a big deal."

However, Tess saw it as a big deal—a deal *breaker*, in fact. Her sad eyes met his. He smiled sheepishly, hopefully, but she said, "You should have told me. I can't trust you." Her eyes stung.

His smile faded into a look of pain as he scoffed, "Obviously."

Arms still crossed, she turned in a slow circle and tried to stop herself from grinding her teeth.

When she turned back to face him, he said, "Actually, yes you can. You can trust me. And you know it. This has gone too far. And maybe, just maybe I'm one of the only people you can trust right now. What if this is a setup, and it's not about me, but *you*? We need to push through this together, not apart."

Her jaw remained clenched as she pivoted and marched toward the foyer. "You can see yourself out." She struggled into her coat, flung her purse over her shoulder, and pressed the elevator button. She had no real destination in mind, just away from this, from him.

"Where are you going at this hour?" Todd yelled after her, but she didn't respond.

She smirked when she heard him say, "Dammit."

"Morning, Dr. Andreas. It's a bit chilly today."

"Morning, Miles. I'm planning to grab a latte on my way to work. How about one for you? What's your poison today?"

"Thank you, but that's not necessary, ma'am."

"I insist." She fought back a yawn. More caffeine couldn't come fast enough for her this morning after the sleepless night she'd had thinking about the argument with Todd. She'd been rude out of anger, and that didn't sit well with her conscience. The truth seemed easier to face in the light of day—he really didn't deserve to be treated so harshly. She knew that deep inside she must have been searching for an escape from the already dying relationship, and she felt bad about how it had rolled out.

Truth be told, things had been strained for a while. He'd been spending more nights at his old apartment near the bar since his temporary tenant had moved out. Of course, Todd claimed that he didn't want to disturb her at all hours of the night when she had to be up for work. However, that had never been the case before, at least not when things were good in the beginning of their year and half together.

Her heart ached, knowing that he'd moved out mentally a while ago. At least it felt that way.

With the sounds of chatter in the lobby, her attention snapped back to the present, and she turned to Miles. "I'll just guess, then." Her voice rang out in a singsong manner, "I'm ordering now," and she gave him a sly grin as she waved her phone.

He chuckled and said, "You win. I'm a sucker for a cappuccino. Thank you."

Happy she'd won him over, she texted both orders to the coffee shop ahead of her arrival with instructions for delivery on the cappuccino. Then she adjusted the collar on her jacket and exited the warm lobby into the breezy street.

"Good day, Dr. Andreas," said Clint, her driver, as he held the car door for her, bracing it open against the breezy air.

"I sure hope so." She winked.

Wearing a smile, he closed the door behind her.

"Clint, could you stop at Morning Brew? Can I pick up something for you too?"

"No thanks, ma'am. My wife sends me with a whole thermos every morning. I'm set for a couple hours. But I'm happy to make the stop for you."

And he did.

Shaking off a shiver, she settled in the backseat with her own brew in hand and began catching up on emails. She rolled her eyes when she read yet another request from her colleague, Dr. Lawrence Glasgow, to participate in a genealogy study for Ludwell's subsidiary, Lineage.

"The answer is no. For the third time," she said to the email. Then she typed—with one hand—a more polite response than the one she'd uttered because she liked Lawrence, but one that delivered the same clear meaning, nonetheless.

B eing the first to the office, Vail Stuart hung his coat in the closet near his assistant's desk and walked straight into the conference room. He skipped the light switch and instead flipped on the screen to play the op-ed video piece that his law firm needed to review for Ludwell Corporation.

What he considered bad elevator music underscored the dull voice-over:

"The American dream for the Ludwell family began many generations ago with the family's arrival in Manhattan about a decade after the sinking of the Titanic.*"*

Vail fast-forwarded through most of the historical bits, stopping again briefly to listen.

"The family's bread and butter, Ludwell Corporation, ranks among the most prominent global enterprises, earning its stripes the old-fashioned way. The company survived both the stock market crash and WWII—no small feat in and of itself."

"Yada, yada, yada." He skipped ahead again.

"Ludwell's subsidiaries span the gamut from financial institutions to industrial farming, to family businesses including wineries, bakeries, and the like, but at the top of the family empire, one company stands out—Lineage.

"Lineage has become the most formidable DNA test-kit company ever mass-marketed to the public."

He paused the video and mumbled, "Here it is."

Scribbling a couple of notes, he thought about Lineage's public image. He knew the test kits had caught on like wildfire from day one, selling to millions and logging as many DNA profiles in just under a decade. From all outward appearances, Lineage seemed fun, useful, and domestic—a way to research family history, find biological parents, discover siblings, trace the origins of great-great-grandparents, and maybe even recover lost inheritance.

However, he remained keenly aware that the real driver behind this subsidiary lay in its other financial potential beyond that of just selling kits.

Behind the scenes, Lineage drove something much deeper, side studies that made a whole lot more money than the kits—and something about that didn't sit right in his gut, especially since one person in particular seemed to have full control over said studies and the related finances: Mr. Norman Montague, Ludwell Corporation's second-in-command.

"That's never good for anything, except corruption." His mouth went a little dry. "We need to get ahead of this." He made a note to touch on the idea that the research served humanitarian medical purposes or anything other than greed. Something positive, a well-dressed distraction, to feed to the media sources when (not if) they came knocking with questions.

Next, he penned a big question mark next to the words *privacy disclosures.*

Vail groaned, knowing that if the kits didn't have the right legal language to cover these offshoot studies, there'd be a lot of backtracking to do there as well.

"Rookie mistake," he grumbled. *Only I'm no rookie. But maybe I am too nice.* He cringed as he thought about a personal misstep he may have made.

He genuinely believed Dr. Lawrence Glasgow to be a stand-up guy, so when the man had asked, he'd quickly said yes and donated his own blood sample for a genealogy side study—the one Tess refused to participate in, which in retrospect probably would have been a smarter career move for him too.

His head fell back against the chair. *Would have, could have, should have.*

~ 6 ~

WEDNESDAY, SEPTEMBER 12

U nder the fluorescents in his Lineage office, Dr. Lawrence Glasgow, a Stanford biosciences graduate in his early thirties, wrung his hands in dread of his eleven o'clock appointment with Mr. Norman Montague, not the easiest of personalities to manage. The man wanted updates on the "genealogy study."

Lawrence groaned. He hated meeting with Montague, and he hated that title.

"Boring and misleading." He meant both.

The study at least deserved a better masthead. And if he could ever get past the latest roadblock, maybe he'd get to rename it. But right now, he had bigger problems.

"I shouldn't have said her name. Mistake one." Lawrence huffed. "And mistake two—saying her blood was the Holy Grail to viral resistance." He put a hand to his forehead in regret. "I don't even know that for sure yet." He had not made that last part clear to Mr. Montague on purpose, and now it was biting him in the *hindsight*.

He leaned back in his chair, squeezing his eyelids tight. He needed to slow things down, backtrack a bit with Mr. Montague.

The whole debacle had started a few months prior when he'd been running tests using data from a cache of deceased subjects. Nothing morbid—the figurative graveyard just served as a safe place to dig for his side studies. For legal reasons.

He'd happened upon an anomaly of sorts in one particular specimen. No red flag there—he often found variations, mundane stuff. Except for that day, the finding didn't seem ordinary at all. More like *groundbreaking*.

Problem was, he needed more data, preferably from someone in the realm of the living. Definitely from someone related to the person with the anomaly, specifically that person's child.

So he took a risk. He broke protocol and searched the internet thinking he could find relatives of the deceased who just maybe were already in the Lineage database, a dream scenario—almost—minus the little issue of privacy laws.

Ask for forgiveness not permission, right?

That was all water under the bridge now. As soon as the search results had flickered on the screen, a real complication arose. As it turned out, the specimen in question just happened to be from an employee's parent.

Specifically, Dr. Tess Andreas's deceased father.

Not ready to violate HIPAA regulations or go to jail, he'd come up with an idea.

A bad one in retrospect.

First, he'd asked Tess to participate, in an offhand, can-you-help-a-colleague-out way. Then, to camouflage his true intentions, he'd asked a few other employees in front of her.

Once he'd hooked several willing volunteers, including Tess's former fiancé, who was also the company lawyer—Vail Stuart—he'd jumped the gun and told Montague about his theory.

Montague hadn't seemed particularly interested, which was his norm when it came to anything Lawrence worked on.

At first.

Why didn't I leave it alone?

But he hadn't. In fact, he'd inflated the findings—a lot.

It worked too well. He'd gotten Montague all fired up about viral resistance, and the old man acted like he planned on ruling the world.

Then the very worst happened. Tess refused to participate.

Lawrence had dangerously overestimated his ability to sway Tess.

Initially, Montague said he'd handle it, get her to submit a blood sample. As far as Lawrence could see, the old man had been equally unsuccessful.

If only I'd gotten her blood before I opened my big trap to Montague.

His regret did nothing to change the facts.

With her blood, he could dig deeper, analyze her DNA, RNA, take a look at enzymes, antigens … basically piece apart the whole gamut of genetic components, everything related to viral resistance. Finally, he'd have the chance to build on what he'd glimpsed in her father's sample.

If she'd inherited the variant.

Lawrence would put money on that being the case. "I just know the secret is in her blood," he whispered.

His breath caught in his throat at the impact a discovery like this could have on the human race, not to mention the possibilities career-wise for him.

I would be in the history books. Forget that … I'd be making history and the future. His ego pulsed.

I. NEED. HER. BLOOD.

His chest deflated with a release of breath as he replayed all the times he'd asked her and how awkward it had become.

I can't ask again. Not after the last response. At least not for a while.

He rapped his pencil relentlessly against the edge of the desk, thinking that there had to be another way, a workaround.

Maybe tell her the truth? He shook his head. No. Montague would not allow that. Side studies were always top secret. He rolled his eyes, but his paycheck depended on his discretion.

He bounced the pencil some more.

Thinking.

"I've got it!" He shifted in his chair, causing a loud creak. He jotted down a new hypothesis. He would show Montague that the anomaly could be more common than suspected. *Not impossible.* He wanted to believe it too.

His thoughts formed into sentences. *Viral resistance is variable, unique to the individual—there could be others. Besides, I know what to look for now. I just need access ... and time.*

He also needed to get around the legal boundaries that had him boxed in where the Lineage customer databank was concerned.

Then another *aha* moment struck. *What if this study fits one of the preconditioned parameters already listed on the Lineage DNA test kit itself?*

"Why reinvent the wheel?" One side of his mouth raised in a lopsided grin. "I hope this works."

Mostly, though, he hoped it was legal. Surely it was. Right?

"It's a genealogy study. Broad title, broad category." Montague's studies always were.

He typed in new search filters—region, eye color, hair color—all based on Tess's appearance and her father's information. "Keep it simple. Quantity is the goal. Increase the odds," he mumbled.

Barely breathing, he watched data fall like snowflakes on the screen.

This should help to satisfy Montague.

Lawrence felt a little better until he realized the amount of work it would take to test every sample. Because really, all he had were more oysters, no pearls. Yet.

Always something.

As usual with Montague's studies, he worked alone, but he knew that was going to have to change. He already felt like a drowning man with this study and two other studies—all with no help, no one to bounce around ideas with.

He thought about his old pal from grad school, the definition of a mad scientist. He needed some of that moxie now.

His fingers flew across the keyboard. *Tap, tap, tap ...*

Done.

Chuckling, he printed a new cover page with a catchy new title. Obviously not a solution, but the juvenile stunt sure made him feel better.

After stuffing the new title page into his backpack among the folders for his meeting, he headed for the lab—last stop before going to see Montague. He wanted to check a couple of things with Tess's father's sample.

The young lab tech, too bald for his age, sat hunched over a microscope, one foot rhythmically patting the floor. He didn't even seem to know that Lawrence had entered the room.

"Bret. Bret!"

Lawrence rolled his eyes. *Why the earbuds all the time?* It drove him crazy. He would think he was having a conversation with someone, but no ... they couldn't hear him because of earbuds.

He forcefully tapped Bret on the shoulder.

Cursing and rubbing his shoulder, the tech craned his neck to make eye contact. "What's so important, man?" he huffed as he removed his earbuds.

Bret only came into the lab three times a week to run DNA tests, grunt work. He knew the young man felt underutilized by the company. What self-respecting scientist wouldn't? *Not my problem.* "Where'd you put those samples I gave you yesterday?" Lawrence asked.

Bret stared at him blankly.

"You know. The *special* ones."

"Ah, right." Bret spun on his stool, launching himself toward the small storage freezer. He opened the drawer and waved his hand. "Here they are. Labeled and ready for the taking."

Lawrence peered into the drawer and grumbled a thank-you. He then removed the tray of vials and traipsed off to his workstation.

He could feel Bret's eyes on him.

"What are you working on with those?" the young lab tech asked.

"It's just a project for one of the higher-ups. Probably trying to find out if he can cut someone out of his will or something."

Bret scrunched his forehead. "Fine ... don't tell me, then."

Lawrence cleared his throat and leaned over the microscope, hoping to cut off any further discussion on the matter.

And it worked. Out of the corner of his eye, he saw Bret shrug and spin back to his own microscope, jamming those blasted earbuds back in.

~ 7 ~

On her way to her own office, Tess noticed Lawrence sitting outside of Norman Montague's all-glass corner office. The scientist's shoulders sagged, as did his face, making him look far older than his years. She wondered what was going on—and if it had to do with her latest refusal to participate in his study.

"Hi, Lawrence. How's life at the lab?" Tess's voice rang out pleasantly across the common area.

Immediately, he shifted to a more upright position in his chair. "All's good, thanks. How are you, Dr. Andreas?"

"I'm not bad. And call me Tess. We've been through this before." She cut her eyes at Lawrence like a teacher scolding a student, even though they both held PhDs. "Are you here by choice, or have you been summoned to the gallows?" She raised an eyebrow and tilted her head in the direction of Montague's office.

Lawrence paled. "Not sure yet."

"That bad, huh?" She took a seat.

"I don't know. Just a snafu with my study." He didn't make eye contact.

"The genealogy one?"

"That's the one." His attempt at putting some enthusiasm behind his words fell flat. His tone was just one notch higher than what she would describe as lifeless.

She truly respected the science as much as the man sitting next to her. Her refusal stemmed from Montague demanding that she do it, touting it as a job requirement, not from rejecting Lawrence or his work. In fact, she'd made that clear the day she laughed Montague out of the room in response to his demanding she hand over a blood sample "for company research purposes." His approach broke more laws than she could count.

She shook off the memory and said kindly, "It's really rather interesting, your study."

He looked down and shifted his feet.

Was he uncomfortable? Embarrassed? She felt obligated to say something else.

"You know, Lawrence, it has nothing to do with you. Why I didn't—"

He waved off her comment mid-sentence. "No. Of course. I get it. Lots of people don't want to participate in research. Really, it's not my style to pressure like that."

"I know where the pressure originated." She cut her eyes toward Montague's office.

"Dr. Glasgow." The receptionist's voice interrupted their conversation. Then she sneezed. A big whomping sneeze. And again ... *ah-ah-choo!* "Mr. Montague will see you now." The stricken woman wiped her nose with an already-damp wad of tissue as she approached.

Tess noticed Lawrence's neck stiffen as he leaned back. She hid her smirk behind a file folder. *No germs for Lawrence.*

"Sorry," Doris said, breathless.

Tess patted her arm. "I hope you feel better soon."

"Thanks. I'm hoping it's just allergies."

An awkward silence fell. From the looks of Doris, it wasn't allergies.

"Can I get you something? Do anything?" Tess offered.

"No, but thank you for offering. I just hope I don't get anyone else sick."

"Allergies aren't contagious." The sarcastic mumble came from Lawrence's lips, and Doris looked as if she'd cry.

Tess attempted to rescue the moment. "Don't worry about that. I, for one, never get sick. Family trait, my dad, my grandma ..." She noticed Lawrence shifting in his chair, another couple of inches farther away from Doris.

"Maybe take a day or two to rest. Chicken soup and all," Tess said.

Finally, a weathered smile flickered under Doris's dark circles just before she sulked away.

Lawrence still looked stunned, jaw agape now.

"Nice seeing you," Tess said.

"Um. Yeah. You too. Uh, so ... you don't ever get—"

The question died on his lips as the sound of knuckles on glass caught their attention, and they turned to see cranky Montague with his fist in the air. He frowned at them beneath his poorly groomed eyebrows. The old man's off-putting personality could enter a room even before the man himself.

Tess let out a huff. "Good luck in there," she said.

With the strangest expression on his face, he said, "Right. Uh, thanks."

"Come in. Have a seat." Montague motioned haphazardly to an empty chair.

Preoccupied with what Tess had said to Doris about not getting sick —ever—Lawrence sat awkwardly, struggling to contain his racing thoughts.

Montague cleared his throat.

Lawrence mumbled, "Oh, right." He plopped his bag on the floor, then leaned down and withdrew a folder, handing it to the old man.

"Operation Alien Blood? What is this? Did I miss something?" The old man pushed his glasses only to have them slide down again as he peered over the rims.

"Oh, that. My apologies. Just a nickname. For lab use only." A flush came over him. The blasted title page he'd printed earlier had stuck to the folder. "Just a leftover habit from grad school—we used to think of the most outlandish titles for studies—nothing more than beer and skittles." He tried to chuckle, but it came out weird.

Montague squinted, apparently waiting for a better explanation.

"Of course, not *alien* in the trite, large-eyed creature way, but alien because the difference has never been detected before, because its purpose remains undetermined, and because it's not found in every human sample." He'd rattled off far too many words, but to his relief, Montague seemed to lose interest.

"Did you get her human blood sample yet?" He pointed to where Tess had been standing earlier, obviously missing, or ignoring, the *alien* play on words altogether.

"No. I asked, and she refused. For the third time," Lawrence said in an enough-is-enough way. He knew Montague had pushed her on it as well.

"So ... ask three more times if that's what it takes," Montague snapped back. "I thought you said her blood would show something big. Can't you see it in the DNA? Get a saliva sample. Use a Lineage kit."

Lawrence breathed as he counted to four silently. Then, he did his best to speak without condescension.

"Blood has DNA, too, and white blood cells ... and anyway, the blood is better in this case."

"Then get it," Montague snarled.

"Here's the thing. I may have oversimplified something along the way. You see, I've collected a lot more samples since then." He bit his lip knowing that he'd collected random samples, maybe illegally, just that morning. "In time, I'm confident we'll find another specimen, several more specimens."

The old man's face went red, and his nostrils flared. Not happy.

"What? Didn't you say her blood was unique, a monumental discovery." His eyes went to slits. "Your exact words, I believe, were 'Holy Grail,' and now you're telling me you can find others. All you need is time?"

"Um. Yeah."

"Really? Exactly how much time?" Montague crossed his arms, calling his bluff, it seemed.

Lawrence's hands went clammy as he tried to think of a reasonable answer. He couldn't come up with even one, really. "Well, I don't exactly know. I'm close, but that's one of the things I want to discuss. Gaining access to more data."

Montague glared at him. "Let me guess. If you had her blood sample, you'd know immediately and wouldn't need others."

"Well, yes, maybe but ..." Lawrence couldn't deny it, especially now that Tess had admitted she and her dad never got sick. The old man had hit the nail on the head.

"Then ask her as many times as it takes!" The man spit the words like venom.

"I'm, uh, not comfortable doing that again so soon." He had trouble standing up to Montague, but he just couldn't ask her again. It had already gotten weird. No, *past* weird. "It couldn't hurt to explore others ..."

Montague cut him off. "No. No. No! This has taken too long already. Look, tell her Mr. Ludwell is asking. And when you do get the results, I need to know as soon as possible. Time is something we don't have." Montague's last words were almost inaudible.

Lawrence tried not to show confusion on his face, but something definitely felt ... off. Why the sudden time pressure? And ... had Mr. Ludwell really asked?

Montague's chair squeaked as he pushed back from his desk. "Let's get down to business. Do you have an update for me on what you've done so far?"

"Uh. Yes." Lawrence took a second to get a handle on his thoughts. Hadn't what he'd already said been enough of an update?

Montague raised his brows. "Let's have it. In layman's terms. I need to be able to speak about this."

He cleared his throat and hoped he could come up with something on the fly. *Thinking, thinking ...*

He rattled off a jumble of sentences about blood cells, genomes, and variants, not really making much sense as he tried to simplify it all. At best, he sounded like a bad textbook.

Montague stared blankly, clearly waiting for more. Lawrence decided to just skip ahead. "Which brings me to the question of viral resistance."

Montague, stone-faced except for a bit of blinking, finally spoke. "Keep the scientific jargon to a minimum, please."

Lawrence took a deep breath. "Um, let me see. An analogy ..." He didn't really have one ready for sharing, so he prepared to speak off the cuff once again.

"I'm waiting."

Lawrence nodded. "Right. Think an accent mark on a word or a sharp on a music note. Just that little change can make a big difference."

Montague's brows drew together.

Not knowing what else to do, Lawrence kept talking. "My hypothesis is that these little variants, the ones I can see in the blood, also result in an altered outcome. In this case, viral resistance." Lawrence held his breath as he surveyed the old man's comprehension. He couldn't tell. Montague's expression remained blank. Not quite confused but not comprehending either. Which was probably just as well. He needed to wrap this up, fast. "You see, that's why Tess's blood is important in confirming all of this."

The last sentence slipped out of his mouth before he realized what he'd just said. He silently cursed himself. He'd just undermined his whole let's-look-for-others argument.

Thankfully, Montague showed no signs of catching on. Instead, he looked like someone awaking from a trance.

No one spoke for a few seconds.

Finally, the old man waved his hands and said, "I've heard enough. Do you have all this on a thumb drive, in a slide show?"

"Yes. Right here." Lawrence pulled out the thumb drive and held it out. When Montague didn't take it, Lawrence slowly rested it on the desk that divided them.

"Good." Then the old man leaned in and said, "Don't forget ... this stays between us for now. Understand?" His beady eyes connected with Lawrence.

Lawrence drew his lower lip between his teeth. He almost asked why Montague needed a slide show and an explanation if this was just between them, but the courage to do so evaded him. He just wanted to get out of that office.

"Is there something else?" Montague griped.

And here stood Lawrence's last chance to capture anything positive from this meeting. He needed manpower—even with just Tess's sample—and this was his opening to push for it. He swallowed the lump in his throat. "Yes. Actually, the sequencing, testing, analysis, all of it is getting a bit much for just one researcher. I could use some help. I'd like to add a scientist to the project." He avoided eye contact, fiddling with the zipper on his backpack.

Montague stayed silent.

Is he considering it?

Lawrence twisted his hands.

"Let me get back to you on that."

"Okay. But I wouldn't have asked unless I thought it was really necessary."

"Is that all?"

Lawrence sighed—not too loudly or obviously, of course—and accepted that he wasn't getting an answer right then and there. "Yes. That's all."

"Very well. I'll see you here next Wednesday morning. Same time, eleven o'clock." With that, Montague diverted his attention to his computer screen.

Lawrence let himself out, wondering again about what Tess had said: *"I never get sick."*

~ 9 ~

Todd counted the minutes while pacing the back hallway of his bar. The clock read 11 a.m., and normally, he'd text Tess about now, asking her where she'd like to meet. Wednesdays had been their one exclusive lunch each week for the eighteen months they had been a couple. He kicked his foot across the floor in frustration. Then, in a moment of courage, he thought, *Why not? It's worth a shot.*

He dialed, surprised when she picked up.

"Hello." Monotone, quick.

Todd let loose the breath he'd been holding. "Hi, it's me."

"What is it, Todd?" she said sharply.

"I didn't think you'd answer." He felt cautiously hopeful, despite her tone.

"I didn't mean to," she snapped back.

"Well, I'm glad you made the mistake."

"I'm already regretting it."

"Come on, Tess. You know I'm sorry about the other night. Listen, I didn't want to fight then, and I don't now. I miss you. That's all. Do you think we could meet for lunch? It *is* Wednesday." He was determined to keep things positive.

"That's not a good idea."

"Can we just talk about this, please?" His voice cracked a little, and he winced at how he sounded.

"No. I'm not rehashing any of this with you. I'm at work. Goodbye."

Todd felt his entire body deflate. She was so stubborn. He rushed out, "Wait."

She sighed. Didn't speak.

"You still there?"

"I'm waiting."

Well, that was something at least. He said, "Look, we both know I was set up. So I've been thinking about who could have done this. I think that's pretty important, don't you?

A brief hesitation, then, "Well, yes."

"Good. We agree on something. It's a start, eh?"

"Uh-huh."

"I've been going over and over everything. And, well, I remembered something."

"Oh really? What might that be?"

"I'd rather talk in person."

"Let it go, Todd. Just tell me what you remembered."

This time, he was the one to sigh. A long, loud one. Then, "Okay, when I *rejected* that woman's advances at the hotel ..." He felt good delivering that one small reminder.

"Uh-huh."

"When I was walking away, I swear I heard her say, 'I better still get paid.'"

"What? And you didn't find that curious at the time?"

"I know. I know. I guess I just wanted to get out of there, forget it ever happened. I mean, did she think I was going to pay her? I don't know. It had seemed so stupid, the whole thing. But now, as I think it over in a new light, I keep landing in the same place."

"Where is that?"

"Someone had hired her, Tess. But why? The only thing I can think is maybe ..."

"Oh my God. Todd. Spit it out."

He knew she was rolling her eyes at that very moment. He pressed forward. "Do you think it could have something to do with your job?" He spoke quickly as if he were running out of time.

Tess stayed quiet.

"You there? Can we at least meet to talk about this? I don't think telling you this over the phone ..."

She cut him off. "I need to think. I'll be in touch *if* I need to or want to. And that's a big *if*."

Click. She'd hung up.

He tossed his phone onto his desk. "Dammit, Tess."

~ 10 ~

S till agitated from Todd's call, Tess reeled as she rode home in the private car provided to her by Ludwell. Her thoughts remained stuck, specifically on the subject of Todd and his *could this have been about your job* comment—not healthy territory, but also not farfetched. It certainly made more sense to be about her than him.

I've exited a lot of employees, lots of bad juju there. Todd may have thrown some drunkards out before closing time, no big deal. The odds are in my favor where revenge is concerned.

She knew Todd's train of thought, and hers now too, screamed textbook for someone who had just been attacked, betrayed, or disappointed, all of those things that ended up defining trauma. The brain processed it on a loop sometimes, looking for someone to blame. A threat felt like a threat. Period.

Her pulse quickened. Was it related to her job? Questions flooded in and took her to a dark place.

What if someone did want to hurt her? Would they stop at this, tempting Todd with seduction? What would that accomplish, anyway?

An answer struck her—she now lived alone thanks to those photographs. "This has to stop," she muttered, half-meaning her line of thinking and half-meaning the whole debacle. She made a fist and slowly pounded it on her leg, closing her eyes, wishing all of it to be a bad dream.

"Pardon, Dr. Andreas, did you ask to stop?" Her driver peered at her in the rearview mirror.

"Oh, no. I'm just talking to myself. Straight home is fine, Clint. Thank you."

"No problem, ma'am." Clint paused. "One of those days, huh?"

She met his understanding eyes. "You have that right."

Right then and there, she made a pact with herself that she'd get real about handling the situation, taking action, instead of wallowing in this endless unproductive stewing.

The car stopped in front of her apartment building, and the driver opened the door.

"Have a good night, Clint."

"Same to you, Dr. Andreas. See you in the morning." With that, Clint shut the car door behind her.

She noted the look of concern in his expression and regretted being so obvious.

Pleasant as usual, Miles greeted her as she approached the art deco doors.

Tess faked a smile, then broke eye contact as she made a beeline for the elevator to her penthouse.

I have to find out who did this and why.

But first, she needed a breather. She kicked off her shoes and plopped herself on the leather sofa facing the window overlooking Manhattan.

Changing gears, she thought about Lawrence and how he had seemed a bit down in the dumps. Maybe for his sake, to boost his mood, she could donate her blood sample—she'd have to bear a little bruise to her ego as far as Montague was concerned, of course. At least the study seemed relatively benign, and she could make sure Lawrence didn't put her profile into the public data bank. He was trustworthy enough. And she certainly didn't have time or patience to deal with emails from distant relatives trying to fill in the branches on family trees.

Her line of thinking shifted again as she thought about Vail Stuart, her ex-fiancé who had made it unashamedly clear that he still wanted her back. Truth be told, maybe she wanted him back too.

He had agreed to offer his blood sample immediately when Lawrence had asked him. Dove right in without hesitation. *Maybe I should do the same. But that's Vail in a nutshell—full steam ahead, not afraid of consequences.* She shook her head thinking how his innate arrogance made him bolder than most about what he could handle in life, and fortunately or unfortunately, he had rarely been proven wrong in his grandiose notions. She kept far more reserved in that aspect.

On a whim, she called Vail.

"Hi. Can I run something by you?"

"Yep."

"Why did you submit a blood sample for Lawrence's side study?"

"Which one?" he jested.

"Very funny. You know the one he's been hounding me over."

"Aw. Don't be too hard on the guy. He's just trying to do his job."

"I know, but didn't it bother you that, after I'd declined Lawrence's request, Montague practically ordered me to submit? It's so obvious— all part of a control game to him. So annoying."

Vail laughed. "Blood sample or not, what would he be controlling? Look, I like Lawrence. He's a nice guy. He's passionate about science."

She felt her lips draw up in a slight smile. "I know that's true. I just don't trust Montague. With him, there are always layers."

"You're overthinking. But that's why I love you. By the way, why is this on your mind right now?"

"I saw Lawrence today. He apologized for asking me so many times. And ... I felt like he could use a little boost."

Vail responded with a faraway "uh-huh."

She frowned. "Hey, what's got you bothered?"

"Well, it's funny ... just today I was going through some legal aspects of the side studies. I mean in general, not just this one. And it's kind of messy. At this point, I'm wondering if maybe I shouldn't have submitted mine, after all."

"Really? You think there's a legal issue?"

"Possibly. But not for you. For me because I'm the legal counsel. Anyway, it's complicated, relating to language used on the packaging, nothing that concerns you. So, if you want to support Lawrence, I'd say it's fine."

"I'll wait and see if he asks again."

"Let's have dinner together."

Did she want to go down this path with him? She thought about that for a few seconds.

She did. "Sure. When?"

"Every night."

Her face immediately flushed. Smiling, she said, "Smarty pants. Goodnight, Vail," and disconnected the call.

Her smile faded when she saw a text from Todd flash on her phone. She groaned. "Not now, Todd." She dropped the phone beside her on the couch.

She had better things to do than battle with Todd. Such as ... using her professional resources to investigate the possibility that she was the target in an endgame of vengeance, and that Todd had been one of the pawns in that game. What was next?

She'd already accepted that someone had hired that woman to wreak havoc in her life. And it had worked.

"Who would do this? And why?" She flipped through a mental Rolodex, taking stock of people she had fired or demoted over the years. Not surprisingly, a few names raised an eyebrow or two, but none triggered outright alarm bells. Honestly, the one person who seemed the most threatening made the least sense—Norman Montague. But what could he gain by destroying her personal life?

She racked her brain, hoping for enlightenment, when suddenly a memory struck her—that time Todd and Montague had spoken at length. The only time, in fact. "At the winery," she muttered. She reached for her phone but pulled back at the last minute. She was just too drained to respond to Todd.

She'd get a solid night of rest, have a nightcap if necessary. Then she would do what she did best: apply her laser focus to a problem and solve it. In fact, all she needed to make the switch from victim to opponent rested on finding out this woman's identity, which presumably would lead directly to who'd hired her. And for that, she knew exactly who to ask for help.

~ 11 ~

Montague leaned his head out of the doorway, peering down the hallway of his grand Westchester home. No sign of his wife. In about twenty-five minutes, at 8:30 p.m. on the dot, she would be doing her usual: pouring a glass of champagne, grabbing a book, and filling the tub. So, he had some time before she called for him to take their Yorkshire terrier, Nugget, out on a walk. He closed the door to his study, made a martini, downed it, and poured another.

He shuffled over to the club chair, grabbing his phone on the way. Sitting, staring into the flames that danced like devils in his large stone fireplace, he combed through his contacts list, looking for the number, grumbling until he found it. Breathing deep, he attempted to calm his nerves and gather his thoughts before putting in the call to his Russian contact.

He cleared his throat and pressed the call button.

A voice with a thick Russian accent responded. "I hope you have some good news for my boss."

"Yes. Of course. That's why I'm calling." To his chagrin, Montague heard a slight shake in his words.

"Let's have it, then. We can't stay on this line all night." The

Russian's arrogance rubbed him the wrong way, and in any other normal circumstance, he would have readily sniped back.

Instead, Montague feigned respect for the foreign lowlife. "Yes. I understand. The good news is we have made excellent progress with the, uh, genealogy study. However, we need to add more scientists." He rambled on a bit, trying to explain with details. Rubbing his neck, he felt flushed, not knowing if he'd even used the right scientific words. Then he shook off the embarrassment, reassuring himself that the idiot on the other end of the line wouldn't know either.

"More people mean more opportunities for compromise. My boss won't like that."

"I'm aware, but there's too much work for just one researcher. In order to speed this along, there must be concessions. We need to add manpower."

"Just one?"

"For now." Montague didn't want to back himself into a corner, so he left the door open just in case.

"You will fund this extra researcher. Understood? My boss isn't going to hand out any additional financing until he gets some real results. And if you are stringing him along—"

Montague interrupted. "No. The research is progressing, I assure you. This is a good thing."

The Russian hung up.

Montague mumbled some choice insults and then began devising a plan to recoup the costs on the endgame payment. Once he had real science to bargain with, he would raise the price.

He checked the mantle clock; he still had some time before his wife would call for him. He rang Lawrence, giving him the green light to hire a researcher. "Oh, and have your new colleague tell Dr. Andreas that Mr. Ludwell himself wants her blood sample for the study." Montague stressed the *Mr. Ludwell* part. Then he ended the call and finished the last swig of his second martini.

~ 12 ~

SUNDAY, SEPTEMBER 16

Tess had flown to London for quarterly Ludwell business; she would be vetting candidates all week for the UK operations. She didn't mind this trip—she'd established a London routine, always enjoying the same hotel in Mayfair and popping in and out of her favorite shops between meetings.

Alone in the hotel lounge, she sipped on a steaming cup of tea, the corners of her mouth turned up a bit. She had to admit she was looking forward to seeing Vail again. As always, he would be here as legal representative for the corporation.

He had sent her a text after they'd last talked, asking to meet up for a "London rekindling." She snickered at his teasing nature, knowing exactly what he meant. True, their paths tended to cross more often than not when it involved Ludwell business—that hadn't changed with their split. However, their late-night dinners and long strolls had stopped once she'd started dating Todd. *And I'm not dating Todd anymore*, she thought, giving herself permission to dive into the allure of her former fiancé.

After a long nap and a shower in her hotel suite at Claridge's, Tess put on a black turtleneck and slacks, adding a steely-blue Burberry scarf for a touch of color. Descending the elegant staircase, she breathed in the sweet fragrance of the private hotel's famous tabletop floral arrangements. The entrance to the cigar-room-turned-bar hid just beneath the mahogany spandrel. She paused, absorbing the timeless feel of this London hotel. As soon as she crossed the threshold of the bar, her vision landed on Vail coolly splayed in a crimson velvet booth with a candle flickering on the table, his hand around a glass of scotch. Their gazes met, and her heart melted a little at the sight of his intense blue stare.

The air between them suddenly turned electric, hinting at unresolved passions, something close to a feeling of the forbidden. In a way, she thought that maybe they shouldn't be meeting at all—not because of vows to others, but due to their own history. She feared an intoxicating rabbit hole could easily open if they weren't careful. But she didn't fear it enough to avoid the meeting. In fact, she'd been looking forward to this very moment with great anticipation.

Vail stood for her approach, pulled her into a brief embrace, and then held her hand, staring at her. She felt a breathless heat rising within her and quickly slid into the seat across from him, if for no other reason than to slow her accelerating pulse.

"She'll have a glass of rosé and a water, no ice," Vail said to the tuxedo-clad server with impeccably slicked-back hair.

Tess smirked a little at his ordering for her, though she turned her head to make sure he didn't see it. Truth was, she liked his initiative.

The waiter returned promptly, placing the sparkling glasses on the table. They sipped with flitted glimpses, falling back into familiar territory.

Vail's next statement shouldn't have surprised her, given his personality, but it did, nonetheless. "Leave him for good, Tess. This is all beneath you. Men don't risk women like you. It's stupid."

"I *am* leaving him—*have* left him—but I need to know what's going on behind the scenes of those pictures. Someone hired that woman to tempt Todd. It's the only thing that explains the photos being delivered to me. I just know it."

Backing off momentarily, he sipped his whiskey, then proposed, "Does it really matter? He fell for it."

She tapped a finger on the table, *click, click, click* before refuting. "He didn't, actually. And, yes, it matters." She sank momentarily into silence. "The *why* probably more than the *who*, but it does matter, to me. And what if this is just the beginning?"

"Of what?"

"I don't know. I've fired a lot of employees. That doesn't bode well for popularity. Revenge isn't out of the question. I can't look like a willing victim." She didn't mention her suspicions about Montague because she had no real justification for the accusation, except for a *feeling*.

"You want to punch back. Trust me—I get it, and I'd want the same thing. But I'm just not sure it's the *best* thing." His stare pleaded with her to listen, to be less emotional about retaliation.

"I know your words are coming from a good place. But I'm going with my gut on this one. I need to know who did this—and why." Her tone left no room for discussion otherwise.

He conceded with a sigh, sitting back against the booth. There was no anger in his expression. "But I get to help you. And when this is all done, you move back in with me." His words tumbled out, once again catching her off guard.

"So those are your demands? I didn't realize we were negotiating." She taunted the smirking man. She knew he didn't mean it like that— like a bargaining chip. His feelings for her had always been sincere. Feelings hadn't been their issue. Their careers, on the other hand, were their personal thorns. She'd mulled it over and over and had come to a conclusion long ago. In order for a relationship to be fully formed, there had to be some flexibility in both the business and the personal aspects. They hadn't been able to achieve that, even though Vail believed there was hope for their future—that they could handle everything, like some maniacal juggling team. Tess wasn't so sure. When she was with him, she felt herself wanting different things ... homey things. She'd struggled between the allure of a family with Vail and the allure of her position in the corporate world. It had exhausted her. And him too, even though he would never have admitted it.

He changed her, he did. He softened her, and she knew he'd try to give it all to her. But ... *no*. It wouldn't and couldn't be done. There just wasn't a way to have it all—for either of them. That had been why, almost two years ago, she'd broken her own heart and his and ended it between them. Tried to move on with Todd, a bar owner who worked most days of the week, and those days turned into late nights as well. She often wondered if those long hours—in an industry she had no knowledge of or even wanted to know—were why she was attracted to him, a safe bet of going nowhere. And she didn't care.

At least not the way she'd cared with Vail.

Vail interrupted her thoughts. "It will be different. I'll put us first. I learned my lesson. I learned it good. Trust me."

Eyeing his slightly disheveled brown hair and puppy-dog expression, she felt more than just a little tempted, and a lot guilty that he still blamed himself.

"Vail ..." That was all she could manage.

He touched her hand. His fingers felt warm on her own.

He whispered, "You've punished me long enough. It's time to come home."

"Just help me get through this first," she found herself saying.

He squeezed her hand. "Baby, I'll do whatever you need. In fact, I'm meeting with someone soon, here in London. I think he could help with this."

"Really? Who? Do tell," she pleaded.

"I will. Just not tonight." He rose and approached her side of the booth, slid in next to her. Folded her into his arms, the prickle of stubble brushing her face.

They kissed.

Tess knew one thing for sure. She had to leave right then and there, or else she would lose her motivation to care about anything but Vail.

L awrence scrambled to find the stack of employee files that he had requested from Lineage's Human Resources director. He shoved paperwork this way and that across his desk until the files revealed themselves to him. He leaned back in his chair and opened the one he hoped would be the ticket.

He'd requested the information after the meeting with Montague, before he'd even gotten the *yes* about adding a researcher, hoping that would make the process faster. To have some candidates at the ready. Lucky for him, he'd placed his bet on the right outcome—funding had officially come through that morning. Though it was Friday, he held out hope that a new person could start on Monday. A long shot, but possible.

And if things continued to go well, that person would be Catherine Wells, Oxford biology undergrad. No PhD, but two master's degrees, one in genetics from Harvard, and she had an impressive research background, including viral research in China. Cathy, as she had requested to be called on their first phone call, had worked for Lineage as a research scientist regarding the DNA kits for four years. That meant she had gone through Dr. Andreas's vetting system as well.

This candidate was a no-brainer.

He glanced at her employee photo. Straight, shoulder-length, light-brown hair. Thirtyish with large, dark-rimmed glasses framing blue eyes. Her appearance, although quite plain, was nonetheless pleasing. Remembering this was about science, not looks, he shook his head, thinking it best not to evaluate her appearance any further. He dialed her number, and after a brief greeting and some chitchat, he offered Cathy the position.

"Thank you, Dr. Glasgow. I'm thrilled to join your team."

He decided to cut to the chase. "Can you start Monday?"

She hesitated, mumbling something inaudible, then said. "I think so. Let me make a couple of arrangements, and I'll get back to you in an hour."

And precisely one hour later, Cathy called. "What time should I arrive?"

Lawrence grinned. "Eight a.m. Welcome aboard, Cathy."

~ 14 ~

B attling jet lag, Tess leaned back in her office chair, facing the New York City skyline, preoccupied with thoughts of Vail and London. She had enjoyed the personal time they'd snuck in after long days of business meetings. The handful of private meals that lingered with bottles of wine and the one afternoon popping in to see the Monet exhibit at the National Gallery all reminded her how time quietly slipped away in his presence.

A warm smile rested on her lips until the persistent knocking on her open office door drew her back to the present.

"Hello," a woman's voice followed.

Tess turned slowly toward the somewhat familiar face.

"Hello, Dr. Andreas. I hope I'm not disturbing you."

"Hello ..." Tess said it almost as a question, realizing she had reviewed the woman's application file and, impressed with her background, had queued her for a possible promotion.

"We haven't met." The woman peered over the top of her glasses.

Tess blinked a few times, realizing that from Cathy's perspective, they hadn't.

The woman wore a frumpy burgundy top with matching burgundy tights, the two of which were interrupted by an unfortunate brown tweed skirt. Her small fingers tightly gripped a thin folder and a Lineage DNA test kit. She held both close to her chest as she spoke. "I'm Cathy Wells. I work with Dr. Glasgow. Starting today, in fact." The lady pushed her glasses farther up the bridge of her nose.

Tess furrowed her brow as she looked at the test kit. "What brings you here, Ms. Wells?" She knew her tone sounded unfriendly, and she didn't try to soften it.

Taking the cue, the woman awkwardly pushed the kit further behind the folder. "Please, call me Cathy." She took a step to enter the office, then hesitated, obviously not knowing what to do.

Tess acquiesced and motioned toward a chair. "Come in. Sit."

"My apologies for the surprise visit, but—"

Tess interrupted with, "But Mr. Montague sent you—urgently, I suspect."

"Not exactly." Cathy hesitated. "Mr. Ludwell did."

Tess's curiosity sparked, and her guard lowered. "I'm all ears."

"As I'm sure you're aware, we've been conducting sideline genetic studies on deceased donors over the past decade. Most of these studies help drug companies and crime labs. And that is all well and good."

"Cathy, let's just get straight to the point." She didn't need the song and dance.

The small woman's face reddened; she cleared her throat. "Dr. Andreas, we would like a sample of your blood. You see, we found something interesting in your deceased father's specimen." She paused and swallowed hard. "I'm sorry. I tend to be too technical in my speech."

Tess stayed silent, hiding her thoughts from the almost-stranger across from her. Inside, her memories swirled in a storm of latent emotion about her parents and their untimely deaths—a car crash on a dark, winding road in southwestern Canada nine years earlier. Her father had been a diplomat and a big supporter of global issues like healthcare; in fact, he had donated his body to medical science. A memory of her father's voice struck her. *"Tess, it's important to support the future generations."* He believed wholeheartedly that being a donor filled the bill.

"How did you get my father's ..." She waved her hand, not finishing.

Cathy suddenly looked caught off guard. "Oh, the government releases caches of files for testing to the Ludwell Corporation every so often."

That had Montague written all over it. So, her father's specimen obviously had been included in one of those file dumps. And now, apparently, his genetic code somehow fell into Lawrence's genealogy study.

Tess pursed her lips. *So that's how I've been red-flagged. Great.*

"Anyway, we've identified markers for the possibility of immune-related variables. But we can't confirm without a sample. Dr. Andreas, if I may ... this study could be the beginning of a pioneer discovery in the biotech field. Maybe even as big as landing on the moon or detecting the first radio wave." Cathy couldn't hide the passion in her voice.

"Look, uh, Cathy ... I just got in from London barely two days ago. This is my first day too, at least in terms of being back in the office. Perhaps I'm not on my A game, because I definitely didn't understand what you just said. Pioneer biotech discoveries, moon landings ...?" She scoffed. No way her blood sample would lead to anything as big as that.

"I'm sorry. I'm not making much sense. Would you like me to start over, explain in detail?"

"No." *Good grief, no.* "The purpose behind the study isn't the problem. I just don't want to be in the Lineage database. I'm an only child. I like it that way. I have no interest in putting my personal information out there for any Tom, Dick, or Harry to find and use as an excuse to grow the long-lost family tree." Tess turned toward the window, remembering Vail's mention of the possible legal implications concerning the side studies in general. He had said it wouldn't impact her, hadn't he? And she had already decided to help Lawrence. So, if this woman agreed to keep Tess's information anonymous, then why not? She gritted her teeth as she thought of Montague's smug face that lay in wait when he got wind of her agreeing to the blood sample.

"Oh. Of course not, that's not at all necessary. Your DNA doesn't have to be registered with Lineage or associated in any way. This is separate. Lawrence doesn't work with the consumer DNA kits." Cathy shifted to the edge of her seat.

"So this would be completely confidential and just for the good of science, right?" Tess quirked an eyebrow, still doubtful.

Cathy nodded emphatically. "Yes. One hundred percent."

"Okay." Tess ignored her gut, which prickled *don't*. "I'll submit a sample. But I want this anonymity clause in writing first." She pointedly looked at the folder and the partially hidden test kit. "What did you plan to do with that?"

Cathy instinctively moved the kit further behind the folder. "Oh, this kit? I was just thinking it would be a quick way to get started; we actually need a blood test. And you'll be anonymous. Absolutely." She looked as if she would skyrocket from her seat. "Thanks. Thanks so much."

Tess offered a small smile. "In writing first," Tess insisted.

"Right. Definitely. I should be going," Cathy stood and shuffled backward. "I'm sure you have more important things to do than fuss with a DNA test kit anyway. It was nice to meet you, Dr. Andreas. Talk soon." In her awkwardness, she dropped the test kit, quickly picked it up, apologized, and then almost ran smack into the glass wall next to the open door.

Tess popped an eyebrow as the walking debacle hustled down the hallway. "I hope I don't regret this."

Back at her home, feet toasty in her cozy socks, Tess placed the call. Several rings in, Vail finally answered with a groggy voice, "Hey, baby."

She cringed when she realized her error. "Oh, no ... the time difference. Totally forgot you're still in London. I'm so sorry I woke you."

"I don't mind. You know that." He sounded more awake.

"Well, now I feel silly."

"Why."

"Because I was just calling to say that I'm going to do it. I agreed to support Lawrence and give him my blood sample—tomorrow, in fact. Ludwell asked this time. So, if I find out I have oil in my veins ..."

"Then we're set for life. Where do we send our resignations?"

"Cute. If this turns out badly, I'm holding you accountable," she teased.

"Me? That's fine. If it makes you feel any better, just think of it as one less thing to worry about as far as Montague is concerned. He'll be appeased for a while. You can concentrate on more important goals ... uh, of a more personal nature."

She picked up on the innuendo, knowing he meant getting the Todd saga over and done with so they could focus on their relationship.

"I doubt anything could appease Montague. I'm willing to put my money on him finding another reason to torture me."

"Hey, give your mind a break. Montague isn't worth the worry."

"Vail?" She thought for a second about revealing her suspicions about Montague.

"Yes?" He dragged out his response, but she remained silent. He waited then said, "I can put things in motion with the guy in London, by the way. Roger said he'd get him the footage and whatever else he already has. This guy, he goes by Red. And he's good. No doubt he'll smoke out who was behind this."

"Then what happens?" she asked, feeling slightly overwhelmed at the thought of actually taking this on. The truth hit her that maybe now that the sting had worn off a bit, she was starting to lose some of her drive to hunt this woman down.

"Let me handle that part: maybe nothing, maybe something. It depends on who did this."

He didn't seem concerned. *Typical lawyer mindset.* "Are you sure? This isn't your battle, and maybe it will just go away." She wanted retribution, but the academic part of her knew that revenge never fixed anything, not really. And she had cooled down a bit since she'd told him the story and her desire to make the perpetrator pay.

"Let's just have a peek behind the curtain on this one, listen to your original gut instinct a bit longer. Besides, I think we're better off knowing the *who* and the *why*—maybe it's just the beginning of something, like you said. I've been thinking ... do you have any other ideas on whether it was to hurt you or Todd, or both?"

She took a moment before answering. "I'm not sure. But Todd mentioned that he'd been thinking about the *who*."

She felt a pang of guilt—like she shouldn't be talking to Todd. She brushed the feeling aside. *Ridiculous.* She and Vail were not officially a couple again. "He called, wanted to meet for lunch. I said no. But then he said something about wanting to talk about being set up."

"Interesting. Did he name anyone?"

"No. But I didn't really give him a chance."

"Then let's stick to plan A and hold tight to see what Red uncovers. We'll decide what to do after that. Hopefully, we'll expose a bit of the motive as well."

"Okay. Goodnight." She still felt apprehensive but told herself there would be no harm in just looking. *Stick with your original gut instinct,* as he had said.

"Goodnight. I'll be home tomorrow—your time, anyway." He chuckled.

She groaned thinking again how she'd woken him. "Sorry."

"And, Tess ... I love you."

Neither hung up. Only the sound of their breathing could be heard. Finally, she ended the call.

She crossed the living room to stand by the floor-to-ceiling window, feeling a tad relieved that Vail hadn't arrived back from London yet. Otherwise, she couldn't be sure she wouldn't hail a cab straight to his penthouse, a mere seven-minute drive away from her own. Staring through her reflection in the glass, she scanned the glittering lights below, searching for some random sign that she should give in—with abandon—to her feelings for Vail.

~ 16 ~

Unable to fall back asleep, Vail slid his legs over the side of the bed and stretched. He thought about his conversation with Tess, deciding to go ahead and call Red now. The less time that went by, the better.

"Can you meet?"

"Yep."

Despite the early morning hour, Red sounded like he'd been awake for some time, ready to go at a moment's notice. Vail envied the guy. He would need a little more time to get to that point. But he'd give it the ol' college try.

After some half-hearted calisthenics, he splashed his face with water, ran his damp hands through his disheveled hair, and dressed. One more look in the mirror, a shrug, and he was out the door, shoving his arms through the sleeves of his coat.

The two met on the dimly lit street just behind Vail's hotel, the Corinthia in London. Red wore a dark pea coat. The collar had been pulled up to cover the bottom half of his face; a hat camouflaged the top half. He looked like two eyes and a nose in the shadows. He puffed a cigarette as he leaned against the damp brick wall. Vail took stock of him for a moment, then scanned the dim street for passersby before approaching.

"Whatcha got for me?" Red kept his voice low and his words to the point.

"Are you up for a trip to the good ol' US of A?"

"Always." Red flicked the glowing end of his cigarette onto the dewy sidewalk, stamping it out completely with his boot.

"Remember that client I mentioned, the one who needs to identify a certain someone?" Vail said the words casually.

"Yep."

"We've got the green light for step one, finding the woman from the photographs and surveillance video. I'll get you what we know so far." He spent a few more moments explaining some details and his own suspicions—mainly that Tess was the target of the setup, not Todd.

"When do you want me there?" Red asked.

"Soon. The incident is already a few weeks old."

"Yep. I agree. Trails tend to dry up quickly in these matters. The sooner the better."

"One last thing. This may turn out to be bigger than it appears. We may need to ruffle some feathers, send a message or two if it turns out to be something more. I'll put you in touch with the hacker who has brought us this far. You can trust him."

"I like to use my own people, though. Keep the circle small."

"I know, but this time I need you to branch out a little." Vail's expression left no room for debate.

There was a pause as the two men locked eyes, sizing each other up. Finally, Red shrugged and said, "Right. I'll get to work on this straightaway. As for how far you want me to take this ..."

"I'll let you know once we get more information. For now, I'll be your contact to the client."

"It usually doesn't end with finding the hired girl, you know." Red lit a fresh cigarette. Just before he sauntered away, he added, "In fact, that's usually just the beginning."

The words haunted the hollow street even after his figure disappeared around the corner.

~ 17 ~

The cool morning air gave Tess a bit of a boost, maybe even a faint glimpse of hope that normal life lay just ahead. She tugged at the collar of her coat as she walked toward the Smith restaurant near Columbus Circle in Manhattan. She had just completed the blood test and had a pleasant chat with Cathy, who seemed like a genuinely nice person. Maybe she also felt more than an ounce of regret about how cold she'd treated her at first. Anyway, today had been more agreeable between them, mostly because Tess had lowered her guard a bit. Now all she needed was to come up with a solid plan to dodge Montague—permanently. She couldn't stand the idea of him gloating. However, she knew it would ultimately be inescapable now that she'd succumbed to the request. He was just that kind of an ass.

Entering the restaurant, she edged by the long line of patrons waiting to be seated and surveyed the place for Roger. From a table near the back of the dining area, Roger stood and waved, trying discreetly to straighten his too-tight Hawaiian shirt that he had layered over long underwear—far from a fashion statement other than maybe a *haven't shopped in years* flair.

A hostess greeted her with a smile. "This way, please. Oh, I'll take your coat and scarf if you like." Tess handed them over and followed the young woman to the table where Roger sat. She then hung both items on a nearby hook.

Tess thanked her, and the hostess dipped her head and replied, "You're very welcome." She scurried back to the front.

Sitting across from her longtime friend, she tolerated his playful eye roll. Then he razzed her a bit. "This isn't a five-star restaurant, for chrissakes—they don't carry personal items to the tables. Unbelievable. Wherever Tess goes, she's treated like she owns the place. I need some of that swagger." He threw his hands up in feigned annoyance and chuckled.

"Real funny. Cut it out. Let's get down to business. You have a new trick to share, don't you?"

"I do." Roger's lips curled as he glanced up through his thick glasses. "It's pretty cool, actually."

"Let's have it, then."

"Here's the deal. Ready?"

Right then, a server interrupted to take their orders. Once that was out of the way, Roger leaned forward and said in a low voice, "I can hack someone's phone from anywhere now—anyone at any time. A perfect stranger. Anyone sitting right here in this restaurant, in fact." He wore a puffed-chest posture.

She leaned back and crossed her arms. "Oh, come on. Anyone, anywhere, Roger?"

"Oh ye of little faith. Yes, I'm serious. Anywhere with Wi-Fi, that is. As long as the target connects or is open to connecting. Secure or not secure. Doesn't matter." He gleamed. "Oh, and I can connect them through a phone call too."

"Such convenience," she teased. "It almost seems too easy for you."

"Yup, easy for a *genius*." He waggled his eyebrows. "Trust me— you're getting your money's worth with my skills."

She tilted her head and shrugged, but she wore a smile too.

Undeterred, he proceeded to remind her that Ludwell Corporation and even Vail's firm often found value in his *hat tricks*, as she had playfully nicknamed his demonstrations years ago. Then in a mischievous tone, he said, "Pick a victim."

"Really? Here?"

He had a big grin on his face as he nodded, looking confident.

"As you wish, Mister Genius." She looked around. "How about her?" His gaze followed her not-so-discreet head nod, and they took a moment watching the soon-to-be victim, a loud, cackling lady with big hair and bright-pink lips.

"Boyfriend?" Tess questioned as she surveyed the lady holding the hand of the man across from her.

"What gave it away—the groping or hair tossing?" He spoke softly as he typed on his laptop.

Tess snickered, relaxing back into her chair as the waiter delivered water, no ice, and a soy cappuccino embossed with a frothy heart.

"For the lady." Then he placed a plate of eggs with a mountain of bacon and a soft drink next to Roger's laptop. "Double bacon for the gentleman."

Tess said, "Thank you. This will be all for now." The waiter shuffled away, having picked up the hint.

A wry smile played across Roger's face just as the big-haired lady's phone buzzed.

"And ... I'm in," he said. "Now for the fun part. So, Dr. Andreas, do you want to embarrass her or ruin her relationship with that poor schmuck?" He spoke as he typed.

"Embarrass, slightly—nothing unrecoverable, Roger. Let's not get carried away. We don't need the wrath of Karma or to become cellmates in matching striped jumpsuits." She waited while he continued to mumble and type.

"Got it. This will work."

She leaned closer to him and whispered, "It shouldn't be this easy to ruin someone."

"Here we go." He spoke nonchalantly, ignoring her comment. Pounding a few more keys.

She sipped her cappuccino, wondering how on earth he'd obtained the stranger's phone number. Just as her lips formed to speak, the big-haired lady's phone pinged, and she looked at her screen. First, the woman's face flushed, almost matching the shade of her hair, which didn't pair well with the pink lips. Then came a piercing shriek, followed by a series of crescendo-ing *Oh my God*s.

Roger side-glanced at Tess with bulging eyes and a big grin.

What had he done?

Oddly, Tess felt little concern about the woman's distress. Like this was an everyday thing. Where had her conscience gone? Her coolness in the midst of the other woman's panic seemed poignant, at least to her psychologist side. *I'm projecting,* she chided herself. *This is not the woman who targeted Todd.*

Roger mumbled, "Huh."

Tess snapped out of her private thoughts. "Do tell. What exactly did you do to the poor dear?" She managed a blank expression while her words rang of theatrical wickedness.

He swallowed hard, as if it had just sunken in the power he wielded. Clearing his throat, he said, "Quintessential bad bikini photo posted across her social media." He paused before letting the whole cat out of the bag. "And a text of said photo to *all* her contacts, work included. Let's just say everyone she's ever connected with will have seen her itty-bitty bikini-clad, not-so-beach bod by the end of the day." He snickered.

"How'd you get …"

He waved his hand, cutting her off, and said, "Child's play. That's not the important part. Wait for it."

Just then, the two fell captive to the sights and sounds of a commotion. The big-haired lady frantically waved her phone in the air, flapping it wildly in front of the boyfriend's face as he barked, "Calm down, will you?"

In response to the man's raised voice and the lady's meltdown, a waiter rushed over, asking if everything was all right and offering to assist in their departure.

Roger waggled his eyebrows.

"Impressive. Trite, but … bravo." She silently clapped.

The lady let out a few loud sobs.

At the same time, Tess reached for her purse and stood. "All right, Roger. I've seen and heard enough. That little tantrum is giving me a big headache."

He winced. "She is loud, that's for sure."

Standing, she patted his shoulder. "Thanks for the entertainment. You never fail to impress."

Smirking, he closed his laptop and stood. "We could do this same thing to that woman in the hotel, you know."

She was confused at first, then understanding dawned. "Oh ... yes. Hmmm. I'll let you know." She could only hope the solution to the woman in the hotel would prove that cut-and-dry, but she doubted it.

He grabbed her coat and scarf and gave an exaggerated wink.

"Goodbye, Roger." Tess playfully scowled at him, but then smiled when she turned her back and walked away.

Roger and his Cheshire grin remained at the table, leaning his chair against the wall and resting his arms behind his head. He stared at the big-haired lady, who was now quietly dabbing her eyes, and relished in his handiwork.

The waiter came over, refilled his coffee, and apologized for the lady's behavior.

Roger had to bite his cheeks to keep from laughing.

~18~

Vail couldn't have been happier to be back in New York. He'd barely even napped on the flight home, thinking about Tess. "I know she felt it too," he assured himself as he headed to his office.

Once settled behind his desk, Vail called out to his assistant, Derek, who manned the outer office flanking his own. The flamboyant young man, who always looked impeccably dressed and beautifully groomed, immediately appeared in the doorway.

Vail did a double take on Derek; he noticed bright-purple socks peeking from beneath his slightly too-tight dress pants. The man's clothing cost a lot more than his salary could sustain, so Vail surmised that Derek's live-in boyfriend must be footing the designer bills.

"Could you set up the conference room for the new client meeting?" Vail asked.

"Done." Derek spoke crisply, batting his eyes.

"Of course it is." Vail grinned.

"Any special requests? We have the usual, of course."

Derek's setup always included a carafe of small-batch coffee, sparkling and flat waters, chilled soft drinks, English teas, and an array of gourmet butter cookies and other delectable pastries—with a side of chilled champagne, of course, for when the client signed the deal.

"A pre-meeting injection of caffeine couldn't hurt," Vail said, pushing against the inevitable jet lag, then turned in his chair and began to mentally rehearse his spiel.

People in power are either good or bad or stupid. And the bad attack the good and destroy the stupid. As is the caveat of human nature, in the end, the good turn on each other too. No one is safe. Your company is powerful and wealthy, and there are a lot of people who either want to stop you, rob you blind, or embarrass you—and if they are determined enough, they may accomplish all three. It's always been the way—attack businesses through personal lives to steer societies, economies, governments, and profit, of course. My firm is your first line of defense ... and your last if it comes to that.

Vail knew the easiest attacks always involved women. It remained the age-old weapon of choice—catch a man in a bad spot with a woman and watch his life spin out of control. Everyone knew the formula, and the wealthy all took turns using it on each other. Vail considered it an unspoken modern-day replacement for the duel.

And suddenly the pieces started to fall into place amid his run-through for the meeting... about what had happened with Todd and Tess.

"She's right," he spoke aloud at the realization.

"Who's right?" Derek said as he placed a steaming cup of coffee on Vail's desk.

"Just a light-bulb moment, and thanks."

"Grab that bull by the horns, sir, and you're welcome."

Vail shook the image of Derek riding a bull out of his head and shifted back to his epiphany.

He'd always thought the photographs had smelled of a setup—that wasn't his revelation. No, what struck him in that moment lay more in the acknowledgement of it being something much more. In fact, he thought about how Red's confirmation almost seemed unnecessary; of course, it didn't end with the hired girl.

Right then and there, Vail made the decision to lead the crusade to repay the culprits behind this scheme. He felt a rush of anger stemming from his innate protective nature that lurked just under the surface, especially when it came to Tess.

He ran through various scenarios, thinking if someone had hired this girl, then the real question became *why*? Todd owned a bar, a nice one, but not nice enough to plot against him. If this was a ploy, it had to be because Tess worked for Ludwell Corporation.

By extension, another thought occurred to him: yes, this could be related to Tess, but maybe not fully. Maybe she was simply a means to an end—a way to get to the Ludwells.

But why?

He considered motives, such as getting the company gatekeeper—which would be Tess—out of the way. She screened all employees and played an integral role in assessing partners, big-dollar players in the pharmaceutical world—and her recommendations had caused friction at times.

But to what end? Why get her out of the way? How would a breakup between Tess and Todd achieve the mastermind's goals?

He couldn't come up with a motive, not right then and not without more information.

"That's why I need Red. He can smoke 'em out like no other."

First things first. They needed to find that girl, find out her identity, her age. He cringed. He hadn't seen the video. *Please don't be underage.* And with that, he deemed the situation a legal issue, untethering his own hands to take the lead on this.

"Derek, could you get me the Ludwell file, please?"

"Sure thing."

He listened as his assistant clicked away on the computer keyboard.

"Email or hard copy?" Derek asked.

"Hard copy."

After a minute or two, Derek appeared with a blue folder containing a stack of printed papers. "Here you go." Then he spun, literally, on his toes. He did a sort of backbend dip while holding on to the doorframe. "Do you still want your usual latte this morning? I have time to cancel the order."

"No. Don't cancel. An IV of coffee wouldn't be too much. Thanks, and thanks for this." Vail waved the folder in the air.

Derek smiled and disappeared back through the open doorway.

Vail flipped the folder open to the first page of the notes his law firm had compiled about Ludwell Corporation when it had signed on as a client. He searched for anything that stood out as possible bait for someone with not-so-pleasant intentions.

The Ludwell family's fortune originated in Europe—England and Scotland, specifically.

Ancient history. He skipped ahead.

Ludwell Corporation strives to be a catalyst for the advancement of science, medicine, and military industries, spearheading projects that will serve to advance humankind and protect global health.

He rolled his eyes.

His fingers flipped through the pages listing the family winery, charities, the global disaster relief program. "Passion projects and bones to throw at the media." He decided these were probably not the source of any coup that may or may not exist.

He flipped back to the pages concerning Lineage, the real bread and butter, especially the side studies.

Montague had done a bang-up job of disguising the studies as humanitarian for sure. However, too many existed, in Vail's legal opinion, and too fast. It wouldn't be long before Montague overplayed his hand.

"Hey, Derek, can you schedule a meeting to discuss the Lineage packaging language as soon as possible?" He shook his head, frustrated that he'd let it slip through the cracks with all of the recent travel.

Barely a minute later, Derek chimed out, "Done. Copy in your inbox."

Vail's thoughts landed back on the inception of Lineage. For starters, in order to obtain enough specimens, the company essentially tricked the public into donating their DNA—actually requiring consumers to pay to do so.

Of course, it hadn't been that hard. Lineage simply marketed to human curiosity, dangling a carrot chockful of aspirations linked with tracing ancestry like uniting with relatives previously unknown. Uncovering family secrets. Finding elusive inheritances.

"Like taking candy from a baby."

Having read enough to make his stomach churn at the thought of profiting from people's desire to belong, he put the papers down. With the wheels turning in his mind, he recognized a nagging suspicion that Montague's insistence on getting Tess's blood sample may mean something after all.

His heart beat a little faster than normal.

He winced, thinking how she'd just submitted it. "It's my fault," he muttered while shaking his head. He should have told her not to.

He called Red, who would have recently arrived in the States. "Red here."

"New information surfaced on that, uh, personal case we talked about," Vail said.

"Yep. On this end too. I've got a name."

Just then, Derek peeked through the doorway, holding the latte. He made a *don't mean to intrude* face and then pointed at his watch.

Ah, the meeting. Vail flashed a thumbs-up, then said to Red, "Let's meet this afternoon, two o'clock."

"See you then. I'll be by that big shiny building."

Knowing Red meant the Chrysler Building, he hung up. Derek wasted no time and tactfully corralled him toward the conference room. Halfway down the hall, Vail patted his pocket. "I left my phone." He had wanted to text Tess. Maybe she hadn't actually submitted the sample yet. There still could be time to stall ... just in case.

"I'll grab it and bring it to you," Derek insisted.

Reluctantly, Vail entered the already chatty conference room.

~**19**~

While passing by Norman Montague's office, Tess moved as quickly as she could without actually running. She was in no mood to interact with the man. "Ick," she whispered to herself as she caught a glimpse of him leaning over some papers on his desk.

"Almost safe." She was within an arm's reach of the door handle to her own office when she heard him call out her name from down the corridor.

Busted. She gritted her teeth and turned around, hoping what he needed to say would be short and not require one of his sociopathic nine-minute, closed-door office sessions. She forced a smile. "Yes?"

"I've been meaning to catch you. Let's chat," he said.

No luck today.

"We can talk in my office." He turned, motioning for her to follow him.

Tess rolled her eyes at his back. Once in his office, she thought how he looked like a little troll crawling into the oversized leather chair. If only she could have shot flames from her pupils, she would have aimed for his bushy eyebrows, scorching them right off his face.

"I was happy to hear you submitted a blood sample this morning. It goes a long way in showing loyalty to the company."

Jaw clenched, she held back the urge to grab his fat neck and squeeze it, watch his face turn red then blue. As circumstances would have it, she wasn't a killer, but she could dig into her psychological arsenal at will. And since Montague had shown his hand—that her agreeing to the blood sample felt like a win to him—she decided to toy with his psyche.

Deliberately removing emotional cues from her face, she spoke deadpan. "My loyalty has never been in question. Is there something that needs to be discussed officially, about how I do my job? Should I set up a meeting with Mr. Ludwell?" She postured her finger over her phone as if preparing to make a call. An Academy Award-worthy bluff.

The old man flailed his hands in a rush to protest. "No. I misspoke. No. We're just grateful you decided to support the company on this project."

"Hmm. Just so I understand ... me doing my job and doing it very well pales in comparison to participating in this side project. This donation of my HIPAA-protected genetic data is the big shining star in my cap." Her nostrils flared with anger, her cool façade quickly slipping.

"Well, yes. In some cases, we must go above and beyond for the greater good," he said.

His pathetic stab at philosophical advice made her flush with anger. A grin erupted on his face, presumably from his perceived upper hand.

She loathed when he did that, and suddenly, she couldn't take any more of his pompous nonsense. "You know what, *Norman*? Just so we are clear ... I gave a sample only because *Mr. Ludwell* asked me to."

The arrogance quickly faded from his face, and he blinked owlishly.

A light bulb went on in her mind. *That rat.* He had played her. Mr. Ludwell hadn't asked. No way. Montague had undoubtedly lied to Cathy and Lawrence, ultimately tricking her into giving the sample.

She couldn't help herself. She fired back and said, "In fact, I'm going to follow up with Mr. Ludwell today. Tell him I gave my blood sample at his request. That's a great way to show my loyalty, don't you think?" She narrowed her eyes at him. Of course, she had no plans to do so but couldn't resist toying with him.

The little man's head swayed a bit as if he were fighting not to lose his breakfast. Beads of sweat formed on his round face. "No need. I'll tell him. I have a call with him in ten minutes. He has a full day with the family. It's better not to bother him."

She slowly shook her head, making sure not to break the stone-cold gaze. "No, I think it should definitely come from me. I'll just send him a note since he's so busy. He can read it at his leisure. If this project was important enough for him to personally request my support, then I think it only appropriate for me to be the one to reach out."

Montague seemed at a loss for words, shifting in his seat.

"If that's all then." She stood to leave, and with her back to Montague, she grinned fiendishly.

"Wait," he called out, sounding desperate.

Her victorious expression flattened as she turned to face him.

"How's your boyfriend? Todd, that's his name, right?"

Huh? An uncomfortable tingle crept across her skin. Had she heard him correctly? Why would he ask that?

Had he just shown his cards?

Just as she started to ask what exactly he meant, his assistant poked her head into the office. "My apologies, but there is a very persistent lady on the line for you, a Gemma Stein. She's called three times already this morning but won't say why. I don't think she's going to stop calling."

Montague's face went through a rapid succession of darkening reds.

His assistant and Tess watched and waited.

When he finally spoke, he stumbled over his words, ending on what sounded like some curse words followed by, "Put her through."

Grateful for the interruption, Tess made a quick exit, a theory starting to form in her mind.

She closed the door to her office and leaned against it, trying to steady her racing heart. Deep breaths.

What are you up to, Norman?

There was a reason he'd mentioned Todd, and she fully intended to find out.

What did he know about Todd? Hadn't they only truly interacted once? Why would Montague even think to bring him up? He'd never asked about him before ... ever.

She stewed on that idea for a few minutes before chiding herself for being overly dramatic.

"Montague asked about Todd because he's creepy that way." She spoke aloud as if the sound of her voice would prove more convincing than a simple thought.

She rationalized some more. He just liked to get under her skin, remove the veil that separated her business life from her personal life —cross boundaries. He'd done it before, and she'd always ended up feeling like bugs were crawling through her skin. This was probably the same tactic, nothing more than Montague's typical MO—to be as weird as possible and make everyone uncomfortable. "I need a sanity check." She dialed Vail, only to reach his voicemail. She rattled on and on in a message, explaining what had just happened.

Then, just before disconnecting, that familiar nudge, a gut feeling, took hold. Her breath caught in her chest, burning her lungs as she held it in too long. She knew exactly what Montague had done. What she couldn't fathom was the *why*. With her lips dry and her pulse racing, she said one last thing.

"Hey, do you think Montague had something to do with the setup? Call me."

Thirty minutes passed. Restless, she clicked her tongue. Her finger hovered over Todd's name on the screen of her phone. No. She wanted to talk to Vail first. "Tea. I need tea. A distraction." She went to the kitchen area. "No Earl Grey." Empty-handed, she returned to her office and noticed a missed call from Vail.

"My luck." She picked up the phone. Eager to hear his response to her question, she listened to the message from Vail.

"I don't know. Maybe he had something to do with it. A stretch maybe, but then again, not exactly out of the question." He made a *hmmm* sound then continued, *"Red has some information. I'm going to see him now."*

She heard his assistant in the background, asking Vail something. Then Vail said, *"I'm sorry, Tess. Have to take care of something right now. But can we recap tonight? Dinner at your place? Send me a quick text, k?"*

She texted him a *yes* along with her suggestion for dinner plans, and then tried to focus on work, but her mind kept drifting.

This is futile. She threw her pen on the desk and grabbed her purse. She decided to get some fresh air and take a walk to the coffee shop down the street.

Along the way, she stopped to watch a jubilant gaggle of children playing on swings behind a school fence. Within seconds, her mood lightened. She spoke softly to herself as her hand grasped the iron post, "I'm not afraid of you, Norman Montague ... or whoever's messing with me." She knew that with Vail's help, this whole thing could be tackled efficiently. As for Todd, she'd need to deal with him at some point—she owed him an apology and some closure about their relationship. *Just not yet ... and definitely not today.*

~20~

Cathy glanced at her watch for the umpteenth time. Several hours had gone by. *It's gotta be in the database by now.* She didn't want to drop the ball this early in her new job path. And truth be told, she was curious to fill in the blanks as to why Lawrence was so excited about this particular specimen. He'd given only the highlight reel on Tess. She spun in the chair to check the screen, bumping a stack of folders on the desk, setting into motion a storm of flying paper.

"No, no, no." She grasped at the airborne sheets until finally ending up on her hands and knees reaching under the desk. As she read the pages, trying to make sense as to what went where, she noticed the letters MsVI.

"It can't be." Her mouth went dry. She knew the meaning of those letters all too well: Moscow Viral Institute, a Siberian facility. She also knew a lot about the institute's jaded reputation from the smallpox study she had researched in college.

As she continued to flip through the documents, Lawrence opened the door behind her, startling her with a loud, "Hey, whatcha reading there?"

She turned to face him, stricken with a sinking feeling.

"Cathy?"

"What is this?" She haphazardly waved several papers.

Appearing a bit confused, he took the papers and glanced at the top one. "Oh. It's just our partner lab in Siberia. Not a big deal."

She wondered if he really didn't get it. "You really don't know, do you?"

"Know what?" Now he seemed annoyed.

"This lab, MsVI ... they store eradicated viruses."

"Like what?"

"Like smallpox, anthrax, Ebola. To name a few. Ringing any bells?" She raised her eyebrows and waited for a more appropriate response.

"So, what's the point?" Frowning, he handed the stack of papers back to her.

Disappointed that he still seemed to miss the magnitude of it all, she dragged out her first three words. "*The point is* ... they aren't allowed to have those viruses stored all together like they do. It's a national security concern. You should know this already." Now she was frowning, and she could hear the anxiety in her tone.

"Maybe you're misinformed. Eradicated viruses are stored in labs monitored by the World Health Organization. Maybe that lab is one of the approved locations."

"Yes. But the thing you're neglecting to realize is that WHO doesn't store multiple viruses in one lab. EVER. What if an incident occurred, a breach? Then what? There'd be ten viruses released at once. And to be clear, Lawrence, I'm not misinformed."

He stood silent, taking it all in, as if her words had finally found a crevice in his brain through which they could enter.

She pressed on. "Can you just tell me one good reason why we would be sending our data to that lab? We aren't conducting viral research; this is immune function research." Her mind was moving faster than her words could be spoken.

"Kind of relates. Immune, viral resistance, viruses."

She gave him a horrified look.

"Don't worry. Listen, I don't know why we're partnered with these guys, but we're getting a lot of great funding somehow, and honestly, I don't see a real problem here. MsIV is a legit lab with renowned scientists. They do real cutting-edge work—eradicated virus storage or not."

She looked at him in a stern fashion. "I need to see Mr. Ludwell. This could put the whole company at risk."

Instinctively, he moved to casually block her path as she headed for the door. "No. I'll talk to Mr. Montague at my meeting on Wednesday. Let me handle this."

Undeterred, she put her hand on his arm and gently pushed him aside. "Fine. But I expect an explanation. Now if you'll excuse me, I need some fresh air."

~21~

Vail was on his way to meet up with Red when he saw a text from Tess confirming dinner plans. He scolded himself, realizing he'd never told her not to submit her blood sample. But it was already too late in the day to worry about it; he'd tell her tonight instead. Right now, his biggest focus was finding out what Red had to say.

Vail rounded the corner to the alley at the back of the Chrysler Building and was pleased to see Red waiting for him, cigarette dangling from his mouth. The two men greeted each other with nods, then got down to business.

Red spoke in short sentences between puffs of his cigarette. "The girl's name is Gemma Stein. Not much to her. Works at a beauty parlor. Earns money on the side through her lowlife wannabe gangster cousin who goes by Ray, just Ray." He rolled his eyes.

Vail looked down. "What about who hired Gemma Stein?"

"That's still pending. Just may have to beat it out of one of them. Here's the girl's address." Red handed over a slip of paper.

Vail stuffed the address in his coat pocket and then spoke low. "Check into a guy named Norman Montague, will you? Call it intuition, but I think there's a good chance he may have his paws in this one."

"Sure thing. And the girl?"

"As for the girl ... hmmm ..." Vail tucked his hands in his coat pockets. His jaw clenched, he was angry, but not beat-it-out-of-her angry. "Mess with her image, personal life, finances, employment. Basically, begin the slow dismantling of her life until she finds herself scraping pennies together to make ends meet just to live in a place that barely has hot water and needs at least three bolts on the door. That should entice her to come clean."

"Problem is society's beat you to it. She already lives like that." Red casually breathed out a ring of smoke. "You know there's more straightforward ways of getting people to talk, right? Faster too." He punctuated the point by raising both eyebrows.

Vail thought for a moment as the expanding oval of smoke dissipated, then an idea hit him. "Yes, I'm sure there are, but I'd like to avoid that path, for now at least. I think messing with her life—just enough—will convince her to fess up. I've no doubt she'll connect the dots. So, I guess we'll have to find a way to make her pathetic life even worse than it already is."

"You're in luck. That's our specialty. Any requests?"

"I'll leave the details to the experts. I'm not sure I can think of anything worse than her current circumstance, though I'm sure there are deeper waters out there to explore." His eyes went wide in a *this is out of my league* way.

Red winked in understanding. "Not a problem. We'll handle the details. Anything else?"

"Probably," Vail paused, "but not yet." Then he stepped out of the alleyway and seamlessly joined the flow of the crowded sidewalk.

Violin music played maybe a little too loud, but it invigorated Tess as she prepared dinner. She put the finishing touches on a small cheeseboard and a chef's salad, then peered into the oven to check on the roasting chicken and vegetables. *Divine.* A feast for two, but she needed the distraction, and cooking had always been her go-to for that. She sipped a light rosé, then spun like the ballerina she had practiced most of her childhood to become. Some dreams just weren't meant to be though, and as it turned out, psychology had become plan B—and had proven to be a good one.

In anticipation of Vail's arrival, she opened a bottle of Caymus cabernet, one of his favorites. She stood watching it flow smoothly into a carafe and reminisced about the trip they had taken to the California winery. She smiled at the memory of the private tasting and how the resident owl had appeared in the tree next to their garden table. According to the staff, the owl had not shown itself to anyone since it had taken up residency on the property a year prior.

At that very moment, Vail appeared in the kitchen, interrupting her reminiscing. "What a beautiful sight. And the wine isn't bad either."

She laughed. "I didn't hear you come in." She floated toward him, as if carried by an easy current of water. He pulled her close. In his embrace, she breathed deep, fitting perfectly in his arms. Their eyes connected and lips touched, gentle and breathtaking, and the familiar softness of his mouth on hers stirred something inside. His was the kiss she lived for—and that was precisely why he was so dangerous for her. If she let him into her heart again and it didn't work, she doubted she could survive that fall. She knew Vail didn't share the same fear. He'd promised that if she let him, he would never let her go again. He had assured her so many times that they were at their best together, an unstoppable team. She wanted to believe him.

"You know my world revolves around you, in this moment and for the rest of our lives."

She pressed a palm to his chest. "I want that too, truly. I just need a little time. So meet me halfway, and let's enjoy this interval?"

He kissed her forehead. Once again, she spun on her toes, this time landing delicately in front of the carafe of red. She poured a heavy glass and handed it to Vail while savoring the intensity of his gaze.

Popping a slice of tomato into his mouth, he spoke casually. "I met up with Red. His guy ID'd the girl."

She hadn't expected that news but was thrilled to hear it. "And?"

"Someone definitely hired her to do that bit with Todd."

"I see." She waited, wide-eyed, hanging on his every word.

"The girl's name is Gemma Stein."

Her expectant expression dropped as she furrowed her brow. *Well, that sounds familiar, but how ...?*

"What's wrong?" he asked.

"I don't know. I think I've heard that name." She stood motionless as she looked across the kitchen into the living room. "When, when, when?" she whispered.

"Hmmm. Are you sure?"

They locked eyes.

"I don't know."

"Anyway, this is kind of funny, actually." He swallowed a gulp of wine and broke her train of thought.

"What could be funny about this? Enlighten me." She said it in a lighthearted way, but there was an undertone of seriousness.

Vail picked up on that right away. "You know I'm taking this seriously."

She waved her hand, gave a little shake of her head. "Fine. Just finish what you were going to say."

He chewed on some cheese. Took another sip of wine. "I'm starving."

"The suspense is killing me." She nudged him playfully.

He swallowed and said, "I told Red to unleash holy hell on the girl's lifestyle—you know, put her in the poor house. Get her to talk that way."

"And ..."

"Come to find out, the girl's already pretty much destitute."

Tess wrinkled her nose. "So that plan won't work."

"But it will," he said, holding his wineglass high in the air. "Never fear. I told Red to somehow make it worse."

"Oh, yikes."

He shrugged his shoulders. "Not sure how it can get much worse than living in a slum apartment, though."

"No violence." Her eyes flickered with uneasiness.

He indicated *no* with a wave of his hand then grabbed a few more hunks of cheese, popping them into his mouth. One, two, three.

Did he miss lunch or something?

"Good. No physical violence. So, he'll probably mess with her mind —make her feel unsafe, violated, basically give her a taste of how she made me feel. Right?" She didn't give him a second to respond and continued. "If he's as seasoned as you say, he may go as far as destroying her relationship with someone she cares about." On some level, Tess felt badly about participating, even remotely, in this game. She wrestled with the idea of just stopping it all—right here, right now —but she decided to let it play out.

He stopped chewing and stared at her. "Sometimes I forget what you do for a living."

She rolled her eyes. "Whatever." Then she grasped for a bit of perspective to keep her growing conscience at bay. "Hey, let's not focus too much on this Gemma Stein." The name tasted bitter in her mouth. "She's a scoundrel, yes, but we need to keep our eye on the ball—find out who's behind the big picture and, maybe more importantly, why. Stick to that, okay?"

He nodded, but she noticed a bit of hesitation.

~22~

THURSDAY, SEPTEMBER 27

Juggling two coffees—a vanilla latte peace offering, to be exact, for Cathy—Lawrence carefully swiped his pass to unlock the lab.

She turned at the sound of the door opening and jumped into action. "Oh! Let me help you."

"Thanks. Your cup has the stopper in it."

She graciously thanked him while gently prying the hot beverage from his grip.

"And I'm sorry about yesterday. I can get a little intense when it comes to research." He smiled sheepishly.

"No worries," she said with a wave of her hand. "Professional pitfall. It's fine."

The two had agreed to meet early to start the analysis on Tess's blood. Cathy had already been running tests for two hours, and it was only 9 a.m. A caffeine boost couldn't come fast enough.

"Perfect timing. I just loaded the B Flu T3 slide." She motioned toward the screen that showed the results.

He leaned in close, his nose almost touching the computer screen. "It can't be," he whispered.

She leveled a glare at him, raising one eyebrow and waiting for more. "Well, are you going to share?"

"I'm a little afraid to look away in case I've imagined it all. I don't want it to disappear." He froze with eyes glued to the screen.

She leaned over his shoulder. "Tell me what I'm looking at here. I don't see anything unusual. What am I missing?"

"That's the point exactly, Cath."

"What's the point, Law?" She emphasized his shortened name as a response to his calling her *Cath*.

"Okay, so ... maybe no nicknames." He shot her a side-glance, then took a step back, finally creating some space between his face and the screen. He pointed at the monitor. "See those cells? They look completely healthy, don't they?"

"Yep. Textbook."

"Well, according to your data, they were being attacked by a live flu virus an hour ago. And now they're healthy."

Cathy leaned in and gave the data another close look. "There must be a mistake. Maybe the virus wasn't viable in the first place."

"That's what I thought. But ... look. The other three tests read the same as this one. Did the virus vials come from the same freezer?" he asked.

"No. I made sure I took three virus samples from three separate cold storage areas."

He grinned, pleased she would think to do that.

"Are you sure this isn't the control sample set? The ones without the virus?" she asked.

He checked and double-checked. "Yes, I'm sure."

"Well, hell's bells ... what happened? We must be missing something." She pushed her glasses farther up her nose, only to have them immediately slide back down.

He raised an eyebrow as he took in her futile struggle. "I think we're actually doing the opposite ..." Before he could finish his sentence, she interrupted.

"How?" She let her word stretch out.

"I'm not sure, but it seems like the virus couldn't attach. There are no antigens either." He remembered Tess's words again: *"I never get sick."*

Cathy let out a low whistle, then said, "This is big. Big. Big." She paced around the room, repeating the mantra.

When she finally stopped, they were eye to eye. He said, "I know. Big, indeed."

His thoughts skipped ahead as questions flooded his mind. What did all of this mean? For science? For healthcare? For him? For his team, the lab? For Tess? He cringed at the last question. It was her blood, after all—and her life that could be hijacked by the discovery.

Who cares? This could change the world. He puffed out his chest, his enthusiasm for the results trumping his negative thoughts.

"Okay, Cath ... er, Cath-eey. Please test all thirty-four of the other marker samples and perform the same viral response experiment. My lab notes are right here." He pointed to the freezer and then tapped the open pages of a folder next to the computer. "Then replicate with each sample and compile a new database."

"You've got it." She hopped into motion, her eyes darting about as she read over the lab documents.

He said, "I'll start running the mutations analysis." He was practically drooling at the possibility of what he might discover next.

Both coffees sat abandoned as the two moved with precision around the lab.

~**23**~

Vail's whole body stiffened as he struggled to make sense of the stomach-churning images on Red's phone. "Dogs, Red? Seriously?" Resting his hand on the cool brick of the alley wall near Grand Central, he felt bile rise in his throat as he waited for some kind of explanation.

The seasoned rogue shook his head. "Not my handiwork. The new guy, Hannibal. It seems he got a little creative. Listen, those dogs—they were killed quick, not tortured like it appears. If that helps lighten the blow at all."

"You sure about that? Because this could cause a full-blown police investigation." He didn't even try to hide the concern in his voice.

"Already handled that. Rest assured, as far as the police go, this never happened. Those records never made it into the system." The man showed no signs of worry.

Vail chewed his lip and decided to take him at his word. What choice did he have, really? "What am I supposed to tell Tess? This is definitely not what she had in mind." He knew, without a doubt, she would be livid. "I think she wanted some financial pain and some fear, embarrassment maybe, but not this. This is some kind of psycho-killer move."

Red's jaw tightened. He said, "I'll make sure it's toned down in the future."

"Good. This is important to me—really important. Don't let your people screw it up." A vein pulsed on his neck.

"I hear you. Rest assured, the only thing that will be screwed up is the girl's life." He cocked his head in an arrogant way and lit a cigarette.

"Let's shift focus from the girl for a moment and concentrate on finding out who hired her. I think your people have done enough fearmongering for now." He took a deep breath to clear his head.

"I'll be in touch." Red rolled the lit cigarette between his fingers as he spoke.

"No more '80s horror-movie stunts. Got it?"

Red gave him the once-over. "I told you it's under control." He paused there, as if waiting for Vail to acknowledge the statement, which he did with a quick nod. Red continued. "Your guy Roger's wiretaps show she's still waiting for a payment. That's a clear trail straight back to the wolf behind all of this."

"Better be," Vail grumbled, still furious about the animals, knowing he'd eventually have to spill the beans to Tess. He turned on his heel and took long strides away from the fixer, trying to distance himself as quickly as possible.

24

Clutching her phone to her ear, Gemma's hands went cold as ice when her mom, Sylvia, told her what had happened. She held her breath as she listened, eyeing the patrons scattered around the coffee shop where she'd been sitting for over an hour.

"Someone broke in to rob me, I think. Nibs was probably trying to protect the house, and they killed him." Her mother sounded heartbroken. Nibs was everything to her. "I called the police, but they haven't gotten back to me, haven't even checked on me."

Listening to the familiar scenario, Gemma rubbed her hand on her thigh, trying desperately to find the courage to speak. At last, she found something just over a whisper and said, "Oh God, Mom. It happened to me too." And as the words crossed her lips, she could feel the color draining from her face. Deep inside, a terror beyond anything she had known before began to fester as she realized that someone had sent a very clear and serious threat.

"What?" Her mother obviously couldn't grasp the parallel.

"Buddy too. Someone ..." She paused to catch a breath. "Someone hurt him too. He's gone." She couldn't say the word *dead* and maintain her already flimsy grasp on her nerves.

"Gemma, what is this all about? Are you in some kind of trouble?" Silvia's tone had quickly become less weepy, more suspicious.

"No, Mom. No trouble. Everything will be fine. I think I know what this is about. I'll handle it." She stopped to look at her shaking hand, balling it into a fist to stop the tremor.

"It's not fine, and you darn well know it. Tell me what you did to get into this mess."

She blew out a breath. "I needed some extra money, and I-I ... did something for Ray." She had wanted to be reassuring—let her mother know that everything was under control—but her quivering voice betrayed her fear. She bit her lip.

"Ray!" Silvia scoffed. "He's no good. He's my nephew, but he's no good."

"I know. I'm sorry. I never should have agreed."

"No. You should not have. If you needed money that bad, why didn't you ask for help? You know I would have helped you."

"I know. That's why I didn't ask." She felt terrible.

"Who would do this? Why?" Silvia's voice carried a shrillness that begged for answers.

"I can't get into that now, but trust me, it'll get handled."

"But, Gemma, our poor little babies. You can't bring them back. Oh, it just breaks my heart." Her words trailed off into sobbing once again.

"Mom, I know. I am so sorry. It's all my fault." Gemma felt defeated, stupid, and careless. How could she have gotten into this much trouble this time? Then a thought crossed her mind, one that she didn't want to address but had no choice. "Mom, go stay with your friend, please. Just for a few days until I know this is handled."

"Why?"

"Just to be safe. Please, just go."

"Oh sweet Jesus. I can't believe this."

"I'm sorry, Mom. I'll be in touch soon."

Gemma let out a pained sob as she hung up the phone. Fighting back a feeling that she'd be sick, she rushed to the shop's restroom, hoping to find it unoccupied. When she returned to the table to gather her coffee and jacket, she noticed a napkin sticking out from under her cup. She picked it up, read it, causing her heart to pound so hard she thought it might explode straight out of her chest. In glaring red marker were the words: *Yes, it's personal.*

Out of reflex, like swatting at a bee, she crumpled the scornful napkin and tossed it in the trash. Frantically, she looked all around her, hoping to see someone, *the one* who had done this.

But there was no sign. No clue. Everyone seemed unaware of, unaffiliated with her circumstance.

Petrified, she left the shop, her feet flying beneath her. Somehow, she had to get this under control—and fast.

She did the only thing she could think of in her shaken state and headed straight to see her cousin Ray. To her frustration, he wasn't at the body shop. His coworker said he'd "gone away for a few days."

Gemma stiffened at the words. "You mean he's locked up again?" When she got no response other than a shrug, she left in a huff and headed to the one place she didn't want to be: her apartment.

Once she had locked and then relocked her door, she wasted no time in making the call to follow up on her dog's murder, but the police said they had no record of the incident.

"What? How can that be?" she screamed at the officer on the phone. Hand shaking, she called the police station in her mom's town to ask about Nibs, only to get the same answer: *"We have no record of an incident at that address."*

That's when she knew in her very core that someone powerful had to be behind this coverup. "Ray, what have you gotten us into?"

Defeated, she fell into a tattered chair that faced the television, dragging her fingers through the long strands of unwashed hair. Why would someone kill her dog ... and her mom's? "We live in different states, for crying out loud," she whimpered.

She absolutely must speak to Ray, wherever he was, because he was the one who'd put that old guy in touch with her to set up the hotel incident. To make matters worse, she was still waiting on her ten-grand payment from him. If that old troll had done this, then why still pay her? Her voice sounded eerie in the empty apartment as she spoke aloud to the dingy walls. "And if it wasn't him, then who? Damn you,

Ray. Why'd you have to get locked up again right now? Because you are an idiot. That's why."

Then she started cursing, all of it directed at Ray, at Montague, at life in general—for giving her nothing but misery and stress and feeling used and useless. She punched at the threadbare cushions of her couch, pounded the walls, stomped her feet, spun in angry circles. The rising fury actually made her feel better.

When she finished, she knew two things for sure: she wanted that money, and now she wanted revenge too.

And she would have both.

25

Lawrence scrambled in preparation for his meeting with Montague. He had big news to share with the little man.

On his way out of the lab, Cathy reminded him to also probe on the Russian lab involvement. "Make sure Mr. Ludwell knows about the possible issues with the eradicated—"

He cut her off. "Will do," he said, then let the door shut automatically behind him.

He arrived at Montague's office and participated in the usual waiting game through the glass wall.

"Come in, Lawrence." Montague's voice called out into the hallway.

"Finally," he muttered as he shuffled in, balancing a stack of folders in his arms. "Good morning, Mr. Montague."

The boss's mouth was set in a hard line as he nodded.

Lawrence began his update, making sure not to mention Tess as the specimen he was presenting. He did his best to keep it scientific. Montague asked for a lot of clarification, which made it clear that most of what Lawrence said had flown right over the old man's head.

"So, Lawrence, cutting to the quick, it sounds like you're saying the blood anomaly that you *suspected* existed does, in fact, exist. And that it has some kind of virus-fighting powers?"

"Well, yes and no. Yes, you have the umbrella idea, but no, there are not special virus-fighting attributes. It's more of a resistance." Lawrence adjusted his glasses. "I need to do more testing, obviously."

The old man waved his hands. "That's all well and good. Test your little heart out. Do you have this information on a thumb drive for me?"

"Yes." He dug in his pocket. "Here you go."

Montague eyed him intensely. "You haven't told anyone about this, outside of your assistant?"

He jolted upright. "No. Of course not."

Montague spun in his chair, looking out the window as if he needed time to process the information. Swiveling back, recognition dawned on his face before he asked, "Is this whole discovery just from Tess's sample?"

Lawrence's heart dropped. And there it was—the one question he had hoped to avoid. He reluctantly nodded. He'd never actually clarified that he hadn't used others as well since that meeting when he'd suggested there could be more people with the anomaly.

"I see." Montague swiveled in his chair to face the window again.

Lawrence pinched the bridge of his nose. Then he remembered Cathy's concern, and he felt desperate to change topics. So he cleared his throat and said, "Mr. Montague, if I may ... I wanted to ask about the Russian lab. My assistant has concerns."

The man turned, eyes boring into him. "What concerns exactly?"

"Well, she's under the impression that the lab we're coordinating with illegally harbors eradicated viruses. That could put the company, our studies, all of it at risk."

Montague scowled. "That is not her concern. Or yours. You should know that."

He kept quiet, waiting for more, hoping for a semblance of reassurance that Cathy's suspicions were wrong. But he got nothing. Montague simply ended the conversation with, "See you next Wednesday."

On the walk back to the lab, he thought of all the things he could have said, should have, and didn't. Kicking himself for letting the old man off the hook so easily, Lawrence stood with his card, ready to swipe to enter the lab. He had a lot to do and needed to get to work, but he couldn't face Cathy without an answer. And he didn't have the one he needed to keep her on board.

He looked down, shook his head, and decided that in the name of groundbreaking research, he'd have to stretch the truth a bit, at least for now. He swiped his card and entered. "Hi, Cathy. Great news."

That night, Norman Montague sipped his martini while waiting patiently in the study of his house for his wife to disappear into her bubble-bath sanctuary. He knew he needed two martinis before making the call to the Russian contact. "If I didn't think my speech would slur, I'd have three," he grumbled.

Finally, he dialed, cleared his throat and, when his contact answered, said, "Good evening."

"Yes. I will tell you if it's a good evening or not after I hear what you have to say." The man nearly spat out the words blanketed in the all-too-familiar Russian accent.

So much for decorum. Not that Montague had really expected it.

"I have big progress to share. The scientist found the suspected anomaly having to do with viral resistance." Norman tried to sound as if he fully understood the words that seemingly rolled off his tongue.

"Do you have the information ready for us?" The Russian didn't even try to pretend that he cared in the least about the science of the deal.

"Yes. I can upload as usual."

"Anything else?"

Montague cleared his throat. "There is one thing. The lab in Siberia … someone mentioned it's housing illegal samples of some sort. If that's the case, we may have a problem." The words hung thick under an uncomfortable silence.

"Who's asking?"

"The new lab assistant." Norman had spoken without thinking. And as soon as the words crossed his lips, he clenched his jaw, bracing himself.

"Not a problem then." The Russian hung up.

Confused at the response, Norman tossed his phone onto a nearby leather chair. He should have known mentioning the Siberian lab wouldn't be a smart move. "I'm juggling too many pins."

He retrieved his phone from the chair and dialed Jamie, the man who sometimes made deliveries for him, including driving Gemma to the hotel that day.

"Yes?"

Without preamble, Montague said, "I need you to make a delivery." He gave the details and hung up feeling like he could check Gemma Stein off his to-do list. It had been too close a call when his assistant had mentioned her name right in front of Tess.

Montague huffed. "She never should have had my name, let alone my number. That moron Ray hasn't done one thing right." What did he expect from a two-bit criminal anyway? He wasn't dealing with Einstein here. He shook his head in frustration, but then reminded himself that the important thing had happened—even if it had happened in a roundabout way. They had Tess's blood sample, and Lawrence had confirmed the gold therein.

The conversation he'd had with Todd at the Ludwell family winery briefly flashed across his memory. That was when he'd realized that Tess had an Achilles' heel. The plan had been to blackmail Todd into forcing her to submit the sample. Except that idiot Ray delivered the photos to Tess instead of Todd. He snarled at yet another sloppy mistake, then shrugged. *All's well that ends well.*

He flipped off the light and closed the study door, reminding himself of a motto he learned as a boy: *You don't have to outrun the bear, just the other guy.*

G emma tapped her foot under the kitchen table as she watched the clock: 3:05 p.m., 3:11 p.m., 3:33 p.m.

She let out an angry grunt. *Where's my damn money?*

Montague's guy, Jamie, had finally contacted her yesterday and assured her that the money would arrive at 3 p.m. on Friday, today.

A knock sounded at her door. Gemma bolted up and rushed to answer.

She paused—just a feeling that she needed to be cautious. "Who is it?"

"Special delivery," a male voice called through the door.

Satisfied with the reply, she unlocked the door and carefully opened it just enough to see who was on the other side. As soon as her eyes met those of the stranger in the hallway, her body jolted backward from the impact of the door being pushed violently inward from the hallway. She fell hard. Pain rang through her right elbow, and she instinctively clasped it with her other hand. The pockmarked man with crooked, yellow teeth moved closer, coming to a stop in a looming position above her.

"So you want ten grand?" he snarled.

"You're not Jamie." Her voice cracked, and fear swallowed her very being like a wave pulling her out to sea. Planting her hand to the floor, she began pushing upright. He kicked her hard in the side. She couldn't breathe, let alone make a sound loud enough to get help from a neighbor.

"Here's your money, minus a delivery fee."

A bent yellow envelope hit her sharply in the face.

She scooted backward on the floor, attempting to put distance between her and the brutal stranger. Even through the panic, though, she reached for the money.

He noticed and stomped his foot on the envelope. Taunting her with dominance—some kind of sick game. Then he bent down and grabbed it, pausing close to her face. She could feel the heat of his stale breath. Cringing, she thought she'd be sick.

He moved his sneering mouth closer to her ear. "If you want this money, then you need to answer some questions."

She shivered, and tears streaked along her face as she attempted to move away.

"We can do this the easy way or the hard way, like your friend outside."

"F-friend?" *What is he talking about?* A stabbing bolt of fear gripped her. *Jamie?*

"He chose the hard way. It makes no difference to me." The man paused, looking toward the door, and then grabbed her by the hair. "I'm only going to ask once. Who hired you?"

Gemma winced from the pain. "For what?"

The guy yanked her hair harder. "Don't get cute. You have ten grand here. Who is paying you?"

"The guy in the hallway." She sneered.

He twisted the wad of hair. "I'll rip it out of you."

She shrieked, not knowing if he meant her hair or the truth or both. "Okay. Okay. Some old guy hired me."

"WHAT. IS. HIS. NAME?" His upper lip snarled as he spoke.

"I don't know."

He yanked the wad of hair. Pain shot through her scalp.

"Ow!" she yelled. "His name is Montague. Norman Montague."

He released his grip.

Then something hit her, landing on her chest. She heard the jingle of the object as it fell to the floor next to her—a bloodstained dog collar.

"No." Gemma felt bile rise in her throat. Her body shook uncontrollably.

The guy backed away. He had his hand on the door when he took a moment to glare at her again, saying, "You might want to text the *old guy* and have him clean up his mess in the hallway before your neighbors see."

Her jaw dropped, and her heart pulsed with such intensity that her chest actually hurt.

He left the door open, and she rushed to close the door, but there in the hallway lay a man with a bloody nose.

"Shit." Gemma recognized him as the one who'd driven her to the hotel. She tried to rouse the guy. "Jamie, Jamie." He stirred, and she coaxed him into her apartment and shut the door.

Montague's man plopped onto her tattered couch as she handed him a glass of water and a few ice cubes wrapped in a towel.

He clutched his head and said, "Got anything stronger? You really should keep your abusive boyfriend on a leash."

"He wasn't my boyfriend." She rushed to pour him some tequila.

When she returned, she noticed his eyes had trailed to the envelope on the floor, and he cocked a curious eyebrow.

Placing the glass on the coffee table, she quickly picked up the envelope. He leaned over and snatched it from her, taking a stack of bills, which he stuffed into his shirt pocket. "Medical expenses." Then he boldly picked up the bottle of tequila from her counter and hobbled out of her apartment.

Once Jamie left, she opened the envelope. Only sixty-five hundred of the ten grand was left.

She clutched the money as she slid slowly into the armchair. "I have to get the hell out of Brooklyn."

~27~

Cathy swiped her card to enter the lab, then using her body weight, she pushed the heavy door open, took one step into the room ... and stopped in her tracks. Her breath turned shallow and quick.

"Bret?"

The technician was slumped over the desk, unmoving.

"Oh my God. Bret. Bret." Patting him on his cheek at first, her attempts to stir his slumber evolved into an aggressive shaking of his body. "Please, please, wake up." Deep inside, denial gripped her soul as she desperately wished to be wrong—that he was indeed alive—and for the opportunity to laugh about her dark imagination later.

But Bret didn't wake up. She noticed something around his neck, a wire of some sort. Her stomach dropped. Fear swooped in. She could feel its grip in her chest as she struggled not to faint.

She backed away slowly, all the while reaching in her pocket for her cell phone. She dialed 911 with unsteady fingers and then reached for the door to retreat into the perceived safety of the hallway.

Before long, what might have been half the building's occupants had gathered just outside the lab, waiting for a tidbit of information. Lawrence stood next to Cathy, his hand resting softly on her back.

"What happened?"

"I-I ... I don't know. Bret is dead, murdered it seems," she whispered as her body trembled from shock.

His eyes grew to the size of saucers. "That can't be. I'm sure it must have been something else. Not murder. Not here." He attempted to peer through the open doorway past the officers.

"Strangled. I saw the wire around his neck." She twisted her hands together, inadvertently demonstrating as she spoke.

"This isn't good. But who would ...? Why?" He continued to look past her into the lab.

"I bet it has to do with that Russian lab," she said, narrowing her eyes.

"I told you Mr. Montague said it was fine."

"And you believed him?" Cathy scoffed.

"Yes. Didn't you? You must have, because you didn't quit, did you?"

She saw a flinch in his jaw. Did he mean to be that cruel? She crossed her arms. "I should have, and I definitely will now."

"Cathy. I'm sorry. I didn't mean it like that. Don't be rash. Take a couple of days. The research we're working on is monumental. Don't give that up. I'm sure this is all a mistake." He spoke kindly now.

She forced a lopsided smile but hadn't really heard his words. She just wanted to leave, but an officer approached them. "Ms. Wells, we just need you to sign a statement and go over your contact information, if you don't mind."

"Sure." She looked desperately at Lawrence as she took the clipboard from the officer.

Lawrence patted her on the shoulder. "It's going to be all right."

As Cathy disappeared around the corner with the officer, she could hear Lawrence say, "I bet he was wearing those darn earbuds."

Mr. Montague's assistant rushed into his office. He squinted over his glasses at the breathless woman, waiting for an explanation for the dramatic entrance.

"Mr. Montague. Oh. I have terrible news. It's just unimaginable."

"Spit it out, Doris." He signaled for her to get on with it.

"A lab assistant has been murdered. In the Lineage lab." The red-eyed woman looked as if she might cry.

"Wha—" Taken aback, his heart pounded from the influx of dread in his veins. He thought he might pass out.

"Mr. Montague, are you unwell? You look rather pale." She approached him with a hand outstretched.

He waved her off. "I'm fine. Fine. When did this happen?"

"Just now. The police are still there."

His mouth went dry, his hands clammy.

"Let me get you some water." She scampered out of his office, clutching her chest.

Pressing his head on the back of his chair and gripping the armrests, he replayed the Russian's words on the phone. *"Not a problem, then."*

"This is bad," he whispered, wiping his sweaty forehead.

Montague filled his lungs with a deep inhale as he grabbed his keys and phone. He then fled the building before the cops came knocking on his door.

Tess stood sipping her Earl Grey in the hallway outside her office when she observed a clearly distraught Doris beelining to the kitchen area.

Catching up with the frantic woman, she asked gently, "Everything okay, Doris?"

"No. It's terrible. Just terrible what has happened." The woman choked on her words as she fought back tears.

"Okay now, try to take a deep breath." Tess led her to a chair. "Sit for a moment. Tell me what's wrong."

"I can't. I need to get Mr. Montague some water." She tried to rush away.

Tess put a steady hand on her arm. "Please, just for a second."

Eyes shimmering with building tears, Doris complied.

"Talk to me."

"Someone at the lab has been m-m-murdered." She lost it then and began sobbing into her hands.

Tess tried to hide her shock as she comforted Doris the best she could. Thudding footsteps sounded behind them, causing Tess to turn her head. She caught sight of Montague leaving the building in a hurry, almost as if escaping a fire.

And he probably was.

~28~

R ed finished listening to Hannibal's description of the encounter with Gemma. When the conversation ended, he dialed Vail's number to give an update.

"Vail here."

"We got a name on who hired the girl. I'd feel better giving it to you in person. Let's just say you won't be surprised. Meet same place as usual."

"I can be there in twenty."

"I'll be there."

At the meeting spot next to the Chrysler Building, Red waited patiently, smoking and thinking. Only a few minutes had passed before he heard footsteps approaching. Vail rushed around the corner, almost running smack into him.

Red held up has hands. "Whoa. Slow down, buddy."

"Sorry, I'm late."

"I'm on your clock. Nowhere else to be."

Vail nodded, and they wasted no time getting into the gist of it.

"It was Norman Montague. He was behind the whole setup at the hotel. The one you suspected." Red studied Vail's expression as he said the name. *Not much of a poker face for a lawyer.*

"I'll be damned. I thought it, but I didn't really expect it to be true."

Red waited a few seconds for Vail to swallow the information.

"Did I mention that I work for him? And so does Tess—well, kind of. And even Roger, for that matter. He's one of the big dogs at Ludwell Corporation."

He skillfully blew out a puff of smoke, being careful to respectfully direct it away from Vail's face. "Yep. I'm aware. You just let me know what you need next."

"For starters, let's start watching and listening to him. I need to know what he's up to—and fast. This guy is powerful, connected, and wealthy. And an asshole." He made deliberate eye contact. "Know what I mean?"

"I do. That's a bad combination." Red stomped out his cigarette. "I'll contact Roger with a heads-up."

"I'll let Tess know."

With that, Vail walked away and disappeared into the crowd.

A lopsided grin appeared on Red's lips. "Let the games begin."

29

Roger shook the last of the M&Ms out of the bag and into his mouth, following the sugar rush with a swig of his room-temperature cola.

He had just gotten word from Red that Montague had been the mastermind behind the hotel *setup*. Feeling a little protective of Tess, he decided to get to work on some retribution. He knew he didn't have the green light on torturing Montague—yet—but that woman, Gemma, the gutter rat ... he could start on her.

He spent the next half-hour hacking into Gemma's email and social media accounts. Petty, maybe, but humiliation often went a long way in his book. Besides, he'd wanted to use some of his parlor tricks for a while as Tess teasingly had called them.

"Brace yourself, little lady." He typed furiously at the keyboard, and as he hit send, a grin came across his face. "No one messes with Tess on my watch." With the way he felt, all he needed was a superhero cape flapping behind him.

Groundwork laid, he pulled up a monitoring screen, kicked back, and waited. He expected his target to try to log in to her accounts shortly. The only thing that could make this better for him would have been a side wager with someone on how long it would take her to notice the pillars of her online world crashing down around her.

30

Gemma's fingers shook as she recounted the remaining money from the job she'd done on Todd at the hotel. She'd never been one to put cash earned the old-fashioned way into the bank, so she rolled up little bundles, stuffing them into hiding spots around her apartment.

Middle cushion

Cake pan

Freezer

Brown boot

Here and there, she stashed the cash, jumping at every noise she heard.

And then something dawned on her. Something pretty obvious, really. She just hadn't taken a moment to think it through before now. All of her recent problems—the dog, the guy in her apartment—they all tied back to that hotel job. Not just her troubles, her mother's too. True, people had been angry with her in the past, and she'd even been roughed up a couple of times as a result of her side jobs, but never to this extent.

"What am I going to do?" She knew her place in this— she was hired to do a job, nothing more, nothing less. She had no real insight into the bigger picture. What she did know, though, was that Ray shouldn't have put her in touch with Montague directly. She huffed. "Lazy jerk. This is your fault." And typically, she wouldn't care if Ray's plans fell apart, except this time … it was affecting her family. Her mother. The dogs.

Exhausted from the events of the day and from all the thinking, she plopped down on the sofa, her task of hiding the cash complete. "I'm just an underpaid actress. I don't care about any of you jerks," she yelled, thinking her apartment was probably bugged. Who knew? And her paranoia had gone up a few notches with the incident at the coffee shop—the note.

Her phone pinged, and before she could even get to it, there were several more pings. When she finally grabbed the phone off the kitchen counter, she read the text from her friend, Chris, and her jaw dropped. "Oh no."

Before she could even check to see what he was referring to in his texts, he called. "Hey … um. Did you drunk-email everyone? Probably want to keep your issues on the down-low, especially at work."

"What? I don't know what you're talking about?" A cold sweat formed on her palms.

"The email you sent to everyone." He stressed the last word.

"I didn't send an email. I seriously don't know what you're talking about." Her heart raced as she tried to switch him to speaker.

"Well, maybe you've been hacked—in a big way. You better check your sent mail."

"Um … just a min."

Chris waited.

"I can't get into my email. What the hell?" She typed her password three times.

"I just forwarded your email back to you. Now it's in your inbox."

"Duh … I can't access my email. Take a screenshot or something. Text it to me. Hurry." Her voice cracked on that last word.

"Oh, right. Texting now."

As she read the text of the email, she gasped and her face flushed.

The message described in detail an embarrassing rash *and* a drug problem. *As if the rash wasn't enough?*

"I don't have a rash, and I don't do drugs. Well, not those kind anyway. Maybe I eat the occasional herb-infused brownie, but I'm not shooting up between my toes."

"Well, you probably need to clear this up."

"How? I can't even see who it was sent to."

In what she assumed served as an effort to be helpful, he started rattling off names.

"Okay, Okay. It's everyone. I get it." Her lips stuck together as her mouth went dry.

"I don't know what's going on, Gemma, but you should email everyone, letting them know you've been hacked. Like *now*. Even if you haven't, this is *no bueno*."

"Thanks ... but like I said, I can't get into my email." She moaned, feeling the weight of the world on her shifty shoulders. "I have to go."

Then Chris said, "Wait. Oh no ..."

"What now? Just tell me!"

"Your social media too."

She let out a frustrated scream. "I gotta go." This time, she simply hung up, not waiting for more commentary from Chris.

Her fingers hammered out her password over and over, trying to get into her social media accounts. Nothing worked. "Shit. Shit. Shit!"

With shaking hands, she tried unsuccessfully to light a cigarette. *Click, click, click.* Defeated, she threw the pack of smokes across the room.

Her mind raced. *This is serious. Who are these people?*

In a panic, she scribbled a quick note and left it on the counter for her sometimes boyfriend in case he stopped by after work. She kept it brief and simply stated that her mom needed her and that she would be back in a few days. She looked at the list of hiding places, let out a grunt, and started collecting the cash she had just stashed.

Last minute, she added a P.S. to the note, mentioning that she had been hacked online and not to pay attention to any emails or posts, not that he was really an online type of guy.

Then she texted her mom: *I'm coming home.*

Across the city, at his desk surrounded by flashing screens, Roger Palmer saw Gemma's text ping on the surveillance monitor he'd set up just for Tess's project. He immediately called Red to tell him the target would be on the move soon, to her mom's house in New Jersey.

Red said, "Keep tabs."

31

M ontague scrambled to erase a minor trail of calls and texts that would tie him to the hiring of the charlatan. Once finished, his crooked finger hovered over the delete icon for calls to and from the Russian contact as well. He couldn't decide if having a record or not having a record would be better. *Either way, I'm probably going to hang.* Hindsight being what it was, he regretfully admitted this whole plan to consort with the Russians had been precarious at best.

"I'm an intellect, not a common criminal," he mumbled, trying to soothe his wounded ego.

He moved to the window overlooking a courtyard off his study. He felt pressure in his chest like he couldn't take a deep breath. The lab murder had him jittery. So, when the phone rang, he jumped. *What now?*

He glanced at the caller ID, and finding none, he knew immediately who it was. "Montague here."

"I solved your *lab rat* problem," the Russian said then broke into a maniacal laugh.

Heat flew up Montague's neck and cheeks. "Actually, you didn't. In fact, you simply put a big spotlight on everything. The police are investigating. Lucky for you, your village idiot killed the wrong guy, so our research can continue."

"It sounds like you are calling me stupid. I think it's you that's stupid."

"It won't matter who gets the gold star here if you expose us," Montague countered.

"Expose us? No. The way I see it, I did you a favor."

Shocked at the twist the criminal had put on the whole situation, Montague went to sit and almost missed the chair. His brow glistened with sweat as he spoke, "Let's just lie low for a few days. I'll make sure this blows over. No more surprises, though. We don't need the complication. The whole deal could blow up over this."

"You better not let that happen, or there will be a new target, and my guy won't get it wrong next time."

Montague understood the innuendo—even in its pathetic representation. He knew the Russians would kill him without a second thought if they saw fit to do so. The two disconnected, and after a few deep breaths, Montague opened the data cache again and downloaded more files from the database for his personal records. He needed an insurance plan of sorts in case things started to go south with the Russians. *Or maybe they already have.*

32

G emma yanked her overstuffed suitcase down the street toward the train station, causing the wheels to smack loudly on every crack. Flustered and breathless, she said, "Ugh. I need a drink. I can catch the six o'clock instead."

With her unkempt, sandy-blond hair blowing in a gust of wind, she flipped her head to avoid being swatted with the loose strands and spotted a bar just across the street. *That'll do.* Once inside, the hostess led her to a two-person booth. She stowed her roller bag in the aisle, but kept her purse closely at her side, the money hidden within.

Her stomach growled. "Hey, can I go ahead and order?"

The hostess huffed but obliged.

"Thanks. I'll just have onion rings and a pint of your house lager."

The hostess grumbled as she traipsed away.

Curious, she surveyed the place. This wasn't her usual stomping ground; from what she could see, locals definitely dressed a lot nicer in this neighborhood. Suddenly, her eyes landed on an all-too-familiar figure, a tall lean man with wavy, dark-blond hair working behind the bar on the far side of the room.

"You have to be kidding me." She leaned forward as if that alone would enhance her eyesight. Fumbling through her purse while still watching the man, she dug hopelessly until her fingers caught on the edges of the creased photograph. Her wild eyes ping-ponged from the photo to the man. *I can't tell for sure. Just turn around. Turn around.*

Finally, he did.

It's him. She couldn't believe her luck—bad luck—and the slow burn of anger grew inside her chest. Even when she tried to unwind for a few measly minutes, the poison of the whole situation still found her.

What were the odds, for chrissakes?

Todd Burkhardt. Her mark for the hotel ruse.

Emboldened by the thought of all the trouble she'd had since the regretful encounter, she raised her voice, calling out to him. "Hey, Todd."

The man stared, but he didn't seem to recognize her. She glanced up to the ceiling while mumbling softly, "I'm not your type, obviously." Raising her freckled hand, she motioned to him. Willingly, he came around from behind the bar and approached her.

"Hello," he said, almost like a question. No sign of recognition crossed his features.

Was she that forgettable?

"Hi, there," she said. "Guess you don't remember me, huh?"

"I'm sorry. A lot of people come in here. I promise, I won't forget next time." He offered a genuine smile.

"You work here?"

"I'm the owner, actually. And you are?"

Her words tasted bitter as she replied, "Really? I have to spell it out? We sort of met at the hotel that day. Remember now? You turned me down."

His expression changed quickly—an *aha* moment, then something darker. He pointed to the booth as a way of asking to sit. She nodded.

He slid in then leaned toward her over the table. "Hey, you caused me a lot of trouble."

"Likewise." She spat out the words. "My life has been a train wreck since that job."

"Job?" He put a hand to his forehead, mouth hanging open for a moment. His next words were delivered with a sharp tone brimming with rage. "I knew it. I was set up. You—" He stopped abruptly when he realized others were looking in his direction. Instead, he just shook his head, his angry eyes boring into her.

"Listen up, Sherlock." She didn't have time for his soap-opera long pause as he processed the revelation. Instead, she laid it all out there in one swoop. "Here's the deal. Someone killed both my dog and my mom's, stole part of my money, used me as a punching bag, and hacked my social media and email accounts. Oh yeah, and let's not forget the threatening note."

Then a new expression from Todd: one of confusion. "What? Look, I'm not sure what you're getting at, but I need to know why you did this. What do you want from me?" He snapped his fingers at her. "Start talking. Now. I'm not kidding."

"What do I want from you? Nothing, except answers as to why I'm being targeted. People are trying to destroy my life, what little there is of it to destroy. I want to know who it is. And for the record, I'm not kidding either."

"Destroy *your* life?" His nostrils flared, and he pounded the table with his fist.

She hadn't expected him to get so ticked off. She held up her hands and said, "Chill out. Here's what I know. Some old guy, gray hair, grouch, the whole bit ... Anyway, his name is Norman Montague. He's the one who hired me to"—she wiggled her fingers around, searching for the right word—"play that trick on you. But ever since the job, things have been going badly for me. At first, I thought it was him or his guy, the one who was sort of the go-between, the driver that day. But get this: it wasn't Jamie, I mean his driver guy, coming after me. At least, I'm pretty sure it wasn't after I found him beat to a pulp in my hallway." She fidgeted with the cardboard coaster as she waited for some sort of response.

His face went deep red as if he might just punch someone—maybe her. But he leaned his head against the back of the booth, staring off into the distance, unmoving, except to whisper the name, "Montague."

"You know him?" She moved her face to connect with his eyes. "Hey, do you think it is him, after all? I'm assuming ... well, since you seem pretty in the dark, it's not you. Because I kind of thought maybe it could be you."

He blinked a few times, and she noticed his jaw tighten. Finally their eyes locked, and he said, "Norman Montague? From Ludwell Corporation?"

"That's the one, yeah." She felt calmer somehow with the shared association.

Just then, the waiter approached with her food, but Todd waved him off.

"Hey, wait." She reached out to stop the young man, but he'd already turned his back. Her stomach growled louder this time as her order floated away, untouched on the tray. "Thanks a lot," she said to Todd, who had a distraught look.

"I need you to tell me everything." Then he stood and said, "Come to the back—we can talk in my office."

A rush of panic filled her empty stomach as she protested. "No. I don't know you. We can stay right here. In the open."

He screwed up his face. "Yet somehow—not so long ago, in fact—you were willing to go into a very private hotel room with me. Your excuse doesn't fly. Get up."

She gasped at the undeniable weight of his words and at the stern grip he had on her arm. Finding herself defeated, she followed him with her shoulders slumped, all the way to his office, away from prying eyes.

~33~

On her way home from the office, Tess's phone buzzed. *Todd*. She sighed. Couldn't he leave well enough alone? Apparently not. She'd call him back later, but within seconds, he rang again.

"I see where this is going," she mumbled. She knew he'd keep calling, so to avoid the whole dramatic back and forth, she answered. Skipping the hellos, she began with a get-to-the-point demeanor. "What is so important?"

"We need to talk. Today. Can you come to the bar? In an hour?"

The psychologist side of her recognized an unfamiliar tension in his voice. "Is everything okay?"

"No."

"I'm actually just a few blocks away. I'll be there in fifteen."

"Thanks." Uncharacteristically, he hung up without a goodbye.

A tinge of anxiety took hold. Something was definitely wrong. She asked Clint to stop by Todd's bar.

A few minutes later, she stood just inside in search of him.

"Tess," he said from behind her, and she spun around. He offered to take her coat, and she allowed it.

"What's the emergency, Todd?"

"We should talk in private," he said, leading her toward his office at the back of the building.

So cloak-and-dagger, she thought. And he hadn't even tried to hug or kiss her. Zero on the affection front. Totally unlike him.

Once in the office, he wasted no time shutting the door behind them. "You should sit for this."

"Really, I'm fine. What is it?" She leaned against the closed door, not wanting to get caught up in a long conversation with her ex, especially when she still had no inkling of what he had to say.

"I think you should sit. Please." He pulled out a chair and gestured for her to take a seat.

Stubbornly, she perched on the edge of the seat, refusing to fully succumb to his direction.

He cleared his throat, dragged his fingers through his hair, and said, "I think we agreed a while back that I was set up—with the pictures and stuff."

Her chest rose as she sucked in a breath and gritted her teeth. She had no desire to rehash this topic, but the way he was looking at her gave her pause. "I'm listening."

"As of today, I know for sure. I have real confirmation."

This was not something she'd been expecting to hear from him. Her interest was fully piqued. "How?"

"The woman, the one from the hotel ... she came here today."

The news caused her chest to constrict a little. "What? Why?"

"Well, I'm not completely sure, but I think it was a coincidence. Anyway, that's not important. Here's the kicker. She said that Norman Montague hired her. Your boss! And that maybe he or someone else was tormenting her."

"Tormenting her?"

"Yeah, well, that part is a little cloudy still."

She plopped down fully into the chair. "Montague. I knew it." A pause, then, "What do you mean by *tormenting her*?"

"Someone's killed her dog, her mom's dog, had her beat up, harassed her online or hired someone to ... who knows? But it's sick, twisted. I don't think she's making it up either."

She didn't blink or breathe for several seconds. The silence became loud, uncomfortable.

She said, "That makes no sense. Did you say dogs were killed?"

"Yep." He shoved his hands into his jeans pockets and leaned back against the desk.

She pressed her lips together until they hurt. She didn't know what to make of the dog slayings, but one thing did sound familiar. The online harassment. That had a *Roger* ring to it. She kept that to herself. "Why would Montague target us or me or do this at all?"

"I don't know. How does one explain crazy? But it's what she said. That he hired her."

Her fingers rubbed her temples. She needed to think. After a few seconds, thinking she already knew the answer, she asked, "What's her name? The woman from today."

"Gemma. Gemma Stein."

Time seemed to stand still. That name again. The same one Vail had told her. Then it struck her where she'd heard it first—in Montague's office. Flustered, she was at a loss for words, but her mind was going at breakneck speed.

"I believe her. I really do," Todd said. "How else would she know Montague?"

She could barely breathe let alone respond.

"Tess, I have no freaking idea what this is about. He's your boss."

She waved her hand. "I know. I know. I'm not sure what he has to gain from doing this either."

"Oh. And there was another guy, a middleman who picked her up for the job, paid her."

A flash of fear carried one word across her lips, "Why?"

Todd kept talking, "You know what? I don't think she even knows why Montague wanted the job done. I'm no expert, but I doubt the hired hand is usually privy to the *why* in these situations." He paused, kicking his foot across the floor, "I should have asked why." Then he spoke again, "Do you believe me now?"

"I do. I don't doubt her involvement with Montague. I'm just trying to put the pieces together ..."

He cut her off, shaking his head, "No, not about that. I mean that none of this was my doing. That I didn't betray you that day." His face wore a mixture of anger and hurt. Yet, she caught a slight tone in his voice, something a bit self-righteous.

"I get that you need validation. I'm officially giving it to you. This was not your fault. I think that's a bit beside the point now, though."

"I disagree. It's exactly the point. You blew up our relationship over this."

With a pit in her stomach, she said, "I'm sorry."

"Thank you." That was all he said, but she could tell he wanted more from her.

"But it wasn't that simple. You know that. There were problems brewing before this happened." Reluctantly, she met his gaze. She swallowed hard as she thought about Vail. Guiltily, she looked away, but could feel him watching her. She changed gears. "Let's just focus on figuring out why Montague is after us. Okay?"

"That's it, really? You don't want to work this out between us first?" His voice rose at the end, and he tempered himself with a deep breath.

She wanted to leave, causing her words to come out colder than she meant them to be. "Not now. Not here. Listen, the good news is I don't think Montague is after you. It's got to be me."

"How's that good news? I'd rather it be me."

"I know. Thank you for saying that." Her heart softened a bit. "Hey, we'll talk about us, just not tonight."

He looked shipwrecked.

She gazed at the floor, chewed her lip. In fact, she almost went to him. For a second, she thought how easy it would be to just erase the past few weeks and go back to their "normal," which had been nice, predictable. She blinked the thought away. No. That was water under the bridge for her now.

A quiet knock interrupted. "Hey, Todd. You in there?"

She shot up from the chair and flung open the door, ignoring Todd's signal to not answer. Within seconds, she slipped past the man in the hallway and escaped straight out the back door. The cool night air rushed into her lungs.

I need to tell someone.

Her first thought was to call Vail. But he always seemed so hurt when she mentioned Todd. No. She needed to tell someone neutral.

Roger.

Roger grinned at his accomplishment. The surveillance install on Montague's office and his devices had been a success and quicker than expected. He'd set everything up in only a few hours. Pleased, he tossed cheese puffs into his mouth as he reviewed the fresh footage. "What's he up to?"

The old man appeared to be literally sweating bullets—wiping his forehead with a handkerchief and plucking at his shirt collar all while pecking at his computer. Primed and ready to catch him at something, Roger cross-referenced Montague's computer usage with the footage.

"He's grabbing data and a lot of it. Whoa." *I think the little leprechaun is up to no good.*

He needed to dig deeper, so he created new code. "And let's establish a little digital logbook for you, Norman. Time stamp and destination file ... mmm, yes." His fingers flew across the keyboard as if he were a concert pianist. He was definitely making his own music.

Roger twisted greasy fingers in a napkin, which he crumbled then tossed at the trash bin across the room. He missed, and it landed among the dozen or so other balled-up papers on the floor. He thought about cleaning up the scattered mess, but his phone rang. So, he gladly let that notion go and answered with, "Hola."

"Cute, Roger, but I'm not in the mood."

"Sorry. What can I do for you?"

"I know who set me up." Tess's words dropped like an iron gate.

"Give me a minute." Roger scrambled the signal. He'd learned a long time ago to never overrate privacy. "I'm all ears." He wondered if maybe he should jump in with an update of his own, but before he could speak, she started talking.

She explained in detail what she'd just learned from Todd about Gemma. Then she said definitively, "It's Montague."

"Yes. I heard similar information from Red. I've already set up surveillance on his devices."

"What? When? You don't waste a second." Then under her breath, she said, "I need to meet this man, Red."

"To be clear, I haven't known long, just a few hours. I'm sure he will be calling you soon."

"It's fine, Roger. I'm not worried about any of that. But I do have some questions. Todd mentioned someone had killed Gemma Stein's dogs, hacked her, physically assaulted her."

"I'm not aware of the dogs or any attack, but ..." He let that trail there for a moment, then he updated her on how he'd been working Gemma over through her social media accounts and email.

She seemed unaffected, thankfully, because all she said in response was, "I figured that was you. I do agree with Red that we need to watch Montague. Besides, I want more than just Stein's word that he's behind all of this. Can you get some solid proof?"

"Hell yeah."

"Good. Do what you need to do. Oh, and ... gracias."

"De nada." He beamed. *She does like my humor.*

~35~

In the elevator on the way to Tess's apartment, Vail spun the engagement ring on his pinky. A lump formed in his throat as he remembered how she'd given it back to him almost two years ago exactly. "Don't push it." He leered at his reflection in the mirrored wall. Now wasn't the time to move too quickly. So, he tucked the ring back into the box and shoved it deep into his coat pocket. He had to be satisfied with the fact that Tess was letting him back into her world again. That had to be enough for now.

Besides, they had more urgent things to think about. Like Gemma Stein. Like Montague's role in whatever game he was playing.

Tess met him at the elevator door. "I'm glad you are here. I was just speaking with Roger. I have news." From the way she twisted her hands, he didn't think the news would be good.

He let out a deep breath. "I have news too. Want to draw straws?"

She said, "It's Montague. He's behind it all. I'm ninety percent sure, I think."

"Yes. I was about to tell you the same thing. Roger beat me to it, I guess."

There was a moment's hesitation. He followed her into the kitchen, where she poured two glasses of wine.

Suddenly, Tess seemed faraway in her thoughts, gripping her glass with white knuckles.

"Hey, is there something else?" He touched her arm.

"It's just ..." Her shoulders dropped. "I feel guilty. It wasn't really Todd's fault. I just ... I don't know. I left things undone."

His chest ached. He tried his best to not seem jealous or hurt, but he didn't want her to lose perspective. "He still could have been honest with you from the beginning."

"I know. But I'm starting to understand a little why maybe he wasn't. Maybe I was too hard on him."

His mind echoed with the sound of her last words as he tried to push away the stinging pain in his throat that accompanied the thought of her ever going back to Todd.

"Anyway, Montague is the real culprit. What he did to those dogs ..."

He winced, realizing he had his own truth to tell.

"Did Roger tell you about the dogs?"

"Oh, no." She paused and screwed up her lips, as if considering something. "I have to be honest."

Oh God.

"Todd's the one who told me about both Montague and the dogs. I stopped by to see him, at his request. He called. Gemma was at his bar today."

Vail knew his face betrayed his shock and confusion at her words. "That snake."

"Have to agree with you there," Tess said. "Montague has always been a bit conniving."

But Vail hadn't been talking about Montague. The snake was Todd. No denying it, he felt threatened. Todd had taken Tess from him once. Vail couldn't let it happen again.

Tess continued. "I talked to Roger right after I saw Todd. Anyway, even though Montague's a shifty sort, a crime like that, with the dogs and all ... it just doesn't fit the psych profile of someone like him."

Feet to the fire, he didn't have a choice; he had to clear this up immediately. Gripping the stem of his wineglass, he paced around. She followed him with her gaze, looking inquisitively at him—or so he thought.

He didn't want to mess things up between them. He tried to force a smile, but his lips quivered slightly. He chided himself for being such a wimp.

"Let's sit," he said, motioning toward the couch in the adjoining room.

"What is it?" She didn't move.

Out of options, he just said it. "The dogs weren't Montague's doing. It was Red's guy." He put his hands up in a hear-me-out fashion. "Before you say anything, just know, it's a bit more complicated than that, and I already told him you wouldn't like it—I didn't either. Oh, and not that this makes it much better, but the dogs weren't actually tortured."

She stared blankly at him, as if she hadn't fully grasped what he was saying. Then, in a whisper, she dragged out the word, "What?"

But what more could he say?

Tess started doing a little pacing of her own. "I think it's time I officially meet this Red character. I thought he was in London, though. He's been trying to manage all this from London?"

"No. Red's here. Yes, I met him in London after our middle-of-the-night phone call. But he's here in New York now. Working on this for us."

"This type of situation can't happen again. This is horrible."

"I agree. Red said this guy is new and clearly a little nuts. A caveat of the business, I guess. But Red's got him under control now."

"Good grief. You know me, and I don't use the word *nuts* ever, but in this case ..." Her words trailed off into oblivion, along with her stare.

The relief that she wasn't angry—at least not at him—soared through his body. He needed to sit.

Tess continued. "Bottom line. I want to meet Red. Soon."

Normally he would argue that it was unnecessary, but no way would he push his luck tonight, and so he agreed with a nod and then gulped his wine to keep from saying anything else.

The doorman buzzed. *Thank God.* Vail sprang at the opportunity to abandon the topic for what he hoped would be the rest of the evening. "Food's up."

~36~

MONDAY, OCTOBER 1

From the street, Lawrence spotted Cathy at a small table near the window at the coffee shop. She didn't look great, kind of smaller than he remembered, and worn down. He suddenly felt tense. They had planned to meet here to ride into work together for her first day back to the office since Bret's murder. She didn't really look ready. He hadn't wanted to press her too hard, but Montague had been almost threatening about getting Cathy back. A "race against the clock." Research needed to "restart, pronto." The guy was like a mosquito that wouldn't go away until he drew blood. Literally.

Lawrence forced a smile as he plopped down in the chair across from Cathy. "Hey there."

"Hi," She had dark circles and sounded really exhausted.

He tried to keep the moment upbeat. "Ready to start fresh?"

"I'm not sure. I've barely slept since ... you know."

"I know. Maybe getting back into a routine will help."

"I keep imagining Bret's chair, the desk, just sitting there, empty." A tear formed in her eye, but somehow it didn't fall.

He handed her a napkin. "No. I moved things around a bit." He couldn't help feeling guilty for pushing her to be over this so soon—she'd been the one to find him, after all. And he knew he probably shouldn't be this okay either, but if he focused on his emotional side now, he may drop the ball and end up with the same fate as Bret.

She dabbed her eye with the napkin and took in a shuddering breath. "I need this job."

"Me too. Look, we can do this." They stared at each other for a moment, and he clasped her hand across the table, adding, "Together." He hoped it wasn't too aggressive a move.

She gave a sad smile and a forced nod.

Not too aggressive, then. Good.

Standing, he gallantly held out his hand, and she took it. "I'm ready, I think."

Something stirred in his soul as he thought about the magnitude of trust she seemed to be putting in him. He hoped he could live up to it.

~37~

T ess studied Montague with a new curiosity akin to observing a
zoo animal in a glass cage. So far, the despicable man seemed to
be keeping a safe distance from her, which proved unusual.

Was it a guilty conscience? Maybe. She was thinking it could be
something else altogether. But what? *Oh the webs we weave.*

She tapped her pen on the desk and decided to create a timeline of
events. Maybe if she laid it all out in black and white, she could put her
finger on what fueled his vendetta against her. But pinpointing the
actual beginning of this witch hunt ... she was stumped.

Tap, tap, tap.

True, they were like oil and water, but could clashing personalities
justify trying to ruin her personal life, even for someone as vicious as
him. It seemed too petty a reason. *The risk needs to match the gain.
Sticking it to me just for kicks isn't worth the risk. What did you mean to
achieve, Norman?*

She began recounting.

"What happened in January, February, March? Nothing really."

She swiveled in her chair, biting the end of the pen. "This is
pointless."

Then she remembered something and began to scribble notes.

June:
Todd and I visited Ludwell winery. Montague attended too. Todd called him a strange bloke after a long conversation. What did they talk about?
Mid-July:
Blood sample requests started.
August:
Montague out of town—Russia for 3 weeks
September:
Incident with Todd. Lawrence gets my blood sample. Montague avoiding me (maybe).

But the big question remained: WHY?

Her thoughts whirred. She needed answers. Reluctantly, she called Todd. He picked up after the first ring.

She jumped right in. "Hi. Quick question."

"Sure." His tone was hesitant.

"Do you by chance remember the conversation you had with Montague at the winery?"

He stayed silent, then, "Wait. I think ..." as if pieces were flinging together in his mind.

"You remember something?"

"Yes. I can't believe I forgot about that."

"What? The conversation?"

"Well, yes. It just can't be."

"What?" Her voice cracked a little.

"I can't believe I didn't see this all along. Montague's the one who introduced me to the sommelier I met that day at the hotel, when Gemma ..."

"Are you sure?"

"Totally. That's what we discussed. A meeting at that hotel. Bloody hell. You think he's been planning since then?"

"Kinda looks like it. I just can't figure why. Are you sure there wasn't anything else discussed?"

He stayed quiet. She assumed he was replaying the conversation in his memory.

Then he moaned.

"What?" she demanded.

"This is going to sound weird. Well, maybe not considering Lineage is a DNA company."

"Spit it out, please."

"He asked if I could help persuade you to submit a DNA test."

"What? And you didn't tell me?"

"Umm."

"Oh, never mind." She almost dished out an insult about his withholding yet another piece of information, but instead she said, "Gotta go," and disconnected before another tiff about their relationship could start.

Fuming, she stood and circled the desk, thinking.

When the *aha* moment hit her, she dialed Roger. "I need you to send an anonymous email to our resident toad."

"Norman, I take it."

"Who else?"

"Not a problem. What do you want it to say?"

Her mouth curled into a grin as she told him what to type.

38

That evening, Vail hopped into a cab heading in a direction that he knew he shouldn't. "I'll just talk to him. Let him know how serious this is. Ask him to contact me with new information instead of her." Vail gave the pep talk under his breath before entering the bar.

He looked around. Todd was nowhere to be found. He still had over an hour to kill before joining Tess at the Ludwell charity event. *What the heck.* He slid onto a barstool and ordered a scotch.

As he finished the last of it, he scanned the area. Still no Todd. "Want another?" the bartender asked. Vail pressed his lips together thinking he shouldn't but nodded anyway.

Well into his second drink, the whiskey stoked the fire in his veins.

Good timing or bad, Todd finally made an appearance, walking right past him, unaware.

For a few minutes, Vail simply eavesdropped. Todd chatted with the bartender first about business, then he muttered something personal about "getting her to listen," "working out this mess," and letting him come home "because she's the one."

Vail's jaw clenched. His hand bore down on the glass. He knew without a doubt that Todd meant Tess. The guy still wanted her back. Couldn't blame him, but he could stop him.

The empathetic bartender offered up some stock advice. "I know that look, man. You just got to wait it out. Give it time. A little Jameson never hurt, either." He slid Todd a small glass of whiskey on the rocks.

A sullen Todd nodded. "Thanks. I'm not sure there's enough whiskey in the whole city to fix this one, though. And I've wasted enough time."

"I've been there, sorry to say. Maybe you just gotta go for broke." The bartender shook his head and wiped the slick wood with a cloth before heading to the back.

Vail chuckled at the exchange, loud enough to catch Todd's attention.

Todd threw a questioning glance.

Vail smacked his lips after a hearty sip and said, "Hey, you know what's worse than knowing you want something? Knowing you will never have it."

"That's dark, man. And not exactly the way that saying goes," Todd said as he started to turn away but then he stopped and eyeballed Vail more closely. "Hey, do I know you?"

"Maybe."

"Remind me."

"You know what, Todd? My name isn't what's important."

He waggled his finger. "I do know you. You're that guy. The one Tess used to date with the cheesy name. Tahoe, or something."

"Very funny. *Engaged to*—way past *date*," Vail clarified, heat rising again.

Todd scoffed, "Whatever, she left you. So it's way past anything now."

"Apparently, she left you too," Vail shot back.

Todd's eyes narrowed. "Says who?"

"Says your pathetic sulking and the cheap whiskey."

"We don't serve cheap whiskey, pal. You must be in the wrong neighborhood. How about you mosey on out of here?"

Vail rose slowly, then leaned over the bar, and spoke in a low, menacing tone. "Listen, *pal*. I'm going to give you a bit of advice. You can consider this your warning. You've stuck your toe in the wrong pool. This isn't your world. I've got it from here." He tossed a few bills on the bar.

"Go to hell." Todd flipped him a low bird, then turned to go down the hall toward the back of the building.

Where is he? Tess wondered as she desperately tried to avoid Montague and, truth be told, any resemblance of mingling altogether at the Ludwell charity event. She peeked at her phone hoping to find a note from Vail that he was on his way. Instead, a text flashed on the screen from Todd that read: *Call off your dog.*

What the on earth was he talking about? She placed her phone back inside her clutch bag and surveyed the crowd. She smiled when she saw Vail approaching with two glasses of champagne.

"One for you, one for me," he said as he sidled up beside her.

"Thanks." She took a sip. "You know ... I just got a strange text." She took her phone out and held it up for him to see.

"Oh. About that."

After the charity event, Montague desired only one thing. Well, two maybe: to sequester himself to his study and to get a handle on the slippery slope with the Russians.

His wife had overdone it on the champagne during the event, and he'd helped her into bed. He stared at her now as she lay there snuggling up with their dog. Quietly, he patted the furry pup then kissed his wife's forehead before slipping down the hallway.

At his desk, he flipped on his computer to check his emails, out of habit more than any real expectation of receiving some important news.

What he saw there, however, was nothing that he could have imagined.

The email read: *I know what you did.* And that was it. He looked for the sender information and got zilch.

The back of his neck prickled as the color drained from his face. *The Russians?* Not really their style. Warily, he leaned his head back against his chair. Moments later, his lips clearly mouthed the word *Tess.* He scowled. She'd seemed smug at the event earlier. This little stunt must be why.

And he knew. Right then and there.

"It's her. That conniving ..." He noticed a slight tremor in his hands as anger, fear, and frustration bubbled within him.

He knew he had pushed Tess Andreas too far, and he wondered how exactly that would play out.

39

TUESDAY, OCTOBER 2

The next afternoon, two coffees in hand, Tess arrived at Grand Central at 4 p.m. for her first meeting with the elusive Red. Not knowing what to expect, she stopped short when she noticed a striking man already standing in the spot she'd designated for the meetup. She watched as his tall figure casually leaned against a column near the busker skillfully playing the cello.

Red's clandestine demeanor evident even from a distance gave her pause. *He looks like Eastwood with a dash of Bond.* She approached, and he coolly turned his head, giving a little nod. For a few seconds, she stood next to him listening to the beautiful cascade of notes flowing from the stringed instrument and wondered if it would be impolite to speak during the performance.

To her relief, Red turned in her direction and said, "Nice to finally meet you."

"You too." She offered him one of the coffees. "I took the liberty of bringing you a coffee. Black. I wasn't sure how you like yours."

"The stronger the better. Thanks." He took a sip. "So, what can I do for you?"

Strangely, she struggled to find her words. A silence fell between them before she said, "I'm not sure of the rules here. What I can say, when, where." Her voice trailed off.

"Rule one: you can say anything to me." He paused and emphasized, "In person."

"Okay." Her voice reached barely a whisper.

"And the basic rule of thumb: never write anything in a text, email, whatever, or say anything over the phone that you wouldn't want exposed."

"Understood." She took a deep breath. "I want to find out why this happened, if it's over, or if I still need to worry."

His brows cinched as if he were sizing her up before he responded. "Not a problem. My guy can handle that. It may take a little push here and there to get information."

"But just inconveniences. No uncivilized stunts." She locked onto his gaze, not even trying to hide the innuendo about the dog predicament.

"You have my word." He closed his eyes briefly as if taking the verbal punch he knew he'd earned. "Inducing paranoia is one of my specialties." His response, although chilling, sounded sincere.

"Good. Paranoia seems fitting." A small smile appeared on her lips. "By the way, expect payment in full on the first assignment. I think we can move on from the woman now."

He clenched his jaw, and then leaned in a little. "Can I make a suggestion?"

"Of course."

"You want paranoia, right? Well, one sure way to ignite that is to mirror the tactics between two targets." He tilted his head and raised his eyebrows.

She raised one eyebrow of her own as the light bulb went on in her mind. "Like with the dogs between the girl and her mom."

He took the second jab about the dogs in stride. "Yep."

She leaned against the large column and thought it all over for a moment, rationalizing that a narcissist like Montague lacked the ability to empathize. This could do the trick just enough to rattle him. Quietly, she said, "You may be onto something."

They locked gazes, and she wondered for a second if he could read her thoughts. He said, "The incidents will be straightforward: flat tires, busted windows, faulty electricity—nothing that will create a police report. Roger's online antics will be intermixed. But the main goal will be that the issues happen to both Stein and Montague."

"But you'll make sure Montague knows the incidents are happening to both him and the girl, right?"

"That usually takes care of itself when the two targets are already in cahoots. Assuming they still are. But yeah, trust me ... we have our ways of keeping paths crossed. Let me worry about the mechanics."

"It's in your hands then, sir." She started to walk away, then stopped and turned back, her hair sweeping over her shoulder. "Your understanding of human nature ... I'm impressed, and rarely do I ever say that to anyone." She looked down and twisted her lips.

There were a few beats of silence. She swore she could feel his stare.

Curiosity winning, she stole a glance upward, catching a slight smile flicker for just a second across his face.

Quickly, she turned to hide her own smirk and disappeared through the arched corridor.

Red's words, *"mirror the incidents,"* replayed in Tess's mind as she rode back to the office. Determined, she scribbled a list in the leather notebook that lay open across her lap. First things first. She needed to bring Roger up to speed on narcissists, give him a crash course in psychological warfare. She didn't think he possessed Red's same intrinsic understanding of the inner workings of the human heart and mind. Once she was sure he'd fully grasped the concepts, then he could start needling both Montague and the woman immediately, using Red's tactic of mirroring—except Roger's attacks would be online.

From a clinical perspective, she knew people like Montague relied heavily on assessing nonverbal cues for emotional information. "Face-to-face is best for you. Tsk. Tsk. Tsk. So, how do I make a weapon through online means?" Of course, Roger would likely have some good ideas of his own. Still, she wanted to offer a few suggestions ...

She flipped to a blank page in her notebook and made a list for Roger.

Some basic hot points:

- *Never use emojis or emotionally leading language (Remove emotional cues)*
- *Be aware that target employs hostile language to intimidate*
- *Target relies on a cache of memorized knowledge to appear intelligent*
- *Actively provoke target toward violence by remaining in control*
- *Impede basic needs: shelter, food, comfort*
- *Expose embarrassing information*
- *Manipulate his finances*

Happy with her list, she snapped the notebook closed and gazed at the blurred scenery that sped by the car window. Her thoughts were racing just as fast, moving from Todd to Vail and then again to the mysterious Red.

40

From the privacy of his rented flat in the old Brooklyn brownstone, Red opened the door to the new recruit, whom he'd nicknamed after Hannibal Lecter for obvious reasons—most recently notable being the dog saga. The two men skipped formal greetings, as proved customary in their line of business.

Red cut to the chase. "The current assignment just got more interesting. There's a second target."

"I'm listening." The guy looked eager. Red thought maybe a little too much so. He'd vowed to keep a tighter rein on this project, and he would. "First, I want to make one thing clear. No more blood and guts."

"I got it—for the second time. Geez."

"The good news is your tit-for-tat playbook will work nicely. So, whatever you do to the girl, you are going to do to the old man. If you slash her tires, you slash his. If you cut his electricity, you cut hers. Got it?"

"Gotcha, Boss. Not a problem."

"And stick to things that won't spark a call to the police." Red realized he was speaking more slowly than he usually did, as if he needed to add some space between each word to make sure his meaning truly sunk in with this knucklehead.

"It'll all be under the radar. I've got this, Boss." Hannibal sounded like a teenager promising not to break curfew again.

Red quirked an eyebrow and watched him for a moment. Then, "I'll expect regular updates and *no surprises*."

"Will do." The guy hopped down from the counter he'd perched himself on and headed toward the back door.

"Just for your information, there will be an online attack happening at the same time. I only mention it so you're aware the targets will likely be agitated from that, which means it probably won't take a lot on your part to push them over the edge. Keep your wits about you if you somehow get approached or caught. Got it?"

"Have faith, man. And for the record, I've never been caught." He scratched his neck, shrugged his shoulders back and forth a few times. Cocky.

"Yeah, yeah," Red muttered as he showed the guy out. Closing the door behind him, he leaned against it, clenching his jaw for a second, hoping that everything would go smoothly this time. He thought about Tess; he'd never met anyone like her—ever. She had a quiet control and precision about her that he couldn't quite figure out. *Keep your head on straight, ol' boy*, he chided himself. Lighting a cigarette, he stepped out onto the narrow balcony.

~41~

Across town, Montague thumbed through the documents the Russians had sent to him about moving forward with the study. He wished he hadn't even told them about Lawrence's theory regarding the anomaly and that Tess had submitted her blood sample, confirming the theory. One good thing, though—he hadn't handed over the actual data yet, or Tess's identity. He'd hold that close to the vest for now.

He knew the Russians wanted to move fast and bring on the deep pockets, and first on their agenda was to form a secret council with funding from benefactors scattered around the globe.

In doing so, they wanted to facilitate a relationship with the blood donor, or at this point, the only donor: Tess Andreas, though they didn't know her name. The plan included meeting somewhere in France, still undetermined.

The idea made him sick to his stomach, so much stress, so much unknown. What had he gotten into? How would he ever convince Tess to go to this meeting? He'd never intended to open a Pandora's box to this level. Hell, if *he* saw this as sketchy, then *she* would no doubt see it as something even worse.

He would have to use smokescreens somehow. For both ends—the Russians and Tess. He clutched his stomach, trying to quell the burning sensation there. To no avail.

Montague's brow glistened with sweat as he read over the introduction provided by the Russian translator. He thought how even the title had a diabolical element—*Blood Secrets: Global Project.*

His anxiety heightened as he read the first paragraph, not really understanding anything fully.

He tossed the papers onto the table, then did some neck stretches, rubbed his temple—trying to ward off the headache that was forming. "Gah! This is too much. I need someone who understands to read this, give me the notes."

And he didn't have to think long about it, for he knew just the poor soul to dump this on, and with his fat, splotchy fingers, he made a call.

Montague grumbled a version of hello.

"How are you, sir?" Lawrence said.

Montague ignored etiquette and jumped straight to the point. "I'm going to leave a file for you with my assistant. Please pick it up this afternoon. I need a summary by tomorrow. It's important. Meet me at my office at eleven tomorrow morning to go over the information."

"Ummm, okay ..." The young scientist dragged out his words, which irritated the old man.

"Do you have another more pressing obligation?" Montague snapped at him.

"No. Well, yes, actually. I have analytics running. That's why I postponed our usual Wednesday meeting to—"

Irritated, he cut him off midsentence. "Isn't this type of situation one of the reasons why I'm footing the bill for you to have an assistant?"

The line went silent. Montague let the uncomfortable moment linger.

"Yes. It's not a problem. I'll be there," Lawrence said quickly, then added, "Could I get some context of what I will be reviewing exactly?"

"It's highly confidential. For your eyes only." Abruptly, he hung up, even though Lawrence had started to say something else.

Montague had no interest in hearing anything other than what the hell the Russian document actually meant. He needed to get a handle on the Russians taking the wheel so aggressively. Losing control of this study, he instinctively knew, would spell disaster for himself—in more ways than one.

P ressing mute on the television remote, Lawrence groaned, crumpled his napkin, and tossed the paper plate covered in taco crumbs to the other side of the coffee table. Reluctantly, he opened the folder that he'd retrieved from Doris earlier that day.

Blood Secrets: Global Project. The surreal words caused a jolt of panic as he wondered what he'd gotten himself into.

With every page, another red flag pinged his brain. Suddenly, he felt split in two. As a scientist, his mouth watered and his curiosity stirred at what he was reading. *Oh the possibilities!* Just the hypothesis of disease resistance made him swoon. Not to mention the funding. "A bottomless bankroll," he whispered. But the human part of him, the part with a conscience and a soul and a moral obligation to his fellow man ... well, that part prickled with dread. He felt a sickness in his gut, as if he were privy to an omen of sorts. He attempted to shake off the negative feelings and focus only on the science aspect.

He looked at his trusty feline friend, Atom. "This shouldn't be a bad thing, right? Can you imagine? Viral resistance is like the Holy Grail to living longer." His thoughts spun as his fingers combed through the feline's soft fur. Then, he picked up the phone and called the one person he felt would understand.

"Hey, Cathy, you still awake?"

"I answered the phone, didn't I?" She giggled.

"True. So ... can I run some existential thoughts by you?"

"Sure. Hang on a sec."

Lawrence could hear her shuffling around. He waited.

"Lay it on me."

"Alrighty, here's what I'm thinking. Without viruses, a human being could potentially live a lot longer, right?"

"Theoretically, yes. I mean, there's other things—cancer, bacteria, car accidents ..."

"Yes, yes. Just indulge me a little."

"I guess without viruses, lifespans could increase significantly. However, that could pose problems for population growth on Earth."

"I agree with all that too. And just a disclaimer, this isn't my line of thinking—it's a bit superhero-villain style, but this discovery could become a commodity for whomever owns it."

"Uh-huh."

"And there's a lot of money in stopping viruses through vaccines already, so imagine eradicating their threat altogether, forever."

"Okayyy. I'm getting a little weirded out here."

"I know. I know. Just hear me out. The process of harvesting, testing, and categorizing viral resistance for the entire human species is a massive project that should take decades if not centuries."

"Technically, yes."

"Unless there is a company that's already been collecting genetic data for a decade."

"Hmmm. I think I know where you're going with this, but I have to admit I don't know why."

"I don't either, not exactly. But I'm concerned we are both about to find out in a very real way."

They stayed silent for a moment.

Cathy cleared her throat and asked, "Does this have to do with the Russian lab?"

He didn't want to answer, but he knew he had to. "I'm afraid it does."

"That's not good news, then."

"Nope."

Across town sitting on a stool in his own bar, Todd fought off yet another late-night yawn. He hadn't slept through the night since the breakup. He missed her even when he wasn't thinking about her, and now he feared he'd alienated her even more with his lashing out about Vail in the last text message.

I'm such an idiot sometimes, he chided himself, referring to not only the whiny text to Tess, but also the entire handling of that day in the hotel lobby.

No stranger to desperate people and manipulative types, he thought he'd seen it all between the bar and the streets of the rough Yonkers neighborhood where he'd grown up too fast—plenty of weird people, weird behavior. Yes, over time, he'd numbed to the shenanigans of people like Gemma. Unfortunately, this particular predicament had caught him off guard.

He shook his head in defeat. Escaping the tainted world of his childhood had been one of the biggest reasons he'd moved to the city—except that hadn't solved a thing, really. The culprits were better dressed and harder to spot. Bad intentions didn't observe zip codes.

Taking a swig of beer, he thought about how he'd let things slip in terms of giving Tess the attention she deserved, knowing he'd taken the lazy route too often. Taken the relationship for granted. He'd made it easy for her to cut him out of her life.

And how he handled the hotel incident had dredged up the old trust issues—he silently cursed his reluctance to commit fully when they'd first gotten together. If only he'd made a clean break with his ex before he'd gotten serious with Tess. He took a bigger gulp of his lager.

His chest ached as he thought about how abruptly she'd shut down her emotions toward him after those photos had shown up on her doorstep. Yes, he had seen her turn ice cold in her professional world, but he'd never felt the effects firsthand. *Brutal.*

One thing poked at him, though. He smelled a rat and couldn't help but think that her figurative door-slam had quite the Vail ring to it, and if he were being honest, he worried that the Ivy League pretty boy would convince her to marry him again.

He swirled the remnants of his beer around the bottom of the glass. Frustration rose within him. "I have to try. I can't give up on her."

"That's the spirit," the patron on the stool said in a beer-fragranced slur.

He needed to get out of there. A decision was made.

Twenty minutes later, he stood in the lobby of the building where he'd once lived with Tess, feeling like an outsider. Miles, the doorman, had always been a bit standoffish, and it seemed he hadn't warmed up any.

"I'll let Dr. Andreas know you are here," Miles said in a clipped monotone.

Todd tried his best to hear what Miles mumbled into the phone, but the doorman was nothing if not an expert at discretion. Then, to his surprise, Miles nodded and motioned toward the elevator. Todd straightened his shirt and ran his fingers through his hair as he rode up to her floor. He wiped his clammy hands on his jeans a couple of times, but it proved futile. Talk about a cat on a hot tin roof.

She stood waiting for him as the elevator doors parted. His heart skipped a beat, and he swallowed hard. When they locked gazes, he sensed that old connection and couldn't help but wonder if she did too.

She invited him in, rather formally, and they sat in the living room, exchanging awkward pleasantries at first. But enough was enough; it was time to put it all out there. Todd scooted toward the edge of the couch, put his elbows on his knees, and leaned in.

"Tess, it's still me. It's still us. We are in control. We can choose at any time to put this all behind us. In fact, we could leave this place, go anywhere in the world. Somewhere we can be alone—away from all of this noise. Reconnect. And I promise you that I will never hurt you again. Just say the word." His heart was beating so hard he swore she could see it through his shirt.

She gently took his hand, weaving their fingers together, but she didn't respond.

"I miss you all the time." He wanted to say much more but couldn't find the words.

She simply looked into his eyes.

He wondered if he should kiss her. Then the elevator opened in her foyer followed by loud footsteps. Todd's shoulders dropped as the visitor appeared.

"What are you doing here? Tess, what is going on?" Vail's angry stare and questioning tone crashed into the private moment like an iceberg.

Startled, she pulled her hand away from his.

Todd jumped to his feet, fighting the urge to lunge at the intruder. "She's fine." The intensity of his words fueled the tension in the room exponentially.

Tess stood too. "Let's all just calm down."

"We're calm." Vail's tone strongly suggested the opposite.

Tess escorted Vail to the kitchen. "Just give us a few minutes."

Voices trickled in from the other room. No way he would continue this conversation with that jerk waiting in the wings, so Todd reached in his pocket and left a coin, tails up, smack in the middle of the coffee table. He knew the meaning would not be lost on her. That had been their game when they needed to make decisions—which couch to keep, which trip to take, which movie to see. He'd always told her she'd turned his world upside down the moment they met. So, in their world, tails always won.

From the kitchen where Tess and Vail stood, the sound of the elevator closing landed brutal in the moment.

"He left." The words escaped shrouded in her breath.

"Probably for the best," Vail tagged on.

Cutting her eyes at him in frustration, she decided to let her emotions about both of them go unresolved for tonight.

Feeling a bit melancholy, she trudged toward the living room, kicking off her red-soled stilettos along the way. From the corner of her eye, she observed Vail pouring two glasses of Macallan 18. As she did quite often, she moved to the floor-to-ceiling window in her living room overlooking Central Park, bracing her hands on the edge of the pane. The lights below flickering with life moved around the streets like fireflies, and she knew that somewhere in the midst of it all, Todd was riding back to his side of town, alone. A deep breath filled her lungs as she tightened her hold on the coin hidden in the palm of her hand.

"Are you mad? I know I overreacted. I'm sorry."

She turned to look at him, feeling a slight sting in her eyes. The pause between them felt strained.

"You know this isn't about him being the bad guy, right?" She spoke softly.

"Yes. For you it isn't, but I resent that he got a year and a half with you that I didn't." He couldn't hide the hurt; she could see it clearly.

"Are you finished now?"

"Yep." He took a sip of his drink.

She turned back to the view, the coin still warm in her grip.

"Tess?"

"No." She knew his question without him asking. He couldn't stay the night.

"I love you." And with that, she heard the clink of his glass as he set it on the table. She turned just as the elevator shut, catching a glimpse of him wearing a slight grin. She heard him mumble, "At least *he's* gone."

~44~

THURSDAY, OCTOBER 4

Tucked away at a back table in a seedy bar at noon on a Thursday in Manhattan, Norman Montague discreetly wiped the sweat from his hands onto his pants as he waited for the Russian to arrive. The rest of the dismal place remained empty, except for a bartender and a couple of goons that he recognized as part of the Russian group he'd been dealing with for months now.

A stern hand came down on his shoulder from behind, startling him. Straining, he craned his neck to see the face behind the action.

"Hello, Norman." The Russian's pinky ring glimmered in the dim light.

"Hello, Mr. Borin. How have you been?" Norman shifted to stand in order to properly greet the man, but the hand on his shoulder pushed down hard.

"No. Don't get up." Rudlof Borin moved toward the other side of the table mumbling, "Relax. Relax, my friend."

Norman gave in to the command and remained in his seat.

The Russian slid roughly into his chair and continued. "I hear you have the sample we need."

"Testing is underway." Montague hoped his ambiguous answer would fly, counting on the language barrier to help in that matter.

"Yes. Yes." The Russian waved his hand. "I want my lead researcher to meet yours. Soon."

The remark sparked a twinge of fear causing Montague to speak before thinking. "That wasn't part of the plan. I can't risk that exposure."

"Plan has changed." Borin's stare lingered. Cold, unmovable.

"What I mean is you'll have all of the research. A meeting isn't necessary."

"You misunderstand my motivation. No?"

Confused, Norman waited for more.

"It's a compliment. Your researcher is quite efficient. The research is beyond what we have seen, and my scientist needs to learn quickly."

"Even so, I don't think we should have the scientists intermingle. It could bring the wrong attention and blow this whole thing out into the open. I need to keep Ludwell Corporation insulated from our business dealings."

Borin picked up his drink and swirled the amber liquid. "You are not a scientist, no?" The question obviously rhetorical, Montague didn't know quite how to answer except with the obvious reply.

"Of course not."

"So, who is going to train my team? If not your scientist?" He paused, then in a visibly angry manner said, "Now, if you do not wish, then ..."

Sensing an overt threat, Norman interrupted, "Fine. I'll set it up." His hands went from sweaty to clammy, and he could barely swallow—his throat had gone dry.

The Russian's face softened, yet he spoke with just a touch of arrogance. "Good. Smart man. Now, we have a lot to talk about."

Montague winced—on the inside—afraid of what the man seemed to have up his Mafioso sleeve.

"The forming of the council. It will be in France. My men, they will take care of the details. You just make sure your scientist and the subject are there. Do you understand?"

"Yes." He had no fuel left to argue another point that would most likely end the same as the first—with him overpowered by the stone-cold Mr. Borin.

Borin flicked his hand in the direction of one of his goons and said, "This is Ivan. He's my interpreter."

Montague tried not to roll his eyes and state the obvious that Mr. Borin did not seem to need an interpreter. From the looks of Ivan, he had other specialties, like brutality.

Ivan snapped to, handing over a file folder stacked with papers to Mr. Borin. Norman eyed the pinky ring as the hand wearing it pushed the file toward him.

"What's this?"

"It's a plan. I've sent it to you in an encrypted file as well. Do not share this information with anyone."

Norman swallowed the lump in his throat and shook his head in agreement.

After a handshake, the men parted.

The hairs on the back of Montague's neck prickled as he rode back to the office, thinking about how this had spiraled out of control so quickly. The original agreement to collect and sell data had long since been lost. In its purest form, the deal had been a simple expansion of what Lineage already did—in a sense at least. And, yes, there existed a slight paper trail through legal, but this face-to-face meeting between scientists and a council in France? Well, it was dangerous territory, plain and simple. Treacherous.

"Is this treason? Espionage?" he asked himself.

Whatever the legal term, he had certainly never planned to cross so far over the threshold. Yet, somehow, he had.

45

Vail answered his phone on the first ring, "Hello."

"It's Roger. Um. We may have a problem. A big one."

"Do we need to meet to discuss?"

"Yes, I think that's best. Can you come here? We should play it safe and talk in a private space."

"On my way." Vail hung up, grabbed his jacket, and called out to Derek, "I'll be out of pocket for an hour or so."

"I've got the helm, Boss."

At his apartment, Roger waited, stewing over what he'd just unearthed from the encrypted file his software had flagged from Montague's email.

A knock on the door, and he practically ran toward it, flinging the door open.

Vail looked concerned, and rightfully so.

The two wasted no time. Vail sat in front of Roger's collection of screens as the professional hacker's fingers floated across the keyboard. Finally, Roger said, "Okay. This is going to sound crazy."

Vail blinked a few times and said, "Trust me, I've been to crazy town before."

"Sorry to hear that." Roger accentuated the words with a singsong tone. "I've been tracking the data collected and cross-referencing it with conversations recorded on Montague's devices. Where it's all leading ... well, it's bad in general. But this latest discovery is next-level conspiracy theory."

Vail cleared his throat. "I'm gonna need more."

Roger cracked his knuckles and laid it out there. "All in all, it appears there's a plan in development, one that will create a powerful secret council of sorts. I'm talking about at a global level." Roger's eyes grew big as he spoke.

"Hold on. Roger, I don't think—" Vail stopped short. Roger's main screen displayed a symbol not unlike the caduceus with wings used in the medical profession, but different, morphed. This symbol sported a protractor-type tool around a pyramid with an evil eye, like on American money. Even stranger, on top of the pyramid rested a staff with eagles.

Vail pointed. "I've seen this before."

"You kidding me, man? Where?"

"In legal documents that my firm has been working on recently. For Ludwell ... well, specifically for Lineage."

Roger shook his head in disbelief before continuing. "What gets me is the mixture of symbols. Medical, American ... and see that eagle? That's Russian."

"It's two eagles."

"Well, technically, it's one with two heads.

Vail nodded.

"Anyway, this is not a new concept ... organized societies or councils," Roger said. "If you think about it, there are plenty of shadow institutions. Area 51, the CIA, the NSA, the NGA."

Vail's eyes grew narrow, indicating he didn't know what the last acronym was for.

Roger elaborated, barely breathing between sentences, "The National Geospatial-Intelligence Agency. It's larger than four football fields and located near DC, but almost no one knows about it. And those are just the *American* agencies. Every super-power country funds its own bespoke secrets. And true, the public seems vaguely aware and often intrigued, but what the public doesn't realize is that there exists yet another level—the organized private entities in the background of those secret agencies. And that's my point ..." He paused.

Vail spun his finger in a *please get to that point* kind of way.

Roger leaned back in his chair. "That's what this really is, I believe —this plan of the Russians and Montague." He wagged his finger in the air. "Their elite council will be one of those entities. In the background, influencing everything on a global level."

"A shadow agency," Vail said.

Roger nodded rapidly.

"For Lawrence's study?"

"It's more than that. It's some kind of control over viruses through the blood. Kind of like software for a computer. I think."

Wide-eyed, staring at the screens in front of them, neither spoke, but somehow their thoughts seemed loud against the silence.

"And Montague is the mastermind behind all of this?" Vail asked.

"That's the thing. I'm not sure he's even aware of the depth of the hole he's stumbled into yet with the Russians."

"Terrific." Heavy sarcasm dripped from the solitary word.

46

The squeak, squeak, squeak of Lawrence's shoes exacerbated the already tense atmosphere of the lab.

"Hey, Cathy, what file name did you use for the viral pneumonia response test."

"PN, then the numbers correspond, one, two, three."

"Got it. Thanks."

He could feel her eyes on him as he leaned toward the computer screen.

"Everything okay?" she asked.

He didn't even turn his head. "Yeah, why?"

"You just seem a little, ah, preoccupied." She swiveled back to face her own monitor. "Or tightly wound," she added under her breath.

"I heard that." Lawrence scooted over in her direction, then dropped his eyes toward his lap while bracing his hands on his knees.

"What is it? Hey." Coaxing, she touched his arm. "Maybe I can help."

"It's just ..."

She leaned in and said in a soft tone, "You can trust me."

"Mr. Montague wants me to meet with the Russian scientists." He paused and added, "In person."

Her eyes bugged out.

Lawrence continued. "I have some real reservations about that, especially after what I read in the file he gave me. The stuff I was telling you about on the phone last night."

Cathy swiped a hand down her face. "Ahhh, geez."

"And then there's my selfish side not wanting to lose control of this project—not to a foreign competitor."

"What do you mean?"

"Well, the way I see it is ..." He stopped for a moment, trying to think of the best way to say it but coming up short. He blew out a long breath and said, "I guess what I'm trying to say is ... if this is going to happen with or without us, then I'm pretty much resigned to sticking with it. And if that's the case, then this is kind of our once-in-a-lifetime discovery, our moment—or at least our country's moment. It could mean such big things for us. I know what I'm saying sounds bad. Sorry."

Her expression changed, but he couldn't really read it. She looked off into the distance, lost in her thoughts.

She stared at the wall; he stared at her. Silence filled the space between them.

Finally, she said, "I know you're a good guy, want to do the right thing. But yes, you're a scientist too, and there's a real draw in this. Being a part of something potentially"—she waved her hands around —"monumental. I get it. I do. Even if it involves working with the Russians." She paused and kept her gaze on him, almost like a mother talking to a child. "There's a bigger question, though. Did we *ever* have any control over this?"

"I think we do have a little say-so—maybe not as much since I shared the data on Tess, which I regret now. But, at first, we pretty much owned this." The angst in his heart over that move was huge. But he couldn't take it back now.

"True. Knowledge equals power," Cathy said. "That's all ancient history at this point. Right now, I'm more worried about going to federal prison for collusion than losing my chance at accolades at the next biosciences convention."

Lawrence cocked an eyebrow and offered a small smile. "An excellent point. Dreams of awards and clapping peers don't seem very important right now."

"When are you scheduled to meet with this Russian scientist?"

"Tomorrow."

Her mouth dropped open. "What?"

"Yeah. They move fast apparently."

"Do you want me to come with you?" An almost smile pulled at the corners of her mouth.

"Yes, but you can't. Montague's orders." He took a breath and gazed softly at her. "And I wouldn't let you anyway."

"So you're going alone with that creepy Montague? Gah! Is it in a dark alley too?"

"Probably."

"This is not weird at all. Not at all." She crossed her arms, clearly unhappy with the news.

At a loss for anything more to say, they just stared at each other.

She reached for his hand. "How about some lunch? Let's get out of here. We can make a game plan. Come on. My treat."

"Thanks. I'd like that."

She smiled, grabbed her purse and coat, then tugged on his sleeve. "Come."

~47~

Norman Montague paced the floor in his office, watching the minutes tick by—exactly ninety-six remained until the meeting between the scientists would commence. He knew this would be a real do-or-die moment for him ... and for Lawrence.

So much risk.

Anxiety built as Norman played out worst-case scenarios. What if the strait-laced Lawrence stormed out or reported it to authorities?

On and on, his mind whirled with dreaded thoughts until he looked up and saw Lawrence standing just outside his glass office.

The old man huffed and flipped up a hand in acknowledgement. "Let's go," he said as he exited the office. "The driver is waiting downstairs."

"Right," was all Lawrence said.

An intense eye contact flickered between them, broken only by Montague struggling with his coat. The two left in silence.

They rode side by side in the back seat, both staring through rain-splattered windows at the gloomy city streets, until the car stopped in front of an old, nondescript brick building. The date 1924 was molded into a stone lintel above the doorway.

Montague peered up at the five-story façade, wondering how he'd landed himself in this spot. He grumbled softly as he tugged at his seatbelt. This definitely had not been part of his plan. He'd only participated in this study for the money ... and maybe a bit of power. There was also some satisfaction in sticking it to Tess, though that seemed more and more trivial every second. Now he found himself caught in this dark web with no clear escape.

Hurrying beneath the black sky, they approached the steps of the building. The only light came from the glow of a streetlamp. A rough-looking man with a scuffed chin and a black eye opened the door before they'd even knocked and escorted them down a hallway with torn, yellowed wallpaper. They entered a stark room with a fireplace, two thread-worn green velvet chairs and a shabby leather sofa. A cluster of crystal glasses sparkled near a decanter of clear liquid— vodka, Norman guessed—all atop a silver tray on a low table. He tried his best not to fidget, but he desperately wanted to wipe the telltale sweat on his forehead. Curiously, he eyed the young Lawrence, who was now perched in his seat like a little kid, moving his head around as he surveyed the strange room.

The door swung open, carrying with it a few loud Russian greetings. Montague recognized the interpreter, Ivan, right away, but a new man followed him. Mr. Borin entered last and took charge of the room, introducing his lead scientist, Nicholai Volkov.

"Please, call me Nick," the young man said in clear English, unlike his Russian counterpart.

The two scientists shook hands and sized each other up, brain to brain. A tension hung over the room. Borin seemed unfazed, however, and he wasted no time in pouring drinks for everyone. He offered a toast to "new friends," then knocked back most of his glass. The others followed suit, though not as enthusiastically, Montague noted.

The clandestine meeting lasted an hour and a half, covering a variety of harrowing ideas for the Blood Secrets project. On the drive home, Montague and a visibly pallid Lawrence rode in silence once again.

As the young scientist moved to exit the car, Montague's crooked fingers grabbed his arm. "Remember, not a word to anyone." The old man's eyes shimmered with threat—or at least that was the look he was going for. Really, he was an utter mess and could only pray Lawrence remained loyal to the team.

With a blank stare, Lawrence yanked his arm away and headed to his car in the company lot.

He's not tough enough for this. Hell, neither am I, Montague thought as he pulled the car door closed. "Take me home," he said to his driver.

A residual burn lingered in Lawrence's arm where the old man had grabbed him, like acid on skin. He truly loathed the man, and even more now that Montague had brought all of them into this horrible game with the Russians. His throat tightened as he realized that even Montague had looked a bit on the sickly side as he agreed to the demands made of him.

He slid into his car intent on driving straight home, but the shock of the present gradually twisted into the dread of tomorrow and so he turned the car in a different direction.

48

The unexpected rapping on the front door startled Cathy, causing her to spill a few drops of tea on the couch with a jolt. She mopped up the hot liquid with a throw blanket while calling out, "Just a minute." She eyed the clock, ten past nine.

From the other side of the door came a familiar voice, "It's me, Lawrence. I know it's late."

She set her mug on the coffee table, and just before turning the lock, she tugged at her sweatshirt and fluffed her hair.

She opened the door, surprised to see her coworker looking frazzled, disheveled, and pitifully soaked from the rain.

"You are a sight. Come in. Let me make you some tea." Grabbing his damp coat, she shook it a bit under the cover of her small porch before hanging it on the rack just inside her entry. "Sit. I'll get you a towel."

Moments later, he sat with a fluffy lavender towel draped over his shoulders, breathing in the steamy aroma of an Earl Grey out of a mug adorned with kittens chasing yarn. She fidgeted with a tin in the kitchen, making a clinking sound before appearing again with a plate of homemade chocolate chip cookies.

"Thank you. With hospitality like this, I may never leave." He winked.

Smiling, her eyes met his and lingered.

"Want to talk about it?" Cathy asked.

Lawrence winced. "Give me a minute?"

"Of course. Of course. Relax for now," she said and turned her attention to the television, which was tuned to the Travel Channel. The pair watched for a while, chatting and laughing over their ideas for the perfect escape to another place.

"Hey." Lawrence's face suddenly turned serious, and she immediately knew time for dreams was over. She turned down the volume on the television and gave him her full attention.

"What's up?" she said.

"I want you to know that what I'm about to say is coming from a good place. You have to trust me on that. So ... here's the thing. You need to quit, leave Lineage. Just say you have a sick mother or sister, or say you're the one who's sick. Anything. Please just get out—now."

Cathy put a hand on her heart. "What on earth happened at that meeting? It's bad news, isn't it?"

"Really bad. And I'm too far in, but you aren't. We can figure a way to get you out, keep you safe."

"Tell me what happened, then I'll decide if I stay or go. I'm not keen to just abandon you now. Not after what happened to Bret." Her hand moved to her throat as she felt a well of emotion rising inside her.

"And that's exactly why you must leave. Because ... honestly, I just don't see how this ends well for any of us."

She shook her head and pursed her lips.

Lawrence continued. "The Russians are mafia or something like that, I'm convinced. They're planning to do testing on people. Like the mentally ill—a captive audience that no one will listen to."

Cathy shivered at the words. "Wh-what? I don't understand."

"Oh, it gets worse. Expansion testing includes using the people in the Mexican slums—a perfect cover for disease research programs. There's going to be some kind of council. I'm not sure what that even means yet."

"No. No. No," she whispered. "This is so bad."

"I know. Way worse than anything I could imagine. And now I'm trapped in the middle of it all. No way out, but for you, there is. There's no need for you to go down with this ship, Cathy."

"No. I can't leave you to deal with this alone. I just can't." She moved closer to him and gripped his hand with both of hers.

His head tilted in a curious fashion as he studied her for a moment. She didn't flinch, allowing herself to be completely captured by his intense gaze. He cleared his throat and said, "Your friendship, you, mean a lot to me."

She realized her hair had fallen around her face, and she brushed it back. "I feel the same."

He scooted closer. "I never noticed before."

"What?"

"Your eyes, the color ... a perfect stormy blue."

She giggled and playfully punched his arm.

The tension broke, and he propped his feet on the coffee table. She did the same, and the two relaxed, shoulder-to-shoulder, staring at the TV again until she drifted off to sleep, her head resting on his arm.

Delicately touching her hair, he whispered, "I'm sorry."

49

R oger looked at the clock every three minutes, waiting. It was almost ten in the evening.

"Finally." He leapt out of his chair, leaving it spinning as he flung open the front door.

Vail, exhausted and damp from the rain, brushed off his coat before entering.

Noticing Vail's dark circles and weary vibe, Roger said, "You look beat, man."

"Yeah, yeah. Running on fumes." He slumped. "And Tess and I fly out soon for Florence ... Ludwell business. So, no real rest in sight."

"Maybe catch some sleep on the flight. You look like you could use it."

"Yep. What's the news? What did you find?" Vail plopped down in a chair in the front room where Roger had his workspace. The two were becoming familiar; formalities slowly vanishing between them.

Roger raked his fingers through his frenzied hair. "Well, it's not going to make you feel much better."

As if in anticipation of the worst, Vail slumped further into the chair. "Terrific. Lay it on me. Is it worse than yesterday's news?"

"I'm gonna go with yeah." Roger spoke at a rapid pace, hoping to minimize the sting. Like ripping off a bandage. "There's a plan in place to collect a lot of data on viruses and immunity through unethical testing."

"Unethical testing by Lineage or the Russians?"

"Well, both." He paused.

"What the hell?"

"Yep. Here's the kicker: I think it all centers around using Tess's blood. Anyway, we will get back to that."

Visibly pale, Vail said nothing as his chest rose and fell more rapidly than it should for someone sitting in a chair. So much so that Roger grabbed a bottle of water from the fridge and handed it to him. "You okay?"

Vail took a swig. "Continue."

"The problem with exploratory science like this is that it involves infecting large groups with diseases. Usually animals. But the Russians have a different plan. They want to test on humans."

"How?"

"Well, for starters in the Mexican slums. And then, mental hospitals, foreign prisons ... you know, for the right price."

"I don't follow."

"From what I can tell, these places will be used as clandestine labs for disease seeding with clusters of inoculation testing that may or may not work."

Vail rolled his arm in a *keep talking* gesture.

"It gets very complex, but it's clear that it's unethical and dangerous."

Vail stayed silent for a moment, resting his chin on steepled fingers. Then, "That's all extremely risky. A lot of people could go to jail, not to mention what could happen if the disease broke containment. Widespread illness. And what about the media? This wouldn't go unnoticed. I don't think—"

Roger cut in. "There's always a way to spin things, to play one tragedy off another, to ignore this in favor of that ..."

"Honestly, you're making no sense. This is outrageous thinking. It could never happen."

"It can and it will," Roger said emphatically. "All the shadow agency needs if the disease escapes is for the public to run wild with some type of media fodder, a red herring—whatever that may be at any given time —to keep the attention away from the real issue. Protests, civil rights movements, border issues, mass shootings, anything that captures the public's focus will work." Roger finally took a breath, his eyes gleaming.

Vail tilted his head left, then right, weighing the words. "I get what you're saying in that respect. But I don't think Lineage or Ludwell is anywhere near that powerful. And shadow agencies?"

"No, but Ludwell is not at the helm. The Russians are." He raised a brow.

Vail ceased all movement as he eyeballed Roger—skepticism and shock and worry fighting for dominance in his expression.

Roger knew in his gut that he'd hit on something big.

Vail rose from his chair abruptly and said, "Keep monitoring. I'm going to need to update Red. And Tess. She may be in danger. Right now, she's focused on the idea that Montague is out to get her because he doesn't like her. I truly wish that was it. This is much worse."

Roger floundered with what to say next. "Hey, it doesn't look like she's in any imminent danger. It's her blood they're after. They need her —" He stopped.

"Alive." Vail finished the sentence.

"Yeah." Roger felt bad for putting that out there.

"Look, just do me a favor. Stick to the facts. Don't try to interpret so much. We need to be clear on what's actually happening—not focused on the screenplay version. I don't want to forecast this and end up getting it wrong."

A bit stung, Roger understood and agreed to tone down the hypothesizing.

As he headed out the door, Vail turned and said, "First and foremost, keep tabs on anything that looks bad for Tess. Her safety is of utmost importance. And second, don't mention any of this unethical testing to her, please."

"Roger that," Roger said, trying to lighten the mood with his play on words.

Vail rolled his eyes but said nothing.

Roger added, "Right. I'll get it done. I'll flag some keywords. I've got your back."

"I need to talk to Tess, tonight," Vail mumbled on his way out of Roger's apartment building. He fought against the tug of fear attached to knowing that her genetic code had served as the nucleolus to this whole scheme.

In fact, she had become a commodity. His thoughts delved into the dark places where something like that could lead—kidnapping, ransom, or ... "Stop it." He couldn't even think it. He needed to get ahead of this. The sooner she knew the truth, the better. Knowledge was power, after all.

Angry with himself, he questioned over and over why he'd encouraged her to submit her sample. Ultimately, whatever had happened or would happen stemmed from that truth. He was to blame.

He clenched his jaw so hard his teeth ached. "I need to tell her before we leave for Florence."

A man walking his dog stared at Vail as he mumbled to himself. Knowing he must look and sound unstable, Vail shrugged and lifted his hand into the night air, hailing a cab and sending the driver in pursuit of her address.

~50~

Tapping her fingers on the arm of the couch, Tess waited for the doorman to buzz Vail up to her penthouse. More than a little intrigued at his vague eleven o'clock text, she eyed the elevator in anticipation. "Finally," she said as the doors opened.

Vail was standing there, deeply focused as he spoke to someone on the phone. "Bad service. Are you there? Can I call you back?" Then he let out a groan, shoved the phone into his coat pocket, and moved swiftly toward her.

His expression was ... what? She couldn't tell for sure. Sadness? Concern? "What is it? Is something wrong?" She reached out for his hands.

Without a word, he pulled her close, nuzzled his face in her hair, and held her tightly. Then he went in for a long kiss. She felt electricity between them mixed with something more intense. The kiss ended, but his embrace lingered. "You are the most important person in my life," he whispered, his voice raw with emotion.

She pulled back and raised an eyebrow, questioning his grim demeanor, "I know something is wrong. Who was on the phone?"

She took his hand, gently pulling him to sit next to her on the couch.

"Red. I lost service in the elevator. I need to call him back."

"Oh, yes. That's right." She reached over to the side table and picked up an envelope, which contained the cash to pay Red for his latest service.

Vail looked confused.

"Oh, no one has updated you, I guess. Well, Red's man works fast. Somehow, he orchestrated an unfortunate flat-tire experience, accented by Roger interrupting the woman's cell service, which left her helpless for hours on a dark road." She chuckled. "I can only imagine how scared she was, stranded with the temperature dropping into the teens."

When he didn't respond, she said, "Don't you find it the least bit entertaining?"

He mumbled, "Yeah, sure."

"What's going on in that head of yours?"

"I have to tell you something. I met with Roger. It's not good news."

She sat straighter. "How serious is this? Should I be worried about my safety or something?" She was starting to piece together Vail's words and his emotional greeting when he'd first arrived. Something was afoot, and it had to do with her.

"Maybe." He took her hands in his, explaining that it was much bigger than just Montague. "From what Roger is finding, the Russian involvement is significant." He left out any mention of Roger's unethical-testing diatribe—best to focus on the bigger picture for now.

"Oh, wow," was all she could think to say. She was shocked, and fear was starting to take hold inside her. She tried to tamp it down, stay reasonable. But Roger's discovery was nothing to easily dismiss.

Taking a deep breath, Vail rose from the couch and stood in front of the window, and she followed. For several minutes, they stood side by side, silent, thinking.

And in that short period of time, Tess's fear was replaced by anger, a deep contempt for those who had her blood on their hands, literally.

~51~

The midday heat reflected on itself from the stone walkway in the piazza outside of the Duomo in Florence, making the fall temperatures feel a little warmer than usual. Tess tried to calm the pounding in her heart. Her body ached from the constant nervousness she'd been managing since she'd found out about what Roger had discovered. She approached the outdoor table in front of the coffee shop. There in a small bistro chair sat Vail, waiting, and staring at her in that intense way she could feel as much as see.

He enveloped her in his strong arms. He must have felt her shaking because he said, "Aww, Tess. We've got this."

Soaking up the safety of his embrace, she lingered in his arms before moving to sit at the small table. And in that perfectly timed European way, a waiter appeared with water and a frothy cappuccino.

"You devil," she teased, relishing the normalcy, the familiar rhythm between them.

He smiled tenderly. "That I am." Then he seemed to study her. "Did you sleep well?"

"Not at all." Even in the warm air, her hands felt like ice, and she cradled her fingers around the steaming cup.

"Please try not to worry so much. We're in good hands with Red.

The plan is in the works, and everything will happen seamlessly." He really did sound calm, and she tried to draw comfort from that.

"I'm sorry I'm such a wreck. It's just ... well, what we're doing ... it has to work." Barely a whisper, the noise from the bustling street swallowed up her words.

"Trust me. It will be fine. I promise. We have the best people executing this. I won't let anything happen to you."

She took a cautious sip of her steamy cappuccino. "He will suffer consequences, right?"

He let out a laugh that had a touch of a sinister ring to it. "My darling, suffering is guaranteed."

"Good." Her eye twitched with anxiety. "The best punishment is for him to live a long and miserable life after what he has put us through. Thinking I would be his golden goose—I want to wring his little neck." Her anger grew at the mere thought of Norman Montague.

"Let's just say he'll have a hard time getting hired at a laundromat after this."

"I want his reputation, identity, everything—his whole life ruined. His finances depleted and his existence to be one horrible struggle after another for as long as he lives." She knew she sounded like some maniacal revenge queen, but that was exactly how she felt at the moment. The atrocity of it all consumed her.

"I know one thing. You're gorgeous when you're on the hunt. Your green eyes are flashing." He stood and gestured at her coffee. "Take another sip, then we have to go. It's time."

She wanted to draw it out, take her own sweet time, affirming her stubborn streak that he often teased her about. Instead, she took that last sip and stood. "I'm ready."

52

Midmorning on Monday across the pond in New York, Roger stuffed his hands into the pockets on his cargo shorts as he waited outside Mr. Montague's office—something he was rarely required to do in his line of work, and he was grateful for that. He started whistling a tune, but Doris gave him the stink eye, so instead he passed the minutes converting the time difference between New York and Italy. Roger suspected Montague's motivation for sending them both to Florence at the same time had more to do with keeping them out of his hair than important business matters. Little did the sinister old man know, but Roger had been hard at work on their behalf; the diversion tactics would prove futile.

Then again, maybe the old man knew about Roger's involvement; hence, the reason for summoning Roger to this meeting. He stuffed his hands deeper into his pockets in a twinge of panic. He chided his overactive imagination. *Stop freaking out.*

Finally, Doris said, "Mr. Palmer. You can go in." She offered him a glass of water, which he politely declined.

"Not planning on being here long," he mumbled, then shuffled into Montague's office.

"Hello, Roger. Please have a seat," Montague said in a casual manner, gesturing toward a chair.

Roger sat.

For what seemed an eternity, there was silence. Montague merely stared at him. Roger shifted uncomfortably in his seat, cleared his throat, and tried to think of something brilliant to say.

Finally, Montague took the reins. "I would like to talk to you about a special project. However, to be clear, this is highly confidential. If that's not something you feel prepared to handle, you should say so now. There will be no repercussions." He paused and darkly added, "At this point."

Sweat formed on Roger's forehead as he wondered what this could be about. He wanted to wipe the back of his hand across his damp face, but he also didn't want to draw attention to his anxiety. Instead he feigned as much confidence as he could muster, "I'm the man for the job. I can assure you. Discretion is my forte—it's a vital factor in any good IT department. The name of the game." He chuckled only to find himself under the deadpan gaze of the other man.

"Uh-huh." Montague leaned back in his chair for a brief moment, then shot forward and pushed a single sheet of paper across the desk. "Sign this. NDA."

Roger's brows drew together as he took the paper and a pen. His eyes scanned the words, but his brain raced with other thoughts.

"Our newest venture involves a coordinated research study with a Russian team of scientists. We need the utmost security on any data collected or shared."

Roger kept a poker face as he soaked in Montague's words. He scribbled his signature on the page and pushed it back across the desk.

Montague tapped the signed NDA. Then, he explained the viral resistance study, but he didn't mention Tess. Montague paused and, to Roger's surprise, said, "Things may go sideways soon on this project we're working on. I need your expertise to contain the bleeding."

Roger tried not to show any of the shock at the forthright comment and what it may mean, but ... *whoa.*

"I need you to box in the Russians. Make them think they have access to a lot more than they actually do. That way, when we need to cut them out, it won't be a rush of madness."

Roger's mouth had gone dry, but he found the wherewithal to nod. Then he offered up reassurance of his skills.

After what was probably only minutes but seemed like much longer, Montague finally ended the meeting.

Upon arriving back at his apartment, Roger went straight to his fridge, downed a can of soda, and then opened another. Checking his face in the mirror, he said, "I knew it." He looked a little flushed. He plopped in a chair and simply stared at nothing at all for the next couple of minutes.

He couldn't believe what had just transpired in Montague's office. The old guy had given him carte-blanche access to the cached data, including the one he knew contained the data on Tess's blood.

"Snooping just got a lot easier."

With renewed energy, he opened a bag of chips. Hours passed as he combed through file after file—not having to cover his own tracks sure saved a lot of time. When he finished, he leaned back in his chair, wondering whom to call first. Vail, Tess, or the White House?

He hadn't been off the mark at all with his theories. *Blood Secrets: Global Project* was as crazy as he'd thought.

Vail had been skeptical. He'd damn sure believe Roger now.

53

A pungent bleach smell permeated the dark pub, yet somehow the table still felt sticky on Gemma's tattooed wrist. "Eww," she whined, wiping her arm with a napkin. Then she went back to waiting, tapping her foot like a jackhammer.

Montague finally came through the doors, wearing a perturbed look. She scrunched up her nose in disgust at the sight of the short man with wiry, gray hair and eyebrows that had never seen the likes of a trimmer. Slightly overweight, he wore pleated khakis and a wash-worn button-down shirt. *The guy has more money than God, so why does he dress like a used car salesman?*

He spied her and shuffled straight to her table at the back of the room. Without a word of greeting, he plopped down into the seat across from her and waved away the waiter who was approaching. The server spun on his heels and went in the opposite direction.

Then the words came, harsh and clipped. "This will be our last contact."

"Hello to you too." She made sure to show a healthy dose of disdain. Besides, he's the one that suggested meeting in person. Something about no more phone records. *Whatever.*

"There is no need for pleasantries. This is business." From the flatness of his tone and lack of expression, she knew he meant it.

"Yeah, well, it's starting to feel pretty personal to me." She boldly stared at his dull blue eyes. The whites were bloodshot. A sketchy face for a sketchy dude.

He leaned in, and she instinctively leaned back. "What do you mean, exactly?" he asked.

"For starters, my tires were slashed, my apartment broken into, my electricity shut off, and my credit card swiped in three countries—all in a matter of days. I don't think that can all be chalked up to bad luck."

The man's red face changed to a sweaty white.

"Hey, are you okay?" She didn't care about his health one bit; she just didn't want to be around if he ended up falling over from a heart attack.

The old man fidgeted, grumbled something about *no coincidences,* and grabbed a handkerchief from his pocket. He dabbed at his face, ignoring her question. "I had nothing to do with all those tribulations. So, I'm not sure what you want from me."

"I want out of this mess. You didn't pay me enough to cover these extra headaches. Whether you made them happen or not, it's *because* of you." She held her breath; she was going for broke here.

"How much?" His voice left no question as to his thoughts—she was a con artist out to squeeze a bit more cash.

"Listen. I'm serious. I just want out. I want a plane ticket and enough money for a new car and a down payment for a new apartment."

"And there it is ... *I want, I want.* Fine. I'll have another ten grand delivered to you by tomorrow."

Gemma started to agree then realized her power in the moment. She decided to take a chance and countered. "Make it twenty and make this all stop. I don't ever want to see any of you people again. Do you hear me?"

His squinty eyes left no doubt that she'd made him angry. Bracing herself, she waited for a rejection or a retraction of the offer altogether, but to her surprise, he upped his original offer.

"I told you, I'm not doing those things to you. However, I'll give you fifteen to go away. Never contact me again. Understand? Or else you'll experience some real problems, and you'll know its me."

Not wanting to push her luck any further, she lowered her head and sputtered, "I understand."

With no further comment, he up and left.

Feeling like she'd won the lottery or something, she waved to the waiter and ordered a glass of champagne, drowning the question—if it wasn't him, then whom?

Red took in the whole scene from across the bar, and he did not miss the self-indulgent show. None of this was supposed to benefit the hustler. *This ain't happening. Not on my watch.*

He texted Hannibal, ordering him to wipe the smirk off Gemma Stein's face, so to speak. The woman was playing outside her league.

Hannibal was happy to oblige and requested that they meet up to discuss.

Red texted back: *Meet in forty-five. Usual spot.*

G lad to be back from Italy—and from traveling anywhere, for that matter—Vail wore a pleasant smile as he entered Tess's building carrying a bottle of Oban 18-year old, limited edition, single malt scotch whiskey, which he'd wedged securely under his arm. From behind the desk and in a thick British accent, Miles greeted him.

"Evening, Mr. Stuart. Tess stepped out. She said to go on up."

"Evening, Miles. Thanks."

Vail readily approached the impeccably-dressed Englishman. He always enjoyed their friendly chats.

As he neared, the doorman's expression brightened a bit. Motioning with a nod of his head, he said, "Forgive my prying eyes, but I notice you have a pretty special scotch in your keep tonight."

"Sure do." Vail gripped the bottle with his free hand only to set it smack in the middle of the reception desk. The gold ribbon tied around the neck of the bottle loosened. He tugged it off, balled it up, and landed it in the small wastebasket behind the desk.

"Bravo, my friend. I do believe that's a three-pointer." Miles then turned his attention to the label, motioning for permission to examine it. "May I?"

"Of course. Be my guest. In fact, maybe you can tell me a little about it." Vail gave the man space to inspect the enticing libation.

"Fancy that. I happen to know a bit about this one. Two brothers founded the distillery in Scotland just before 1800. I visited once and had more than my fill. Let's just say it's very possible I stumbled out of there with a cheesy grin." He chuckled. "In fact, one of the most distinguishable tasting notes of an Oban distillery production is the salty tang of the sea air that infiltrates the smoke and oak backdrop."

A Cheshire grin appeared on Vail's lips. He had an idea. "Hey, what time do you finish up tonight?"

"Let's see." He looked at the time. "I'm due to head out in about twenty minutes, sir."

"Perfect. How about joining me upstairs for a bit of a tasting after you clock out?"

The man beamed at the invitation. "How kind. I'd love to stop by for a little nip. Thank you."

"See you in twenty, then." Vail patted the desk decisively before disappearing into the elevator.

Before Miles started for Tess's penthouse for the impromptu scotch tasting, he opened the bottom desk drawer with his key. His expression moved from pleasant to somber as he pulled out a sealed envelope and tucked it neatly into his lapel pocket. Grumbling a little, he did not want to tarnish the evening, but he felt an obligation to share the information he had. In fact, he was a little relieved that Vail was there. Maybe he'd share it with Vail first, get his take on it, before presenting the info to Tess. *I hope this proves a right decision,* he silently prayed, knowing he risked his actions being seen as betraying her privacy.

As the elevator doors opened to Tess's foyer, a jovial Vail called out, "Come in, my friend."

"Thank you, Mr. Stuart."

"Tonight, it's just Vail."

"Yes sir. Vail, sir. Thank you."

"Have a seat."

He followed his host into the living room. The beautiful bird's-eye view of the city and park at night captured his gaze as Vail carefully positioned the glasses on a little table between two comfortable armchairs. The pair swirled the amber liquid that filled the snifters, toasting to Scotland and to New York.

"Smooth. This is exquisite. Just as I remember."

Vail tilted his glass in agreement.

For several moments, both enjoyed the burn of the scotch as it lingered in their throats.

Then, Miles made his move. "I have something to share with you." Gently placing his glass on the table, he opened his jacket, reaching for the interior pocket. However, his timing proved to be a bit off, and just as he handed the sealed envelope to Vail, the elevator door opened.

"Well, hello, boys. Am I interrupting?" Tess's voice echoed with a deliberate note of playfulness.

With generations of ingrained manners behind him, Miles immediately stood and said politely, "Evening, Dr. Andreas."

"Evening, Miles. Please, there is no need to get up." She plopped her purse on the entry table and removed her coat.

Vail said, "Come, join us. This scotch is one for the books." He half-stood before she motioned for him to stay put as well.

"Sit, sit." She grabbed a glass from the bar. "So, which of you wants to tell me exactly what we're drinking?"

For the next few moments, the three happily sipped the scotch while chatting about visits to Scotland. Then Vail happened to look over at the table and caught a glimpse of the abandoned envelope. "Oh, yes. I forgot." He picked it up, tearing it open quickly.

Miles leaned forward with his hands extended, trying to stop him. Too late.

Tess asked, "What is it?"

Miles interjected with, "I must explain. That's from me. I regret having to tell you this, but someone came by today, er ... well, snooping and trying to pry information out of me. About you, ma'am. I wanted to tell you sooner, but I ... well, I wanted to find the right time. So, I hope you don't mind, but I decided to give the information to Vail instead. Only, I hadn't a chance to explain it to him yet."

She looked confused.

Vail looked alarmed.

Miles continued. "The photo there, it's of the gentleman who came in earlier today. He asked a lot of strangely personal questions. That's what made me think to grab security footage for you."

"Quick thinking. Thank you. What questions, do you remember?" Vail asked.

"Yes. About your job," He looked to Tess. "Your comings and goings from this building, where you're from originally, do you live alone …"

She nodded robotically, seemingly numb from what he said.

"Of course, I didn't answer and readily turned him away. In fact, I threatened to call the authorities if I saw him again. I hope I did the right thing."

She took the photograph from Vail's hands and examined the man in the picture. "Thank you. Yes, you did all of the right things."

Miles felt relieved, but regretful as well—for putting a damper on the evening. Sensing the tension in the room, he offered his thanks and said goodnight. His stomach rolled at the thought of anyone wanting to hurt Dr. Andreas. He vowed to up his doorman game and be hypervigilant. That guy wouldn't get past him.

After a brief silence, Tess faced Vail and said, "I don't recognize him. Do you?"

"No." He took a screen shot and texted it to Red along with an explanation.

Within seconds, Red rang. Not waiting for a hello, the fixer jumped right in, "Looks like a hired punk—I'll float the picture."

"Thanks."

Red added, "I think it's time we put a detail on Tess—for her safety."

"I agree. Let's do it."

Tess gave him a questioning look and mouthed, *"Do what?"*

Vail ignored her question for the time being as he listened to the voice on the other end of the line.

"I'll send someone." Red paused. "Soon."

Vail hung up and wrapped his arms around Tess as she stood surveying the view of the city through the window. She leaned back into him, and just like that, it seemed to him that no time had passed since they had been a couple over a year ago. They stood for what could have been seconds or hours, their focus switching back and forth from their own reflections in the dark glass to the flickering city lights below. Time didn't seem to exist.

Tess tilted her head up to face him. Vail didn't need more than that. He kissed her softly.

"I'm not leaving you alone tonight. Or ever."

"I know." Her breath flowed in sync with his. "But you should stay in the guest room. I don't want to rush this."

Vail nodded, though he wished it could be different. "I have all the time in the world. And starting tomorrow, you'll have a security detail following you when I'm not around. I didn't like the looks of that guy in the picture."

He thought she would protest, but she said, "Me either."

Vail sipped on a pint of Guinness as he sat at the bar in the Oscar Wilde pub. Out of frustration, he flipped a paper coaster over and over a few times before he noticed the Oscar Wilde quote on one side, *"The very essence of romance is uncertainty."* He laughed aloud and stuffed the coaster in his pocket. Tess defined uncertainty to him. He knew he loved her; now he had to wait to find out if she felt the same. He thought she did—was pretty sure, in fact—but getting her to take a chance on them again would be the real hurdle.

There was a light tapping on his shoulder, and he turned to see Red standing behind him. He gestured at the stool next to him and said, "I saved you a seat."

Red slid onto the stool. "Thanks. How are you holding up?"

Flashing a tormented look, Vail said, "Can I order you a drink?"

"Doing that well, huh?"

"Yep." Knowing Red to be a man of few words, he took advantage of not having to explain any further.

"I'll have what you're having, plus a shot of whiskey."

Vail put in the order, and the bartender quickly delivered the frothy beer and the whiskey. Red picked up the shot glass, which was etched with another Wilde quote: *"The world is a stage, but the play is badly cast."*

He stared a little too long because Red followed his gaze, read the quote, and said, "Bloody hell, if that ain't the truth."

"Did you find out who that guy in the photo was?" Vail asked.

"Yep. One of Montague's thugs, the cousin Ray. Hannibal's on it. Ray's slick, but he won't be a problem much longer. You can trust that." Red downed the whiskey in one gulp.

"Good. I expected no less." Vail felt a million miles away and tried not to imagine why the guy wouldn't be a problem anymore. He didn't need the added guilt.

Both remained quiet for a few seconds.

"You okay?" Red said between sips.

"Yes. Just a lot on my mind."

"Does it happen to be named Tess?"

Vail smirked.

"Look, I don't claim to know much about love, but in my experience, the best thing to do is to not give up. Let her know how you feel." He finished his beer and set the glass on the bar, then he rose from his seat, groaning a bit as he did so.

"Thanks." Vail meant it.

"I know you want us to keep Montague under watch, but you give the green light, and that problem goes away too, permanently." Red's eyes darkened with intensity.

Vail shook his head, waved him off. "Let's just watch for now. And keep that detail on Tess."

"Rest assured, we'll keep watch," he said, and then casually left the bar.

Vail read another coaster. *The heart was made to be broken.* He rubbed his jaw. "I have to get out of this place."

56

Chomping furiously on a piece of gum, Gemma marched straight into Todd's bar. She scanned the area, looking for him. Almost empty at 10 a.m. on a Wednesday, her arrival didn't go unnoticed for long.

"Can I help you with something?" the bartender offered.

"Yeah. I'm looking for Todd."

He squinted suspiciously.

"So, is he here?"

"I'll check."

She rolled her eyes. "Okay, yeah. You do that."

Within seconds, Todd appeared from the back hallway. His expression darkened as he laid eyes on her.

Suddenly, she felt self-conscious at how much he didn't seem to like her, but she shook it off. She needed his help more than his adoration. The sting of humiliation would have to take a back seat today. She spit her gum into a napkin at the bar and left it there. "I need to talk to you."

He signaled for her to follow him to the office.

Quickly shutting the door behind them, he turned to her and said, "I really don't think we need to meet anymore. I'd prefer to keep the past in the past. I'm finished with this."

"Well, what a luxury that must be to have the option because I'm knee-deep in all this muck, and it doesn't look like it's going to wash off anytime soon." Her hands flailed as she spoke, and she suddenly felt awkward.

"I don't see how that has anything to do with me." He leaned back on the desk and crossed his arms.

She twisted her cold hands together and then tugged on her too-short skirt, which now, for some reason, made her feel exposed, embarrassed. "Look, somebody is out to get me, and it's not Montague. And, well, I kind of think maybe it's your girlfriend—Tess, isn't it?" Her stomach flip-flopped as the man's face went red with what looked a lot like anger.

He jolted upright, taking an intimidating step toward her.

"Don't ever say her name. Do you understand?" He then said something under his breath that she thought sounded like, "You don't deserve to say her name."

She was shocked at his rudeness. He'd seemed like a relatively harmless guy, but now she wasn't so sure. "Jeez. What should I call her, then?" She broke eye contact and tried to hide the fear that was creeping in. She'd had experience with angry men and experience told her not to play into the brewing rage.

"Call her nothing. Don't even think of her. She's none of your business."

"Look. I get your Gallant White Knight stance, but you need to tell her to stop messing with my life." She regretted the words as they crossed her lips, and braced herself for an aggressive grab, or slap, or worse.

But he did none of those things. Instead he moved behind the desk, putting more distance between them, then pressed his fingertips to his forehead. "And just what exactly do you think she's doing to you?"

"Turning off my electricity, slashing my tires. Killing my dog." She choked up on the last one or else she would have kept going.

"I heard this already—last time. Remember? You told me Montague did all of that."

"Well, it's not"—her breath caught in her throat—"him."

He furrowed his brow.

"I'm just trying to get out of this. My life is crumbling. My boyfriend's always gone. I just want to forget about all of this and start over."

"You have a boyfriend?" The look of shock on his face dehumanized her, and any self-esteem she might have had just melted away.

She fought back her reaction to his words. "Yes, I do. That's not the point. This has been an ongoing thing. Some of it happened just recently."

"Okayyy?" He shook his head. "Again, I ask you what this has to do with me?"

"If she's not doing it, then who is?" Gemma whined, surprised at the emotion in her tone. She was losing it, despite her efforts not to.

"Calm down. I don't want a scene here," he said with some steel behind his words. "What would make you think I know about any of this? Maybe someone else that you've backstabbed for money is behind it."

She glared at him. "You better tell her to stop, or I'll send my own guy to tell her."

That did it.

He came at her. She shrunk back, covering her face with her hands, bracing herself. He stood close, his hot breath on her face. He didn't touch her, but his words remained sharp and testy. "Don't threaten her. Now, you listen to me. Get out of here and forget all of this. And if you do anything to Tess, so help me—" He stopped.

They maintained a stare-down, not moving for several breaths. She fought to control the shaking that plagued her. Without a word, she backed away, flung the door open, and stormed out of his office. As she raced through the bar in search of the fresh air and freedom of the street, she noticed a guy following her with his eyes. Out of reflex, she snarled in his direction, "What are you looking at?"

The man didn't respond. In fact, he barely reacted except for an increased intensity in his eyes, which clearly exuded danger. The hairs on the back of her neck prickled. She couldn't get out of there fast enough.

She bolted for the exit.

Red's nostrils flared; he was becoming more and more annoyed with this girl. *What a pain in the ass.* He took the last swig of his beer, leaving a twenty on the bar. In the shadows, he followed the fleeing girl for a few blocks while making a call. A few blocks in, his guy confirmed he'd caught up to her, saying, "I've got it from here, Boss." Red stopped his pursuit.

And he cursed the girl. He'd been in this business a long time—he could feel in his veins that she could become a real problem.

He dialed Tess. "I saw the girl at Todd's bar. They had a powwow of some sort in his office. Then, she stormed out. One thing is for sure; she didn't look happy. Are you sure Todd's not in cahoots with her?"

"He wouldn't do that. I'm sure. I don't know why she went there, but he wouldn't. No way."

He didn't respond to that, so she prompted, "Is there something else?"

"I don't usually theorize. I'm usually a *what you see is what you get* type of guy. But I have a hunch this girl may become a real problem. Maybe we need to think about removing that complication in the near future so we can focus on the big picture."

"You mean Montague."

Red started to say something, but she interrupted him. "I know he's the real concern, and she's getting to be a distraction. But I don't want to hurt anyone. I think we need to talk in person."

"I hear you." Red wanted to say that he hadn't meant Montague, but instead the Russian involvement. He had dealt with the Russian mafia before, and it hadn't ended well for the client. No way he was going to tell her that now, over the phone. So, he didn't say anymore.

"Thanks, Red."

"Yep." He hung up and pulled out a cigarette, took a big inhale of smoke. He needed to get ahead of this, and fast. He called Vail and got his voicemail. "Looks like the Russians could be playing roulette. Call me."

57

A cross town at the Lineage lab, Lawrence balled up the sandwich wrapper and pumped his wrist a couple of times as he aimed for the bin across the room. He let loose and hit the mark perfectly.

Cathy cheered and said, "Good shot!"

"Thanks. I wish the rest of my day would be as simple to conquer."

She walked over and put a gentle hand on his shoulder.

He relaxed a little under the power of her touch. "I have another meetup with the Russians later today." He whispered *the Russians* part.

"Oh, goodness." She frowned. "Hey, why don't you come over for dinner after the meeting? Unwind."

They locked eyes, and he said, "Yes, I'd like that. Thanks."

The corners of her mouth turned up as she dropped her head a little but not her gaze. He felt a little jolt in his heart at the sight of her.

A few hours later, after burying himself in work, Lawrence quietly left the lab. Cathy's concerned stare followed him out the door.

While waiting for the Russian counterpart at Lineage lab's new remote biosafety facility, he discreetly put a finger to his wrist, taking his pulse under the cover of the conference table. He'd never been here before. His heart raced, and he couldn't keep count, which caused him to feel sick. Struggling to pull air into his lungs, he somehow found it easier to breathe out instead. Fighting the instinct to stand and leave, he clasped his hands tightly—so tightly his knuckles had gone white.

Once he'd regained some control over his emotional state, he took a glance at the sweaty, pasty-faced Montague, noting the old man looked like he was feeling much of the same.

The Russian team, three in total, all entered wearing lab coats. He wondered where Mr. Borin was as he watched the lead scientist, Nick, guide the other two. At the far end of the table, one of the Russian lab assistants set up the presentation. Within seconds, the screen on the wall displayed test results. And that was when the larger, bald Russian started talking.

Lawrence listened intently as the man explained what was on the screen. What he said sounded sinister in nature—specifically, a study expansion plan with shady overtones. Lawrence shifted the collar of his shirt in an attempt to cool a rising heat. Time passed in a haze, the meeting came to an end, and Lawrence abruptly left the room with a flimsy excuse that he was needed elsewhere. No one tried to stop him.

Once in the parking lot, he texted Cathy, "On my way." He raced through the streets, gripping the steering wheel all the way, counting the minutes. He couldn't get there fast enough.

She greeted him before he had a chance to ring the bell and winced when she laid eyes on him. "Yikes, you look a wreck. Come in, come in," she coaxed. "I'll pour some wine."

Lawrence settled himself onto the couch and waited in silence.

Cathy fussed in the kitchen, yammering on and on probably to fill the gloomy quiet. She called him to the table, where she had laid out plates of pasta and the wine. They dug in, Lawrence first taking a large gulp of the red. She continued her chit-chat, and he found himself saying "uh-huh" numerous times.

When the conversation landed on the topic of the meeting, Lawrence discovered he was having a difficult time explaining just what he had learned. He tried to keep it simple enough, but even so, he wondered if he'd somehow gone insane in the course of a few hours.

"So, the Russians believe there's a link between Tess's immunity and her O-negative blood type. And they used alarming terms like *royal blood*. It was really just so strange. I don't know how else to explain it."

"I agree. The terms they're using are a bit weird, but maybe it's just clunky English translation. Let's hope."

"Maybe. But that's not all. They want to harvest her eggs."

She dropped her fork, which made a terrible clank as it hit the plate. "No. What? That's crazy. And illegal."

"I know. At least in this country." He raised an eyebrow, swallowing hard before delivering the next doozy. "And, apparently, I'm the lead American scientist." His voice cracked, and a slight tremor appeared in the hand that held his wineglass, which he was bringing to his lips as fast as possible.

Cathy's jaw dropped. Her pupils grew large as color drained from her face.

He continued. "My first assignment is to get Tess to agree to the egg harvesting. Since her life is not on the line for obvious reasons, guess whose is if I don't succeed?"

"What? They said that? That's criminal, Lawrence! How on earth ...? What are we going to do? Let's call the police." The words tumbled out of her as tears welled.

"I don't know what to do, but I'm sure calling the police is not the answer. I'd probably be dead by morning."

"Well, we have to do something."

"I know. I have to go along with it for now, I think." His shoulders slumped. If he'd had enough energy, he would have cried too.

58

Tess scrambled to find her buzzing phone.

"This is Tess." Kicking off her shoes and plopping on the couch, she answered without checking the caller ID, which resulted in surprise at hearing Todd's familiar hello on the other end.

"Todd?"

"Yes. Listen, we need to talk."

Annoyance immediately kicked in. "Todd, you need to hear me. I'm not ready to get into this. However you want to spin it, the trust was broken permanently. Loyalty and honesty are everything to me. Believe me when I tell you this is not something I am willing to work through —at least not yet." She paused, then added, "Or maybe ever."

"What on earth, Tess." His voice cracked. "That's not why I'm calling. You need to hear me out. Now."

His tone resonated so she stayed quiet, regretting her initial overreaction. She seemed to be doing that a lot lately and yearned for that calm and reasonable person she used to be.

"Listen. That woman, Gemma Stein, the one who started this whole nightmare ... well, she came to see me again. Here, at my bar, today."

"I know," Tess responded sheepishly.

"You know? Good grief. Honestly, I don't know what's gotten into you. Are you stalking me now or something? Not your style, Tess."

"I'm not stalking you," she said, not sure she wanted to tell him how they'd been tailing Gemma.

There was silence for a few beats, then, "Anyway, I thought she was crazy. But now..." He paused, seemed to reset, and said, "She thinks you're—and I quote— 'messing with' her life. Something about having no electricity and her tires slashed. Oh, and then she brought up the dog murder again. She's definitely not over that. I mean it is pretty sick, really sick actually."

"For the record, there is a bit more to all of this than you know, and some of these things are a symptom of that." Tess said the last part with bated breath.

"What the hell? I don't know what to think right now. But I guess that's beside the point. Here's the reason I'm calling. She said if I don't tell you to stop, then she'll send her own guy—"

She cut in before he could finish. "And you told her you would do that—tell me to stop."

"No." He sounded angry and stung. "What's wrong with you tonight?"

"What did you say, then? Because—"

"I can't believe you even have to ask. I defended you, of course, and told her to forget your name, to move on. I basically threatened her, and I'm not proud of that, but I'd do it again. I'm not going to let anyone hurt you. I know you know that. Deep down."

"I do." She breathed into the phone. "Listen, I appreciate you telling me, your support, but I'll take it from here."

"What are you going to do?"

"For starters, she won't bother you anymore."

"That's the least of my concerns. I can handle her myself. Let me help you."

Silence lingered.

"Tess, really ... what's going on? I don't even feel like I'm talking to the real you."

"Everything's fine. I'll handle it. I have to go." The last words erupted under the weight of her agitation. "Bye, Todd." She ended the call with an inkling of foreboding.

She grabbed the cashmere throw at the end of the couch and burrowed her legs beneath it. As she endured the loneliness of the moment, she realized Red needed to know about the woman's threats. She texted him, asking him to call her, and he did in less than a minute. She gave him the scoop.

"I can handle this problem today," he said.

"Nothing permanent," she reminded him.

"Understood."

"Just point the trail in a different direction—away from here."

"Done."

Next, she telephoned Roger.

"Good evening," he answered with a mock formality.

Tess skipped the greeting altogether. "The hotel woman is onto us. Can you confuse the situation?"

"Roger that."

"Funny." She had to admit, the guy was consistent—always his corny self no matter the circumstances.

"I'll unleash the identity-theft virus today. It will look like she's been hacked by someone overseas. Let's say ... Russia."

She could almost hear the grin in those words. "That's good."

~59~

THURSDAY, OCTOBER 17

Stewing over yesterday's conversation with Tess, Todd hurled his beer-tasting journal across his office and huffed as it landed with a thud just under the edge of a chair. His head dropped into his hands. He had always known this side of her existed—he'd seen glimpses—but he just never thought he'd see it from this angle.

How could she just turn off her feelings so easily?

A lump formed in his throat. He swallowed hard, then shifted from sadness to something just short of anger.

Walloping his fist on the desk, his veins pulsed faster with every breath. He needed to get out of there, get some fresh air. After grabbing his jacket off the hook, he left through the back door, walking fast through the alley behind his bar, trying to escape his pained heart.

After a few blocks of moving on autopilot, he realized he was heading straight for the Ludwell building. He then knew what he would do next—he'd confront Montague himself.

His fists and jaw clenched as he thought of the old man sitting behind a posh desk on the top floor. He stopped right in the middle of the street in front of the giant glass building. Horns honked. People yelled, "Hey, watch it." Brakes screeched as a cab swerved around him.

The angry driver brushed the back of his hand underneath his chin and yelled, "Get lost."

Gathering his wits, Todd snapped back into the present and hopped to the safety of the curb. He took a moment to gaze up at the tall building, thinking, thinking, thinking. What would he say to Montague?

He couldn't come up with anything in terms of an effective confrontation, and he didn't want to go to jail for assault.

"Hey, you all right?" a familiar voice called to him.

Following the sound, his eyes landed on Tess's driver.

"Clint," Todd said. "Hey. Yeah, uh … I'm not sure."

"Come sit in the car. Take a moment. I have some water." The kind man opened the door of the vehicle, and Todd practically fell inside. He drank the entire bottle of water in a rapid series of gulps and tried to regain a steady breathing pattern.

"Can I take you somewhere?"

"No. That's okay. Thanks. I feel much better." With that, he exited in a flash, turning from a few steps away to wave to a visibly concerned Clint.

Once around the corner, he thought about going back, seeing Tess. He didn't have the energy for another disastrous interaction. "I need to cool off."

Norman Montague waggled a veiny finger at Lawrence from across the desk.

"I'm not asking. I'm telling you." Montague's gruff voice filled the room like a million stinging wasps.

"This isn't the military. I don't have to follow orders," the young scientist snarled back through an angry glare.

"Well, with the Russian involvement, it may as well be. Don't forget that both our necks are on the line. That's reason enough." Threat rang clear in his words.

Lawrence shook his head back and forth. "No."

Then Montague threw down the gauntlet. "Cathy's too."

"Leave her out of this. I'm not kidding." Eyes flashing, Lawrence peacocked his stance, towering even further over his boss.

A strange calm seemed to creep over Montague. Then a sly grin edged across his mouth.

Lawrence's jaw tightened. Had he shown his cards revealing the spark between him and his coworker? Would Montague use that to his advantage later? Of course he would. Lawrence silently cursed his mistake.

"Just save us all a lot of trouble and get Tess to that meeting and on board," Montague paused and peered over his glasses, adding, "With all of it."

"That's a ridiculous expectation, and you know it." Lawrence's voice cracked and he gritted his teeth.

The two glared at each other as if the next move could result in ten paces to guns drawn.

Lawrence dragged his clammy hand across his pant leg and looked away. "Fine. I'll do my best. You better craft a plan B, though."

"How about you better just succeed with plan A?"

A few minutes later, Lawrence left in a huff, quickening his pace as he passed Tess's office. He took note of her tidy desk. No coat or purse or morning coffee in sight. With a sigh of relief, he continued to the lab. He didn't want to have to face Tess about the weird secret council meeting or the egg harvesting. He could hardly even think the words. He needed more time to think about his approach.

He swiped his card at the lab door and stepped inside.

Cathy looked over with a soft smile that, to him, reflected a sliver of hope. "How'd it go?"

"Not great. I have to convince her to come to the secret meeting. He threw up angry air quotes. And I really don't want to get into the egg harvesting aspect, but I also feel like she should know about the full extent of their plans." Bile rose in his throat.

"This is so bizarre, Lawrence. You know she'll never agree to any of this. She barely agreed to submit her blood sample. Harvesting her eggs? There is absolutely no way that will go over well." She paused. "At all."

"Yep. The odds aren't good. So, maybe I don't mention that part at first. Break it down. Start with step one."

She nibbled on her bottom lip.

"But it feels so dishonest."

"You've been threatened, Lawrence."

He didn't want to mention that she had too.

"So ..." He dragged out the word. "What am I going to say to her to get her to the meeting?"

"I have no idea."

"Maybe the truth is the only way. It's definitely the right way, maybe not the safest way, though. I don't know."

Cathy didn't blink or speak for what felt to him like the longest time. "You mean tell her about the Russians, the veiled threats on your life, Montague ... *everything*?"

"Yes." He didn't blink either. "And, Cathy, the threats are not veiled."

Roger inadvertently hit his can of soda and the liquid sprawled dangerously close to his computer equipment. He grabbed his hoodie from the back of his chair and wiped it up. Then he went back to listening to the recorded conversation that had just taken place between Montague and Lawrence on his surveillance feed. "Holy collusion, Batman."

He called Tess. No answer.

"What to do, what to do." He clicked his tongue.

He called Vail, who simply said, "Hello, Roger."

Roger jumped right in, explaining the macabre details of Montague pressing Lawrence.

"This is out-of-control crazy." A clatter sounded behind Vail's words. Roger guessed the man had lost his cool and thrown something. "She'd never agree to be a part of something like that. It's twisted. Illegal. Inhumane!"

"I know. And that's not all."

"Oh God." Vail groaned.

"Well, this is just my thought—"

"Another one of your wild theories, I presume?"

"Not so wild. I mean, if she's the crux to the success of the project, and if she won't go peacefully, then ..."

"Then what?"

"I'm just saying things could take a turn. You can't trust the Russians."

"Can't trust that idiot Montague either. For crying out loud, Roger.

Are you suggesting kidnapping or worse? Did anyone actually say that?"

"Not overtly. I think we need to warn her."

"Warn her of what? The meeting or your conspiracy theory? Which thing? No, you stay out of it. I'll handle this. She's leaving for Rome tonight. In fact, she may have already boarded the flight." After a pause, he said, "Can you check?"

"Sure thing." Roger's fingers clicked the keys. "I'll text you when I know if she's aboard the flight. Also, I need to switch out her phone. I have a contact in Rome that can do it."

"Why the phone?"

"Just in case she's being tracked."

"Do what you have to. I have to go. I need to get Red on this."

With that, Vail hung up, leaving Roger to battle between his need to take action and Vail's request that he stay out of it.

"Is she in danger?" Vail's mouth went dry. He couldn't believe she'd asked Red to remove the security detail or that Red had listened.

"Not sure, but better safe than sorry. I'll go to Rome tonight." Red paused, "Try not to worry."

"I'm going with you." Vail scrambled to put his phone on speaker while typing a text to Derek, asking him to book the firm's private jet for Rome, pronto.

"Not necessary. We don't want too many irons in the same fire," Red advised.

After a brief discussion, they came to an agreement.

Reluctantly, Vail decided to stay back. His skills could be much better applied at home. "I'll dig up as much legal information on all of this as possible."

"She won't be in danger. I have a contact there. He'll keep watch until I arrive. I've got this."

"I'm putting my whole life in your hands." And Vail meant it. She was his life.

F rom a small table partially hidden by a large column in the hotel lobby, Red kept a guarded eye on Tess. "She's up early."

They'd already planned to meet up in about two hours, but he'd arrived in Rome earlier than expected. So, he'd checked into the hotel and planted himself near the entrance to do some surveillance. He thought about going to her, but she exited the hotel, so he hurried to keep up with her.

"Hmm. Maybe it won't hurt to watch for a bit."

She'd probably be angry later if she found out, but he was all about the value of quiet observation before diving into a thorny scenario like this with the Russians possibly on her tail.

Tugging his trench collar up to cover the bottom of his face, he plopped his hat atop his head. Once on the street, he discreetly followed as she paused here and there, browsing the window of a chocolate shop, then a small bookstand. A sense of sadness crept over him at the sight of her. She seemed so alone, vulnerable.

"I've got your back, tiny dancer," he mumbled.

She picked up her pace, pausing briefly to slide large sunglasses over her eyes. She snatched furtive glances all around her as if she felt his presence. Or *a* presence. He scanned the area himself, seeing no one suspicious, no one overly attentive to the beautiful Tess Andreas. *Except me, of course.*

When she wrapped her scarf halfway up her face, he realized she had indeed noticed his tail but hadn't recognized him. He almost lost her as she unexpectedly darted down a side street. Breathing harder at the quickened pace, he rounded the corner catching a glimpse of a slow-closing door of an old stone and stucco building.

What's she up to? Lighting a cigarette, he huddled up against a wall. He'd hold back and let things play out.

Tess meandered down the hallway of the old building until she reached door number three. She knocked, and a shadow darkened the peephole.

"Who is it?"

She cleared her throat before answering. "Roger sent me. You have my order, I believe."

The creaky door swung all the way open, yet the occupant remained unseen.

"Enter, enter, hurry." A hand flashed out from behind the door, waving inward toward the musty interior.

She hesitated for just a beat, then stepped inside, leaving her sunglasses and scarf in place. The sight of the small man on the other side, with greasy hair and days-old stubble on his face, took her aback. To add to her repulsion, he smelled of stale coffee and salted ham. Not a good combination.

Without preamble, he grabbed a burner phone from a stack and handed it to her with a weathered hand. His movements appeared routine, mundane. His disinterest in her identity was blatant as his eyes darted here and there but never landed on her.

He said, "That one is fresh."

"Thank you. Could you clear this one for me?" She handed him the phone she'd been using for the past month. "Now, please."

He reacted with a scurry toward the vise mounted to a table across the room and crushed it to bits.

"Thank you." Tess handed the man an envelope of cash and turned to leave.

Neither said goodbye. He simply locked the door with a loud click as she stood in the hallway contemplating where to go next. She had a meetup with Red soon and a business obligation later in the day—she would be assessing some new hires—but until then, she wasn't sure what to do with her time. Hopefully, Red would contact her soon.

She left the building, instinctively adjusting her scarf and glasses. It just felt safer to be under the cover of accessories at the moment.

———

Red continued to follow Tess, having made a note of the address of the building she'd just visited. When she entered a boutique, he used the reprieve to text Roger, asking him to check it out.

In no time, the computer wiz wrote back that the address belonged to his guy—a resource for a clean phone. Red shook his head and mumbled, "Rookie." With a roll of his eyes, he thought how he should have been notified of that beforehand.

Eventually, she returned to the hotel, and once he knew she had disappeared to the safety of her room, he texted her: *I'm here. Meet?*

She responded in the affirmative.

He texted: *Lobby in ten.*

He ordered a scotch and kicked back in a cozy leather chair, staring at the flames in the fireplace, trying to decide how to tell her that the Russians may be upping their ante. He'd play it by ear. He couldn't deny he felt the need to protect her, maybe a little beyond it being a paid gig. His emotions could become a problem if he didn't keep them in check. "Not going there." He downed the rest of his drink.

I n her tattered Brooklyn apartment, Gemma sashayed in front of the mirror, checking herself out. Her cousin Ray slumped in a nearby chair, rolling a cigarette.

"I look like I'm going to a costume party." She tugged on the maid uniform, trying to get it to come at least to her knees. "Do people still wear these types of uniforms?"

"Who cares?" Ray sniped. "Listen, if you want this broad to stop using your life for her personal entertainment, then you need to get something on her. Blackmail her. Two birds, one stone. She stops hassling you, and then she pays you to boot."

"I don't want her money. I want my life back."

"Well, once you have your life back, you'll want money to live it. Trust me."

"Whatever. By the way, how am I supposed to get into her place?"

"Easy. The cleaning service has you on the books. They've already cleared you with the building manager. She's out of the country anyway. May as well be on the moon."

"I don't even want to know how you know." Gemma met her own eyes in the mirror's reflection. "It's now or never."

Stowing the cigarette behind his ear, he stood. "Let's go."

Less than an hour later, Ray dropped her at the back of Tess's building before parking down the street.

"Don't go anywhere near the front lobby," he'd said.

Gemma entered through the building's service door, checking in with the clerk at the desk. His name tag read Dwight. Her hand shook slightly as she signed in, her mouth dry.

The slender young man who appeared sallow, as if he hadn't seen the sun in months, didn't seem to notice her nervousness. He kept one eye on the small television screen behind the desk as he handed her the key. "Oh, and do NOT forget to return the key." His eyes darted sternly in her direction momentarily. Apparently, this was a common problem.

"I won't forget," she assured him.

"Hang on. I'll take you up." He pointed to the elevator, then turned the volume down on the television as he stood.

"That's all right. I can go alone. Just tell me which floor, apartment number."

Dwight looked at her questioningly. "You need an access card to get to that floor. We don't give those out." His last words blared with condescension. "Her apartment is the whole floor."

Gemma gulped, eyes bulging a bit as she nodded. She clutched the bag of cleaning supplies for dear life.

The two rode silently to Tess's floor, and once the door opened, he pointed to the end of a dimly lit hallway and said, "You can use the service door there. The other entrance is through the main lobby elevator. Do not use that, please. It's for residents and guests only."

"Okay. I won't. Thanks." Gemma bobbed her head up and down in quick succession several times, feeling more than a little out of place. This pricy place had so many rules.

She let herself into the apartment using the key. Once inside, she made her way through a laundry room into the gourmet kitchen, illuminated by under-cabinet lighting that glowed a soft yellow. She could see that loads of natural light brightened the adjacent living room, where the floor-to-ceiling windows took her breath away. "Wow."

She ran her hand across the back of the dark leather sofa, taking note that everything appeared deliberate, right down to the vintage books displayed on a silver side table. *I'm never going to find anything in here. Look at this place. It's like a museum.*

She searched for the master bedroom hoping for at least some type of disorder, anything personal. However, the same situation awaited her in there. Neat, sophisticated, everything in its place. Flustered, she turned to leave, stomping back through the living room.

She spotted an envelope on the coffee table. *How did I miss that the first time around?* She picked it up, gently sliding her fingers inside and withdrawing two similar photographs.

"Ray!" She easily recognized her cousin in the pictures; he appeared to be talking to a doorman, maybe? But why? Not sure what to do, she tucked one photo in her pocket and the other back in the envelope on the table.

Noticing a desk in a nook just past the dining room, partially hidden by a freestanding wall, she started over. She passed by a large painting, stopped, and studied it, trying to guess its worth. She had no idea.

Moving on, she searched the nook, opening a few desk drawers. The computer screen flicked on, and there in front of her flashed an image from what looked like a security feed. Leaning in, she gasped. "Is that? No way. It is! It's Montague. In his office?" She took a picture of it with her phone.

Suddenly, a soft ding filled the quiet space, and she remembered the main elevator opened directly into the apartment. She watched in horror as the doors opened, momentarily frozen in place. Then she cursed and ducked beneath the desk, pulling the chair in close. A male voice called out, "Hello? Is someone here?"

She tried not to move a muscle, pressing her hand over her mouth as the footsteps came closer. Whomever it was roamed around the space until finally the elevator opened and then closed again. For over a minute, she stayed motionless. Her breath came easier as she slowly accepted that whoever had been there was now gone.

She stood with shaky legs, and when her eyes fell to the coffee table, she saw that the envelope had disappeared.

Her heart raced. She needed a drink, a stiff one.

She made a beeline for the service door, hopped on the elevator, then ran into the lobby, practically throwing the key at the clerk.

The shocked man called out, "What about your supplies? Did you leave them upstairs? We have lockers ... Hey!"

She didn't turn around. Instead, she picked up her pace, clutching the pocket that hid the stolen picture.

~63~

First thing Tuesday morning, Lawrence trudged along toward Tess's office. He'd waited to meet with her until she returned from Rome, but today he needed to face the music. And, oh, how he wished that a minor catastrophe would occur to prevent him from reaching his destination. He considered some half-baked ideas as he walked. *Maybe a tree could fall and knock out power to the building or there could be a false gas leak, causing everyone to clear the vicinity.*

But no catastrophe occurred, and he found himself standing at her office door. He knocked softly.

"Come in."

He stepped inside, waved nervously. "Hey, Tess."

"Oh, hello, Lawrence. How nice to see you. What brings you by?"

He gestured toward the door. "Okay if I close it?"

"Absolutely. What's up?"

He shut the door, then plopped down into the chair she offered him in a small conversation area of her office. She sat on the couch, crossed her legs at the ankle, and watched him expectantly.

He struggled with how to start things off. "I, uh ... have to tell you something."

She smiled and tilted her head. Her eyes were kind, and Lawrence had never before felt like such a complete ass for what he was about to do, what he'd already done.

He pushed onward. "I don't know how to say this, and if it were up to me, I'd never even ask. So that being said, here it goes ... Would you be willing to donate more of your blood for the study?"

"Oh?"

"Yeah, and, uh, possibly a tissue sample?" He just couldn't say the egg-harvesting bit, so he'd improvised.

Her expression was blank. She didn't speak, didn't grimace, didn't laugh, did not even blink.

His heart sank to the floor, as did his gaze. He'd offended her. *Well, how else would she feel, you idiot?*

"Are you asking on behalf of Mr. Montague or Mr. Ludwell this time?"

He dared to make eye contact again. "As far as I know, Mr. Montague."

"Hmmm." She pursed her lips.

"I'm sorry." He flinched, almost doubling over as his stomach churned.

She waved off his apology, and her expression changed to one of concern, for him. "Are you okay?"

"Yes. Just too much coffee, I think."

"You seem like there's something more weighing on you. You know that you can talk to me confidentially, right? It's my job."

Shaky and apprehensive, his eyes darted from hers to the floor, wanting to blurt it all out. Instead, he kept his answer short and sweet, "I'm not doing great. No."

She leaned over, putting a friendly hand on his. "Tell me about that."

And with those words, he threw in the towel.

"Well, the truth is, I'm in over my head. This project"—his voice caught for a moment— "It's taken a turn that I never could have predicted. I'm torn. Well, not really torn. It's worse than that. I'm stuck. Yes. Caught right in the middle of something that I'm not sure I want to be a part of anymore. I mean the science is, uh, groundbreaking to say the least, but the rest of it … gah. It doesn't seem right. Morally right."

"Lawrence, you're clearly under stress, and stress is serious business. I can help you manage through it. But I need you to be straight with me. Is Mr. Montague doing something illegal? Are you in some kind of real trouble?"

"I think he may be. I'm pretty sure, but I'm not a lawyer, so I don't know." He felt like a drowning man.

"Let's try something. I'll ask questions that require just a yes or no answer. What do you say?"

"Sure."

"Does this stress you're feeling have to do with my blood sample?"

"Yes."

"I'm going to take a chance here. A big one, but I'm pretty good at judging character. It's my job, after all." She smirked a little. "So, I'm going to ask you if you'd like to pick a definitive side in this whole mess."

"Wh-what do you mean?" He couldn't really say yes or no to that one.

She cocked an eyebrow. "Would you like to join me in figuring out and maybe even putting a stop to Mr. Montague's dealings?"

Wow, she really was the queen of negotiation. He perked up, and for the first time in weeks, he felt a welcome window of hope had just opened in front of him. "Yes, yes. I would like that very much. I'm in a bad spot here."

"Understood. Let's shake on it. Partners."

"Partners."

He found it odd, strangely formal or antiquated, but he stood and shook her hand. She asked a few more questions. He did his best to fill her in on the whisperings of some sort of secret council meeting. Then, he stopped talking. Bit his lip and pushed away the words *egg harvesting*.

"How does the end of this week look as far as meeting with my team?"

Her team? "Open. Just tell me when and where. I'll be there." He had so many questions.

"Good. I'll set it up and be in touch."

"Can I bring my lab partner, Cathy? She's pretty involved already. You can trust her. She's been my only confidante and ... well, my friend during this."

To his relief, she agreed.

"You're not alone in this, Lawrence. Not anymore."

As he plodded back to the lab, he allowed a smidgeon of positivity to take up space in his heart and mind. It had been so long since he'd felt this way. His instinct toward honesty just may have paid off, finding him a way out of this nightmare after all.

G emma rapped loudly on the back door of the bar several times. It was well before opening time—morning, in fact—but finally she heard the telltale signs of someone unlocking it from the inside.

Todd stood in the doorway, looking stunned at the sight of her. "What are you doing here? I thought you were a delivery person."

"I'm trying to be discreet."

"Why?"

"Well, if you let me in, I'll tell you."

He stepped aside as she passed through, walking straight toward his office with overstated familiarity. She turned back to find him motionless, still holding the door open. She waved for him to follow her.

His jaw tightened but he complied. "I thought I told you not to come back here."

She ignored the comment and took it upon herself to shut his office door behind them. "I was in Tess's apartment, and I found this." She tossed a picture across the desk to him.

"Wait. You were where?" His brows furrowed as he tried to comprehend her words. He hadn't even looked at the picture yet.

"Tess's apartment. Anyway, that's not the important part." She pointed at the picture. "Look at this picture."

Todd eyed the picture. "All I see is some guy talking to Tess's doorman Miles in the lobby. So what?"

"That guy is my cousin Ray. The idiot who set up the whole deal with Montague. You know, to trap you or whatever. He's the reason we're knee-deep in this pile of—"

Todd put up his hands. "Whoa. First off, there's no *we*, and second, what does this prove?"

She looked dumbfounded. "Well, I guess it proves she knows it's us, I mean Ray and me."

"Um, she knows with or without this. I told her it was you." He shook the photograph.

"And that's not all," Gemma said. "On her computer, there was some kind of screenshot of Mr. Montague. I saw him sitting in his office —like it was taken from live feed or something. Really weird." Her eyes grew large.

"What?" His voiced cracked. "Let's back up. I need to know when and why you were in Tess's apartment."

She explained the whole plan, her cousin Ray, his blackmailing scheme, and finally about leaving the supplies behind by accident.

"So, this cousin Ray ... this is him?" His finger tapped the photograph.

"Yep."

"Continue." He raised his eyebrows, egging her on.

"Well, that's why I am here."

"Still not following."

"I think he's into something bad, in deeper than just setting you up. Do you understand now?"

"No, actually I don't, but I'll take your word for it." He landed in the chair in a heap.

She took a seat as well. "Anyway, I don't want to go to prison, and with all the complications, it kinda seems maybe that's where this is leading." She chewed on her nail.

He leaned back, closed his eyes for a moment, then said, "You did the right thing by coming here. But listen, don't go in her apartment again, you hear? Or I'll call the police myself."

"Geez. Don't worry. I don't want another close call."

He couldn't believe his ears. "Close call?"

"Yeah, some guy came in looking for her. Sounded like a friend. Anyway, he left. Never saw me."

"Holy— What the hell is going on?" He held up his hands. "Let's refocus. What about this video of Montague?"

"Not a video." She twisted her lips. "Live feed screenshot. So creepy."

"Okay. Let me look into this. In the meantime, keep me posted as to any new developments." He jabbed a finger in her direction. "No more snooping and definitely no blackmailing schemes."

"Got it."

"Don't forget for a minute that you were the one who threw the first punch here. You hurt her *and* me. No one owes you."

She saw his jaw clench, anger apparently rising. Hoping to ward off an outburst, she broke eye contact and fiddled with her bracelet.

"Did you show this picture to Ray?"

"No. I didn't."

"Why not?" His face shown with disbelief.

"Because I don't trust him anymore."

He stood. "I'll walk you out."

She followed him to the back door and stepped out into the alley.

"What are you going to do?" she asked.

"Right now, I'm going to think." He let the door shut in her face.

~65~

Just after five o'clock, Todd left the bar for some fresh air. His feet pounded the sidewalk, but he couldn't escape his thoughts.

"I have to talk with Tess—in person." He had to tell her about this Ray guy and about Gemma snooping in her apartment. She was going to be livid, but she had to know. Looking at his watch, he took an educated guess as to where she might be. He hailed a cab and headed to Blair's pastry shop.

When he got there, Todd looked around for Tess or any sign of her driver. Seeing nothing, he paid the cabbie and got out, positioning himself slightly behind a lamppost across the street from the shop.

Before too long, Tess's driver pulled up in front of Blair's.

Rubbing his hands together for a bit of warmth, Todd started across the street. "It's now or never," he mumbled.

He stopped in his tracks at the curb when he saw a guy wearing dark clothing and a cap pulled down, shading his face, peeking several times into the coffee shop, but he didn't go in. Then he stared with purpose across the street, in Todd's direction.

Todd hustled to the nearest alcove and ducked for cover. Breathing heavy, he took a cautious look around the building's edge. *What's the deal with this guy?* Todd's hackles were up. *Is he looking for Tess? Waiting for her? Why?* He swiped his hair back and shook his head to clear it. He was probably being overly suspicious because of the new Ray information. The stress was getting to him.

Just then, Tess appeared holding a pink box tied with string, and her driver opened the car door for her. Todd's eyes flipped back to the man, who backed into an alcove just down the street from where Todd was.

What the ...?

The driver pulled away.

Todd decided to take a closer look at the man. Just in case.

He marched straight to the alcove where he'd seen the guy seek refuge. However, the space stood empty. He peered up and down the street—the man was nowhere in sight.

Perplexed at the man's swift disappearance, Todd waved for a cab. He knew Tess's next stop would be the ballet studio and that she'd be in there for the next two hours. The staff knew him. He'd give it a shot and try to go in. He looked at his watch and decided to give her twenty minutes to settle in. He parked himself on a bench just outside the studio.

Then ...

The same man in the dark clothes and cap appeared, lit a cigarette, and lingered just past the studio door.

Todd had seen enough. "Hey," he called out to the mystery man.

The guy gave him a once-over before turning and heading in the other direction.

"Hey." Todd started after him. The guy darted down a side street. Todd started running, almost taking out a lady with groceries as he rounded the corner. "Sorry," he said to her. Gathering his wits after the near head-on collision, he searched for the man.

He was gone.

Thwarted, Todd headed back to the studio. He entered.

The girl recognized him, smiling as she pointed to the hallway, "She's in studio three."

"Thanks." He feigned confidence in his response, which faded instantly as he stood just outside studio three. For a moment, he listened, catching just the faintest sound of classical music floating through from the other side of the door.

He squared his shoulders. "Time to face the music, literally." He pushed the door open ... and there she was, every elegant bit of her.

"Todd?" Her voice rose in surprise, almost to the point of concern— or at least he thought so.

"I need just a minute of your time. Please." He waited for her scowl, her rejection. But none came.

"What's up?" she asked, gliding over to him.

With a silent *thank you* to whatever higher power existed, he realized she must have noticed his tortured expression and was willing to give him a chance to explain.

"I know I'm probably the last person you expected to see. But ... you're being followed."

"Obviously. By you," she deadpanned.

"No." Waving his hands, he continued, "I mean, yes, I followed you here, but I mean ... you're being followed by someone else."

Her demeanor shifted as her stare fell to the floor. Her shoulders dropped. She whispered, "I know."

"Well, who is it? And more importantly, *why*?" Walking closer, he gently put a finger to her chin, guiding her gaze to meet his once again. Staring long and deep into her eyes, he said with conviction, "I'm not leaving without an answer."

A long sigh rode the wave of her breath as she grabbed her cardigan from the ballet bar. "Let's go somewhere, sit. I'll fill you in. I need to change. Meet you in the lobby?"

Tension left him. "Yes. Thank you."

She nodded ever so slightly.

After a few minutes, they left the studio together, walking side by side a few blocks to the café. They shimmied into a private booth, ordered tea and hot sandwiches Then came her explanation.

He didn't know what to say, how to respond to all that she'd just revealed.

She reached over and touched his hand. A warmth, an electric charge sparked in his veins.

"I miss you, and I'm worried as hell about you."

"I'm sorry. It's been too long. I should have talked to you sooner. It's just been … a lot. Across the board." She pulled her hand away and twisted it with the other in her lap.

"This is crazy. You know that, right? This situation. It's not normal."

"Yes," and then a quizzical look crossed her face. "Hey, how did you know?"

He raised his eyebrows.

"That I'm being followed."

Offering a slow nod, he said, "Well, for starters, I saw the guy outside the pastry shop." He caught her perturbed look. Waving his hand in protest, he said, "Before you jump to conclusions, I had planned to stop you there to talk about something else."

A slow "okay" escaped through a whisper from her lips.

"So, who is he?" he prodded. "The *guy*."

"He's one of my hires. Security detail of sorts. He's just supposed to watch—not interfere."

"Good grief. That's not disturbing at all." He paused this time with one raised eyebrow. "Because of Montague?"

"Technically speaking, yes. Now, your turn. What did you want to talk to me about, originally?"

"This." He gingerly withdrew an envelope from his pocket—it contained the photograph. He detected a flash of recognition in Tess's widening eyes.

Breathless, she managed, "How? Why do you have this?"

"You are not going to like this." He explained the best he could what Gemma had done.

"What?" She spoke too loudly, and heads turned.

Todd leaned toward her. "Hey …"

She waved him off. "I need some air." She stood and tugged at the neck of her blouse.

"Of course."

"I'll call you later," she said. With that, she exited the café.

66

Once outside, Tess gulped in the cool air as she walked one block, then another, desperately trying to clear her head. Finally, she stopped. Her insides felt like ice. She looked around, and to her relief, Clint pulled the car up next to her. She opened the door and quickly slid into the back seat, sitting on her hands to warm them. Her thoughts ran deep as she caught glimpses through the car window of the fading sunlight flickering along the gaps between the buildings.

"Dr. Andreas. We're here."

She hadn't realized they'd arrived at her building. "Oh, sure enough. Thank you, Clint."

"Ma'am, you okay?"

"Yes. Just a long day."

Holding the door, he stared with his mouth in a tight line, no smile, just showing what appeared to be concern. She looked away and hustled inside the building.

She sat cross-legged on her couch, jittery. She tried deep breathing. Her phone buzzed and her whole body jumped, catapulting the phone to the floor. "Get it together," she scolded herself as she leaned down to retrieve the phone.

"Hi."

"Hi. Where are you?" Vail sounded worried.

"I'm home." She hoped he didn't have more bad news.

"Good. I have a question for you."

"What is it?" She squeezed her eyes shut and braced herself.

"Do you happen to have the other photograph of the guy? I went to your place to pick them up, but only one ..."

She cut him off. "Yes. I have it. Long story. I'll fill you in when you get here."

"See you in a few."

Twenty minutes later, sitting across from Vail, she spoke in clipped sentences, explaining. "Gemma Stein took it from my apartment."

Silence loomed for a few moments.

"How do you know this?"

"Todd told me. He gave it back to me tonight."

"What?" he spat out. She thought he sounded a tad wounded, maybe about her having met with Todd, but he definitely looked more angry than anything.

"When?"

"While I was in Rome. She and her cousin Ray planned it. Anyway, it explains the abandoned cleaning supplies."

His face wore a mask of alarm.

"What is it?"

"I don't know. It's just that day when I stopped by to get the photographs while you were gone, I felt like someone was here. I called out, but I didn't see anyone. I wonder."

Her heart stopped, then she said, "That woman and that cousin of hers ..." Her voice cracked, stopping her words as her cheeks flushed. She watched his hand tighten into a fist then release.

"There's something else too." He slouched a bit.

"And so it goes; when it rains it pours."

He leaned over the table, eyes intense. "Something weird is going on. Really weird. I haven't figured it all out yet. I've been digging and well, the Russians are more involved than I realized. There's an off-site lab and a lot of paperwork coming in for funding."

She jolted upright, "Oh, I almost forgot. I spoke with Lawrence too."

"You've been busy."

"Yes, but this may be just what you need to make sense of things." She then explained how Lawrence wanted to help stop Montague. At least so it seemed.

Motionless, Vail listened.

"It's a lot to digest," she said woefully.

"Tell me about it." His blinking seemed erratic, almost like an aftershock from information overload.

"We need a record of some sort. To keep everything straight." She floated on the trail of her words to the desk drawer to retrieve a pad and pen. Wasting no time, they huddled on the couch and began hashing out a list of what they knew, including who, where, and what specific events had occurred thus far.

"The common denominator always seems to be Montague," he said.

"No big surprise there." She meant it too.

"I think we need to put all of our heads together. Everyone involved on our side of things, that is."

"I agree. A meeting of the minds."

Together they determined the guest list.

"Roger and Red, of course." She jotted the names on the paper.

"Yes." He poured a scotch. "Want one?"

She shook her head and said, "And after today, Lawrence and Cathy."

"Are you sure about including Cathy?" He questioned her with raised brows.

"Yes. I'm sure. She's going to know everything from Lawrence anyway. He made it clear she's his confidante. It's far better if we have a closer eye on her, form a relationship with her. Making her part of our team is at least a safety net."

He agreed and sipped the scotch as she wrote down the two names.

"And ..." She dragged out the word.

"I don't like the sound of that."

"No. You're not going to like it at all. But I think it's important. Todd should be at the meeting."

"No." His glass clanked hard against the glass table as he set it down.

"He's the link to the girl. He was Montague's first target." The words sounded harsh as she tried to justify his being included.

"I disagree. You were the first target, and besides, the girl doesn't seem to know anything except how to steal." He scowled.

"I see your point. But ..." Their eyes met. "She is kind of an important source of insight since she's related to the thug in the photographs. She's also our only link back to Montague's criminal dealings at this point. And Todd is our only link to her."

Closing his eyes briefly, he shook his head and said in a strained voice, "I know I'm going to regret saying yes to this."

She jumped right in, not giving him a chance to change his mind. "So it's set, then. Now ... when to meet?" The pen *tap, tap, tapped* on the notebook in her lap.

Her fingers scrolled through her contacts, then she dialed.

"Wasting no time, I see." Vail put a foot on the coffee table, leaning back as he finished off the last swirl of amber liquid in his glass.

"Todd. Hi. It's me." As she said his name, she swore she could feel the tension in the room grow tenfold.

67

M ontague incessantly twisted the monogrammed ring on his right hand as Ivan, the so-called Russian translator, revealed the exact location of the impending council meeting.

Under his breath, he repeated the translator's words, "The Louvre."

Mr. Borin's brows furrowed as he looked at Montague. "The exact location is to remain secret. Understand?"

He swallowed hard, "Yes. Of course. But if I may ask ... why?"

Borin narrowed his eyes. "We do not need uninvited guests."

Montague broke eye contact and prayed for this meeting to end. It was late and he wanted to get home.

Borin glanced at Ivan. "Please continue."

Ivan went on with his presentation. "In 1989, when I.M. Pei's pyramid entrance was erected, it gave way for covert construction to take place in an older part of the massive Palais. A secret conference room, a bunker of sorts, came to fruition outfitted with the best of the best in technology. The room is devoid of windows and has fortified walls impregnated with Wi-Fi caging and ballistic protection."

Next, Ivan discussed the matter of the guest list, being elusive at best. This only served to catapult Montague's agitation.

Borin looked to Montague, "And you, of course, will bring the guest of honor?"

Montague fought the paralysis of dread that fell over him. How could he forget the Mount Everest of a task of convincing Tess Andreas to join them?

Borin continued to glare at him, so he diverted his eyes and took a swig of his vodka.

When the meeting ended, Montague pushed away from the table, stood, and started toward the exit. Borin caught his arm on the way and said in a low voice filled with spittle, "There is no tolerance for failure. If you do not bring her, it will be your death, and I will get her anyway, my way. Understand?"

Montague pulled away and left the building as quickly as possible, practically diving into the back seat of his private car. "Go, go," he instructed the driver.

His mind was embroiled in thoughts of disaster. The whole of this project's success fell squarely on his shoulders, as did his life—and he had no idea how he, or anyone, would get Tess to agree to this sham.

He so badly wanted out of this, but he knew he was in too far. That part of him that cared too much about power and notoriety—a place in science history—was slowly diminishing in size.

He dialed Doris, instructing her to book the private jet for himself and a few others, including Tess Andreas.

He had to stay positive, after all.

Next, he dialed Lawrence. After a brief update on the upcoming council meeting, omitting the Louvre and sticking just to the meeting being in Paris, he jumped right to the main point. "You need to get her on board. Now."

"I'm not a magician. I'm a scientist."

"Well, in this case, you'll need to find a way to be both."

Lawrence hung up the phone, wondering if he should call for an ambulance since his heart felt as if it were about to explode. He rubbed his temples. Should he tell Tess now? Tell her later? He went back and forth until, finally, his shaking finger pressed the call button on his phone.

"Hi, Lawrence. What's going on?"

"I have an update." His mouth went dry.

"What is it?"

He swallowed hard. "Remember the council meeting I mentioned?"

"Yes."

"Well, I just spoke to Mr. Montague, and, uh, he informed me that you needed to be at the meeting. It's in Paris. It's my job, apparently, to make sure you come." He listened to her silence as if it carried a hidden message. He added, "I'm sorry, Tess, to burden you with this. But he issued a not-so-veiled threat to my safety. Add to that the Russians, and, uh, it's just not good." *So smooth, Lawrence, so smooth,* he chided himself.

"I need to put you in touch with someone. His name is Red. Tell him everything. He's working on my behalf. It's going to be okay."

Desperate and confused, he agreed. What else could he do? He trusted her far more than Montague.

~68~

V ail cringed at the fact that not only had his archrival for Tess's affection made the guest list but had somehow become the host of the secret get-together at his bar. Reluctantly, he rapped two knuckles against the back door of Whiskey Tales at his assigned time: 9:15 a.m. Without delay, the metal door inched opened to reveal one of Red's stone-faced henchman, who grumbled, "Passcode."

Vail pushed away how ridiculous this felt and forced his own compliance by uttering the password, "Antivirus." He knew without a doubt that the brainiac idea for the word had come from the depths of only one mind—Roger's. He bit his lip. What could he do? Red had insisted on the clandestine style of this meeting. No one had the desire to argue it. Even Tess agreed it would be easier to just play along. So he bit his tongue as another goon appeared to escort him into a private section of an already empty bar.

Roger knocked with a tight fist on the back-alley door. His heart raced and his nerves buzzed, keeping his entire body in a constant state of motion, even as he stood stock-still, waiting for a response.

The door opened at a snail's pace, and a man that looked as if he had recently escaped from Alcatraz said, "Password."

"Antivirus." His voice cracked as he spoke the word, feeling silly now for selecting it.

The shifty guy peered left and right, and then stepped aside for him to enter.

Roger scooted past the rotund man, their thick frames brushing awkwardly. A thinner criminal-esque figure approached and said, "Follow me."

The two entered the main room of the pub. Tess and Vail stood in the center of the room. Todd was at the bar, lining glasses up on a tray. And leaning against the bar was the man Roger had met only once—Red.

Roger thought to himself how intimidating Red had looked the first time he laid eyes on him, and now after having entered into the alternate underworld, he knew he hadn't been wrong in his assumption. Pulling out a chair, he took a seat next to Tess. Seconds later, Lawrence and a petite woman entered the room. Her name was Cathy, according to Vail, and she looked like a little mushroom under the tall tree that was Lawrence.

Tess said, "Please, everyone ... order some drinks, snacks, whatever you need. Then let's all sit at that table over there." She pointed at a large round table with enough chairs to seat them all.

They shuffled toward Todd and placed drink orders. Seemed no one had the stomach for food.

———

Once everyone had been seated, Vail took charge of the meeting. "First of all, thank you for being here." His eyes found Tess. She cut her glance toward Todd, prodding for an acknowledgement of some sort. Reluctantly, he swallowed his pride and said, "And thank you, Todd, for allowing us to meet here."

Todd's cheeks flushed.

Vail continued. "We're all here for the same reason, and I believe there will be strength in our number."

As he summarized what had been discovered so far, his gaze shifted among the group members. He remained keenly aware that everyone at the table knew large portions of what he'd presented already, so he made sure to keep things succinct. Regardless, hearing everything laid out in an organized way just heightened the tragedy of it all. From his vantage point, each person's expression was a mixture of awe and fear, something beyond normal shock—something born from glimpses of pure evil. The bottom line was everyone in that room now knew that Montague, the Russians, and the Machiavellian plan to use Tess as a human lab rat for power and money must be thwarted.

"And for those of you unaware, the Russians and Montague have planned a secret council meeting in Paris. Details still need to be addressed, but the goal is for as many of us as feasible to attend." Vail paused then added, "Under the guise of cooperating with the enemy, of course." His words filled the space like storm clouds, bringing in a morbid sense of doom.

Of course, Todd was the only one unaware of the secret council meeting in Paris. The shock was written all over his face, his jaw hanging agape. "What?" he whispered, looking at Tess. She simply shrugged then directed her attention back to Vail.

Vail hurried through the rest of the pertinent info, not wanting to hear anyone's opinions on the matter just yet—especially Todd's. He just needed to get it all out there. When he finished, he said, "Now that we are all on the same page, let's take a quick break. Be back at the table in ten."

Chairs scraped against the wooden floor as they were pushed away from the table, and the small group scattered toward the bar or the restrooms. In the meantime, fresh libations filled empty glasses, and from all appearances, the drinks seemed a little more potent this time around. Vail scanned the room for Tess. He didn't see her—or Todd, for that matter.

"Have you seen Tess?" he asked Roger.

Mid-sip, Roger blinked owlishly.

"Where?" Vail demanded.

Roger swallowed, smacked his lips, then tilted his head in the direction of the hallway that led to the back.

Vail spun on his heels, stomping away. When he entered the hallway, he saw no one, but heard faint voices and noticed Todd's office door slightly ajar. He moved closer and listened quietly.

Tess said, "I need your support."

Todd responded with, "I *am* supporting you. I don't want you in harm's way."

"I will definitely be in harm's way if I don't deal with this. Head-on."

"Tess, I can't be the only one who thinks going to this meeting in Paris is a bad idea." Todd's voice sounded louder, like someone had turned up the volume on a radio.

"Hmph."

Vail could imagine Tess crossing her arms and lifting her chin defiantly.

"You do not need to go to Paris. You already know everything." A thump like a hand hitting a desk followed Todd's words.

"Do we? How do you know that?"

"Just answer me this ... Why you? Why can't someone go on your behalf? Tell me. Give me one solid reason?"

"I don't have to justify my decision to you or to anyone, but if you must know, I need to stop this. It's my issue. And people could get hurt if I don't go."

"Who? And by the way, maybe no one will get hurt *if none of you go*. What about just calling the authorities?"

"We're past that point, don't you think? I'm pretty sure I'd be in the cell next to Montague. Tires and other regrettable things, remember?" Her voice shuddered on the last part.

"Still, you don't have to go."

"You know what—this was a mistake."

"What was a mistake?"

"This. Meeting here. Asking for your help."

Her words rang cold even to Vail as he loitered in the hallway absorbing the silence that had befallen the pair. After a few more seconds, he backed away, and just in time ... because within a moment, Tess and Todd silently returned to the table.

It was time to regroup. Vail said, "If I could have everyone's attention. Let's all gather round." Shuffling commenced, and Vail motioned to Red. "The floor is all yours." For the first time since the gathering had begun, Vail welcomed the opportunity to be a part of the audience and not the main speaker.

Pushing back the sleeves of his flannel shirt, Red moved from his chair and said, "Now that you've all been schooled on the facts, it's time you become familiar with the dark side of things. If what I say scares you, then we're probably in the right place because fear in my world means you stay alert—and even better, alive."

The group stayed motionless, taking in his words as if hearing a scary tale around a campfire. Even to Vail, who had heard and seen a lot in his time as a lawyer, the things Red divulged about the Russian mafia seemed inconceivable—murder, torture, kidnapping, all of it involving guns and bloodshed. "So, now you all should understand why Tess will appear to play ball with Montague and the Russian counterparts." He paused for a sip of whiskey.

Todd mumbled, "Not really."

Licking his lips, Red aimed his piercing stare at Todd before speaking again. "Now, down to the nitty-gritty. For starters, my team will provide itineraries—or, as I prefer to call them, playbooks—for those of you attending the Paris powwow. And for those of you not attending, you'll have clear game plans to follow from wherever you are." He looked at each person in turn, finding Todd's disgruntled stare last. "This is a team effort. Understood?"

Nods and mumbles of agreement peppered the space. "Good. Now, during the trip overseas, all of us will be working as if our lives depend on it. And make no mistake, they do."

The residue of his words stuck to the energy of the room like gum to a shoe until one by one the group dispersed, leaving the bar as empty as it had been just hours ago. Only Todd remained.

Tess and Vail rode the elevator up to her apartment.

She looked at him. "I feel overwhelmed."

"Me too."

Once inside, he poured a small whiskey as she plopped down on the couch.

"I don't know who to trust outside of our team," she said.

"That's better actually, according to Red. He said it's good to be guarded." Vail held out the glass, offering her a sip.

She waved it away. "I know you're right. It's just not easy to maintain this level of awareness for so long. I almost feel like I'm living a parallel life—and having to keep track of a million lies on top of it all."

"It's torture, I know, but if we can pull this off ..."

"I know." Her words caught in her throat.

He sat, gently taking her hand. "Look, let's just focus on one step at a time. Break it into mini-tasks. First, Montague needs to believe you're resisting and then, at the last, on board. Second, we need to figure out the Russian side of this. And if fate is on our side, leave Montague holding the bag and Ludwell Corporation and our lives intact."

"I hope you're right."

"I am. We will get through this. It'll all be a distant memory. Almost like it never happened."

She took a jagged breath.

He leaned in and lightly kissed her lips.

She took the glass from his hand and sipped.

Alone after the meeting, Todd leaned on the slick bar top, downing a shot of whiskey in one burning gulp. He reached for a clean bar towel, his hands robotically shining the washed glassware as his thoughts whirred. Out of the blue came a rapping at the door. Not wanting to deal with anyone at the moment, he called out, hoping to deter the fancy of the hopeful patron.

"We're closed. Opening at three today."

To his dismay, the rapping unabashedly grew louder.

He tossed the rag aside and marched to the door.

"I know you're in there."

He recognized the voice and shook his head in defeat, unlatching the lock.

"Gemma. What—"

"I saw all those people. I know you're open. Or at least had a private party." She angled her head as she tried to see past him and inside the bar.

He stepped forward to block her, and a wave of concern hit him as he did so. Were there others around, watching her? Watching them? He looked behind her to the street but saw nothing to justify his worry. He was on edge, plain and simple.

"Come in. Hurry." He drew her in by her arm.

"Hey, hands off." She shook loose.

"What do you want? I told you not to come back here."

"Well, for starters, I saw your girlfriend leave here. You patch it up? Oh ... except she left with another guy. He's a looker too."

He waved off her prickly comments. "What happens here is none of your business."

"Oh really? Well, I disagree. Let me ask you this. If I were to go to Montague with a description or, say, these pictures ..." She flashed her phone, and he caught a glimpse of the image on the screen—Roger exiting the bar with Lawrence behind him. She continued in an arrogant, mocking tone, "What would Montague pay for these babies?"

Todd's reaction surprised even himself as he raised his hand and slapped the phone right out of her fingers. Violence had never been his style, but he was over the threats, the blackmail, the danger—and all the people who were a part of that danger. She'd picked the wrong day to threaten him.

"You jerk!" Her stringy hair lashed his arm as she leapt to retrieve the device. "Lucky for you it's not broken." She brushed off the screen with her shirt and started to tuck the phone into her purse.

But Todd was faster. He grabbed it out of her hand, the picture of Roger still on the screen.

"Hey!" Her shrill word echoed in the empty bar.

She reached toward him as his fingers swiped and pressed the screen. He moved away and proceeded to delete the telltale photos, then erased the delete folder. Stuffing her phone in his pocket for safekeeping, he dialed his own.

"Roger here," said the voice on the other end.

"Hey, it's Todd. I didn't think I'd need to call you so soon, but I think we have a bit of a problem."

Gemma's eyes bugged out. "What are you doing?"

Todd turned his back to her.

Roger said, "I'm listening."

Todd explained.

"I'm on it. Texting Red now."

Within a few minutes, the front door flung open.

Gemma gasped when she saw who it was. "You—the dog killer."

"That's not all I do." Hannibal's voice lacked emotion, unless coldness counted.

Todd clenched his jaw at the reminder of the dog debacle, and then he wondered just a little if he actually knew Tess at all. *No way she okayed the dog thing, right?*

All heads turned as the bar door swung open again. Instinctively, Hannibal pulled a gun and pointed it, as if it were the most natural thing to do.

"Whoa." Roger stopped in his tracks, raised both hands, and stepped back a couple of paces toward the door.

Hannibal lowered the gun. "Sorry, man."

Gemma looked from one man to the next, finally landing with desperate eyes upon Todd.

He refused to give her any solace and shifted his attention instead to Roger, tossing him Gemma's phone. "Here it is. She took pictures of people leaving earlier."

Roger peered through his glasses at the cowering girl. "Did you send any of these out? And don't lie because I will eventually find out."

Hannibal grabbed her arm violently. A whimper escaped her lips as she vehemently shook her head no.

Roger set up his laptop along with other various devices and got to work.

"What are you going to do to me?" Gemma's voice was meek and pitiful. She tried in vain to get out from under the ruffian's grip.

Todd flashed a concerned look at Hannibal just as his phone buzzed. Breaking eye contact with the goon, Todd looked at his phone screen. It displayed a message from Red, instructing him to meet him in the back office of the bar.

"Gotta take care of something right quick. I'll only be a minute," Todd said as he moved down the hallway. Cigarette smoke assaulted his nostrils when he opened the door to his office.

A relaxed Red sat behind Todd's desk, puffing a ring of smoke. "You ready for this, son?"

"No. Actually, I'm not."

"Well, that's a good sign."

Todd frowned, his frustration rising. "None of this is the least bit good in my opinion. What are you going to do with that girl?"

"Not sure."

"We're at a crossroads, then. We can make the right choice, or we can go down a path that—"

Red interrupted. "There is no *we* in this. You're the only one at a crossroads, son. I made my own choice before you were ever born."

Reality struck Todd as he observed the older man casually extinguishing his cigarette with the tip of his finger. "I don't want to know what happens to her." He waved his hands and dropped into the chair opposite Red.

"Smart man. So I assume I have your word that none of this ever happened?"

"Shit. Yes." His mouth went dry, and his stomach churned.

"The security cameras, are they ..." The man waved a finger toward the ceiling.

"Still disabled from Roger's setup for the meeting."

With that, the older man stood, leaving through the alley door.

Todd closed his eyes, hoping that when he opened them, this would all have been a bad dream. No luck. Like a prisoner to the gallows, he trudged back to the main room.

Taking in Gemma's trembling lower lip and tear-streaked face, he knew the terror she felt. Without another word between any of them, he did nothing as Hannibal escorted her past where he stood, into the hallway, and out the back into the alley.

Todd shut his eyes, but all he could see was Gemma's terrified expression. He popped them back open and said, "I need a drink, another one."

Roger stopped typing, and the two locked eyes. Neither could find the strength to speak in the enormous hollowness of the moment.

~70~

Cathy put her hand on Lawrence's as they sat on her couch, which had become a nightly routine.

"What a day." She plopped her sock feet on the coffee table.

"No kidding." He stared straight ahead at the flashing television screen.

"Come on. You must feel better. We aren't in this alone anymore."

"Yes, but I'm not an actor. There's a lot riding on my performance to Montague and the Russians. I don't know if I can do this."

"Oh, I know you can do it. Remember what Red said at the meeting —you just have to keep your story consistent."

"Yes. I know. I know. Make it look like she doesn't want to go—like I have to coax her."

"Right. Otherwise, it could raise a red flag if she agreed with bells on from the get-go." Cathy pulled her legs in and crisscrossed them as she turned to face him. She placed both hands on top of his. "It'll work."

He offered a soft smile despite the uneasiness in his chest and said, "I really hope you are right."

SUNDAY, NOVEMBER 10

Two weeks after the meeting at Todd's bar, Vail and Tess waited in her apartment, suitcases stowed by the door. Montague's assistant had scheduled the flight once Tess had finally agreed to attend the meeting in Paris, after a week and a half of pretending to resist.

"Clint should be here soon. It's quarter after five." Vail looked at his watch. His nervous energy showed in his movements.

"It's a private jet. And, apparently, I'm the crème de la crème. They'll wait." Her voice held an ounce of contempt woven seamlessly with sarcasm.

He nodded and checked his watch again anyway.

She eyed a text on her phone. Vail popped his eyebrows.

"Oh, it's Red. He and his two guys are leaving on their flight soon. They'll land before us. We will meet them at the flat he's rented; he's calling it home base, by the way." A smirk flitted across her lips. Vail didn't respond.

The doorman buzzed. "Your car is here, Dr. Andreas."

"We'll be right down, Miles. Thank you."

They walked through the lobby with Vail pulling both suitcases. Miles said, "I will keep an eye on everything here. Don't you worry."

She smiled and put a hand on the doorman's arm. Then, to his obvious surprise, she leaned in and kissed his cheek. "You are a true friend."

The blushing man tugged at his lapel. Vail offered the man a sharp nod of approval, and the two travelers left the building.

Across town, Lawrence knocked on Cathy's door. He heard her scurrying around inside. She called out, "I'll be right there."

A few seconds later, she flung open the door, flushed and balancing two tote bags and one suitcase. She started over the threshold, then exclaimed, "My purse!" She darted back inside, the totes on her shoulders hitting the doorframe. Lawrence grinned in amusement.

Returning in the same fashion, she said, "All set now," and locked the door behind her. "I'm so nervous."

He grabbed one tote and her suitcase. "You're not the only one."

At half past six, Tess, Vail, Roger, Lawrence, and Cathy waited in the private hangar to be escorted to the plane. Nary a peep was said among them. Tess eyed her buzzing phone. A text from Todd read: *"Be careful."* A tinge of guilt poked at her for leaving him behind to worry.

After they'd boarded and settled into their seats, Tess noticed that Montague had yet to arrive. She turned to Vail. "Where is he, for chrissakes?"

"I don't know. Fashionably late?" He gave a slight flick of his hands.

She pursed her lips.

Ten more minutes passed before the horrid little man made his entrance. His gruff chatter invaded the cabin before the man himself entered. Those who were already seated rolled their eyes at each other, undoubtedly dreading the long flight with the devil.

"Welcome all," Montague said, waving his hands around theatrically. "It is my pleasure to welcome you on this trip hosted by

Ludwell Corporation. You are the elite, part of a groundbreaking study that has the potential to change the world."

"Showboat," Roger muttered.

Montague's head swung in his direction. "What's that you say?"

"Let's get the show on the road," Roger said with mock enthusiasm, pumping his fist in the air.

"That's the spirit! I am thrilled—"

Finally, the captain's flight announcement interrupted the speech, and Montague begrudgingly took his seat at the front of the plane.

"Thank God," Cathy whispered.

Halfway into the Paris-bound flight, Montague snored loudly, giving way for the others to speak privately. Roger moved to a seat facing the two that Vail and Tess occupied. "The Russians are driving this. Montague is not in charge, whether he believes so or not. It's dangerous for us all, but especially for you, Tess. They will stop at nothing, absolutely nothing to be the biggest winner in this whole thing."

Vail looked at Tess, whose face had lost all color. She grabbed Vail's hand and closed her eyes.

"I think we get it, Roger," Vail said. He tilted his head toward Tess.

The techie turned crimson. "Oh, right." He got up and headed toward the restroom, and Vail followed.

They met at the back of the plane. "What exactly do you mean 'dangerous for Tess.' Isn't that obvious? That's why Red and his team are joining us."

Roger winced, scratched the back of his neck. "I know. I know, but ..."

"But what?"

"Well, what if this whole thing is just a ploy to take her captive?"

Vail spun in a circle, exasperated. "Where do you come up with this shit? Seriously."

"I've had time to think."

"Well, stop thinking." With that, he hustled back to his seat next to Tess.

"Was coming on this trip a mistake?" she asked. "We'll be on foreign soil. Anything could happen."

"Red will be there the whole time. He won't let this get out of hand. We have an escape plan, remember?" Vail swallowed his own doubt with a gulp.

Roger shuffled up the aisle with a glass of water in hand, sloshing it a bit as he navigated between seats. "For you, Tess. Sorry to add to the worry."

Vail leered at Roger.

"Worries? What worries?" she deadpanned. She took the dripping glass and sipped.

For the rest of the flight, the five players sat under a cold blanket of quiet, accentuated only by the grating snores of Norman Montague.

~72~

MONDAY, NOVEMBER 11

V̲ail paced the marble floor in the rented Paris flat as Red lit a cigarette. The group—minus Montague, of course—positioned themselves in various places around the room, all looking disheveled. Tess's state of mind, in particular, concerned him as she sat with hands clasped tightly on her lap, her knuckles white.

He slid in and sat next to her on the small French sofa, putting his hand over hers. She looked up at him with a glint of angst in her green eyes.

Before long, Red began briefing the group. "Now, as you all are aware, we still don't have the meeting's location here in Paris." He looked to Roger for confirmation.

Roger shook his head and said, "I've combed through everything, but there's no correspondence or footage revealing the location."

"It's a complication for sure, but we'll be ready. Don't worry. I've got all the goods needed to keep us in touch and as safe as possible during this ... whatever this is."

He paused and signaled toward his henchmen, who handed out burner phones, trackers, and earpieces along with unsolicited advice for the day ahead.

Roger showed everyone the ins and outs of the devices. "Like this, push the earpiece all the way. Yes. Like that." He went into another room of the flat to test it all out.

Lawrence snapped to attention with his hand to his ear, nodding, "Yes. I can hear you."

Once satisfied that everyone knew what to do, Red wrapped up the session. "Leave in a staggered fashion—that's standard protocol when we all get together like this."

Vail studied an exhausted Cathy and a doting Lawrence.

"We're headed for the hotel," Lawrence announced.

He lowered his stare to the floor, wanting much the same.

"Time for some shut-eye," Roger mumbled as he shuffled out the door next.

Finally, it was their turn. "Tess, you ready?" Vail asked, offering his hand.

Wearing a tight smile, she grabbed hold and let him lead her back to the hotel.

He saw her to her room. "Are you sure you're okay staying alone?"

"Nice try," she said with a sly grin. "Yes, I'm fine."

Vail fought a small smirk, thankful to see some of her feistiness return. She was going to need it. "I'm right next door," he said.

"I know." She kissed her fingertips, placed them against his lips, then slowly shut the door.

73

TUESDAY, NOVEMBER 12

E arly morning, the group gathered in the Paris hotel lobby at the request of Norman Montague.

Chatter filled the small alcove until the porter alerted them that their cars awaited.

Tess peered through the open doors of the hotel to see three shiny vintage cars lined up in a row, doors ajar. Next stop would be the still-undisclosed meeting place. Her nerves zinged and her heartbeat zoomed, no matter how much she tried to quell her anxiety.

From the flat, Red monitored Tess's tracking device and spoke to the group through their two-way earpieces, working seamlessly, courtesy of Roger's technical magic. "Tracker is a go. Remember the plan at all times, no improvising. We will be right behind you. Stay calm at all costs."

Lawrence nodded and said too loudly, "Okay," in response to Red's commentary. That earned him an elbow to the ribs by Roger. "Why'd you do that?"

Roger leaned in and whispered, "Listen, Captain Obvious. Just keep it cool."

"What do you mean?"

"Stop nodding and answering your earpiece."

Lawrence rubbed his side, exaggerating the pain as he sniped, "Sorry, I'm not experienced at espionage."

Tess's heart rate sped up even more.

Once the cars left for the undisclosed meeting spot, Red and his team hopped into their van and started the pursuit. Winding through the Parisian streets, he realized the entourage seemed headed in the direction of the 1st Arrondissement, home to the Louvre.

"The troops just got company up ahead," his driver called back to him. Red leaned forward to peer through the windshield. Several blacked-out SUVs fell in line behind the vintage cars.

"The Russians," Red said.

"Should I put more distance?"

"No. This is expected. Stay the course. I don't want to risk losing our line of sight on our people." He sat back down but stayed at the edge of the seat, his hand gripping the front headrest. He counted the number of vehicles that had joined the procession. Three of them.

The black SUVs turned off onto a side street as the glamorous cars glided up to a side entrance where two uniformed men waited. The first car, which held Montague, slowed to a stop while the guard spoke with the driver. After much pointing and head-nodding, large iron gates creaked open. The cars slowly entered one by one, driving a short way to an open breezeway-type tunnel, where they parked in an angled row, as if orchestrated. The riders exited and lingered in the shadow of an archway. From all outward appearances, they could have been royalty arriving for a grand tour of the Louvre.

If only, Tess thought.

She saw Roger nudging Lawrence, who frowned and said, "What? I'm not doing anything."

Roger said, "Shhh. Look." He pointed. Tess looked in the direction he was indicating and saw a small lady dressed impeccably and wearing a museum guide lanyard, approaching. She was carrying a sign on a pole that read, *Ludwell Corp: Champagne with the Artists.*

No one spoke except Montague, who clapped once, loudly, before announcing, "Welcome all. Please gather near our guide. She will lead us to the reception room."

Roger muttered, "What kind of circus act is this?"

Vail shrugged. "Beats me."

"Where's Red? That's what I want to know," Tess interjected.

In her ear, Red replied, "I've got you covered. Don't worry. Everything is under control."

She squeezed Vail's hand as his eyes landed on a clearly concerned Lawrence. He was watching Cathy, who seemed more rattled than any of them at the moment, clutching her purse as if her life depended on it.

"If this were a real tour, wouldn't the guide be saying something about the history of the building itself?" Cathy whispered to no one in particular.

Lawrence responded. "It's not a real tour, Cathy."

"Then why pretend?"

He looked around at the scattered groups of people across the courtyard inside the Louvre grounds, answering with just two words and a sweeping hand at the crowd. "For them."

She nodded. "Oh, right. I'm new to this."

Tess patted her shoulder and offered her a reassuring smile. "Yes, aren't we all?"

On the street, Red and his men donned tactical vests as he listened intently to the nervous chatter of the group already inside the Louvre gates.

"Where do you think those SUVs went?" Hannibal asked.

"They took another entrance. To be expected." Red grabbed the handheld monitor for the trackers, which showed dots representing

Tess and Lawrence. He watched the dots move across the center courtyard of the Louvre. He had decided to put the trackers only on the two most at risk in this messy business——the scientist and the test subject. That way, if something went down, he'd know which to follow. While his goal remained always to leave with the entire group intact, the reality of the situation took precedence. There were only two real commodities in the pack, with Tess being his top priority.

Undetected, Red and his men entered the property, staying out of the main area where the tourists mingled. They watched from the shadows as Tess and the others entered the glass pyramid.

Going right through the front door, Red noted. *Hiding in plain sight.*

He then noticed something else—something that alarmed him not just a little bit. Once Tess had descended beneath the pyramid, the dot representing her disappeared from the tracker. Within seconds, Lawrence's dot disappeared as well.

"Roger, do you copy?" Red waited anxiously for a response.

Radio silence served as the only reply. Sweat formed on his back, which proved unnatural for him. Not much rattled him, but this glitch seemed to be doing the job.

"Time for plan B," he said to his men. As experience dictated, he'd devised an alternate operation in case of a communication break. "Trackers are dark," he added, motioning for his men to follow.

The threesome entered the museum through service corridors, and once on the lower level, the dots reappeared. "Trackers are live again." He released the breath he had not even realized he'd been holding.

Then Red heard the telltale signal from Roger. "Masterpiece."

"Ten-four," Red confirmed through the earpiece, then to his men he said, "Subjects are at destination."

And just like that, the two dots disappeared again.

"Trackers dark again."

Roger's voice came through Red's earpiece. "It's possibly a caged room. You won't have contact with us. I'm going in."

"Copy that." Red waited to hear the dissipating sounds of group chatter through the comms. "Comms dark." He looked at his men. "We'll go to the last known position. Now."

74

Tess peered around, taking in the exotic dark wood paneling, priceless artwork ... and the complete lack of windows in the room. And just one door, the one through which they'd just come.

"What is this?" she whispered, leaning toward Roger. "We're trapped."

He cut his eyes at her, doing the *zip it* signal.

She clenched her teeth then turned her gaze to Cathy. The ashen woman appeared utterly terrified.

Feeling unsteady herself, she rested a hand on the large inlaid wood table. As she stared, it struck her that this room had an air of permanence to it that only came from surviving the ages. In fact, the whole space had a weight to it, one that made her feel powerless.

"The chairs are labeled with plaques. Look. King Louis XVI, 1754," Roger was saying to Vail, but she overheard his whisper.

Vail mumbled, "Impressive."

She gave him a cold stare.

"Oh, right. Sorry. I forgot why we were here for a second."

She shook her head in disbelief.

A deliberate clearing of the throat caused them all to look toward the end of the table. Rigid except for an excessive rubbing together of his hands, Montague said, "Please take a seat."

Tess noticed Cathy giving Lawrence a nudge. He looked as uneasy as she felt at the moment. She guessed they were all feeling that way—a mix of stressful emotions packed into one suffocating box of a room with just one exit. And she doubted it was an exit they could use freely.

Gripping the edges of her seat, Tess realized several chairs remained empty across the table. But not for long. In walked what she presumed was the team of Russian scientists and their leader, a Mr. Rudlof Borin, who took a seat next to Norman Montague. She'd learned his name from Lawrence, who had met him previously. Without a word or even a nod of acknowledgment to those already there, the Russians dropped into their chairs, backs straight, expressions blank. The table sat evenly divided—Americans on one side, Russians on the other. Then, as if tensions were not high enough, two militant-looking men joined, holding sentry by the only exit.

Tess tried to breathe in, then out slowly, but she felt dizzy and couldn't calm the pounding in her chest. She wondered how long a person's heart could hold out at this rate.

The meeting began with the opening remarks being made by a young Russian named Ivan with impeccable English. As he spoke, the foreboding that had been hovering in the room grew larger. The words were sinister shards, piercing Tess's skin like a thousand hot needles. Her fellow Americans looked confused, worried. She knew they were feeling it too. She glanced at Montague and was shocked to see the same panic showing on his face as well.

Was this some sick joke?

She could only dream it was so.

The scheme hit Tess's intellect hard—disease control with preliminary testing on socially vulnerable people, using her blood as a harvesting ground. She caught a knowing glance between Roger and Vail and wondered if they'd kept this from her.

The orator's voice rambled on and on, causing her head to throb. And just when she felt she couldn't listen anymore, Ivan looked directly at her as he spoke. To invoke guilt? Social obligation? She couldn't be sure.

"Your contribution through egg harvesting has the potential to fuel medical advancements beyond the imagination," Ivan said.

Oh, hell no.

Did the Russians and Montague think she'd be manipulated into this morally corrupt plan? She glanced at her boss again, wondering if perhaps he, too, had been duped. How much did he know? How long had he been playing God with the Russians?

Just when she thought Ivan had hit rock bottom with his sick monologue, the focus moved to hidden equity, payouts, exclusive access to the medical benefits.

Her stomach rolled, and she moved a hand to her belly, willing the turmoil to cease. She shifted in her seat, ready to run. She didn't think she could hear anymore.

"And none of this would be possible without you, Dr. Andreas." Ivan slow-clapped, followed by applause from Montague and Mr. Borin, then the remainder of the Russian team.

Tess's group remained motionless, seemingly dumbfounded, until Vail began to clap. All eyes landed on him, and he returned the gaze, smiling, nodding ... *He's encouraging us to do the same, to keep up the façade in this dangerous game we're playing.* While Tess understood his motivation for doing so—their safety—it angered her nonetheless.

"That's enough!" Her words flew from her lips. She bolted out of her seat and raised her hands, pumping them in a *stop* signal. "No more. No more. Stop all of this. I mean it. This has gone too far."

Barely an eye fluttered as shocked faces stared up at her. She felt a soft grip on her arm. Vail turned his face away from the group, whispering in her ear. "Tess, listen to me. Hold it together. Now is not the time to take a stand."

She ignored his plea. "No." Her voice ricocheted in the windowless room. "This is not going to happen. Not on my watch. Not now. *Not ever.*" She glared at Montague. "What have you done?"

The room went quiet, and the guests shrunk in their seats—all except Mr. Borin, who appeared to grow bigger to match his voice. He sprang from his seat, inflicting a resounding *bang* on the massive table.

"Who are you to refuse?" he bellowed.

She lifted her chin. "I'm Dr. Tess Andreas, a human being, an American, a person of free will."

Borin looked at Montague. "What is this nonsense she speaks?"

A petrified Ivan looked at Tess with glassy eyes that seemed to plead for her to take it all back or, at the very least, say something, anything less obstinate.

Instead, she stood her ground, finding no mercy for the young man or Montague. She waved in his direction. "Well, Norman. The man asked, tell him."

The rims of his eyelids went red as words failed to come.

Borin's nostrils flared, and he snarled in a way Tess had never seen anyone do before. "You, you ungrateful ..." Then he waved a finger at her and mumbled a word in his native tongue, the meaning of which did not elude her. "The money is not enough for your American greed? Huh? The protections we offer you and your family, not enough? What is it that you want, then? You want me to gift you the whole world?" His tone struck her, igniting a whole new level of fury within her.

"How dare you ... you vile, corrupted, soulless being void of any accomplishment in this life that is honorable." She slammed both hands on the table and leaned in his direction. "How dare you speak to me in that manner, let alone try to intimidate me into becoming the center of your villainous scheme. I won't have it."

Borin's angry expression changed to one of shock as he turned to Ivan then to Montague.

Ivan's jaw hung agape as he remained frozen.

Montague looked much the same.

She yelled, "Cat got your tongue, Norman?" and smacked the table again.

Ivan spoke rapidly then, in Russian, to Borin. The old man roared and lunged, not at her, but at the sweat-riddled Norman Montague, who sat like a stone in the chair next to him. In a flash, Borin grabbed

Montague by his collar and shook him so hard that Montague's glasses jumped into a cockeyed position across his nose.

From the corner of her vision, Tess watched as Roger made use of the chaos. He appeared to be hacking into the computer screen on the table. She surveyed the Russian team—no one seemed to notice. They were too preoccupied with the altercation and the theatrics of Mr. Borin's violently growing temper. Tess put a hand on Vail's and signaled with her eyes toward Roger. He caught on and moved his body to block the view as much as possible.

Suddenly, Red's voice sounded in the earpieces. Roger winked. Lawrence's hand flew to his ear, and Cathy immediately swatted it back down. Tess remained motionless as Vail turned his back to the table and in a low voice said into the comms, "Two armed at the door."

She eyed the goons guarding the entrance, worried they might have overheard, but they seemed oblivious, focused instead on the melee. They had hands on their hips, and she knew there were weapons hidden there somewhere.

Within seconds, the door to the room burst open, and Red and his two men entered, guns at the ready. They knocked the startled guards against the wall, the force so hard they sank to the floor and stayed there, where they were quickly disarmed. Red kicked the door closed again.

"I thought this room was a bunker?" Lawrence said.

"I unlocked the door when I disabled the Wi-Fi caging," Roger whiffed back.

Disorder ensued, shouts filling the space, some fists flying. Cathy hid beneath the table while Lawrence ran around the room aimlessly, arms flailing, calling Cathy's name. Red stayed close to the door, keeping any Russians attempting to escape at bay.

Vail brushed past Tess, jumping in to help restrain a bruised and bloodied Russian while one of Red's men headed to the back of the room, cornering Borin. Not surprisingly, Montague attempted to slither toward the safety of Tess's crew, but an eagle-eyed Red thwarted his escape, shoving him back into the band of enraged Russians. "Oh no you don't, old man."

With guns pointed, Red's two men held the others off while Tess and her team escaped to the safety of the public area outside. As quickly as possible, they scattered into the crowded streets. Each listened intently as Red instructed through earpieces the next steps. "Take side streets, taxis, public transportation, anything that's difficult to track. Meet at the flat as soon as you can get there. Let yourself in—the door is unlatched." Tess and Vail locked gazes. She caught sight of Roger hopping onto a tour bus. Lawrence held Cathy's hand and with the other hand flagged a taxi. Vail put an arm around Tess and said, "Come on." They strode at a quick pace past a hotel and onto a street full of tourists seeking French pastries and souvenirs. Vail grabbed a scarf and a hat, tossing two American twenty-dollar bills at the vendor. "Here." He handed her the scarf.

She tied it around her hair. "It's not the 1950s."

"No. But it is Paris." He winked and plopped the hat on his head as they disappeared into the crowded street.

75

Within the hour, the entire group had reconvened, arriving in staggered fashion at Red's rented Paris flat. A visibly distraught Cathy sniffled with her hands cupping a glass of water while Lawrence perched on the arm of her chair, gently rubbing her back. Roger tapped rapidly on the keys of his laptop. Red stood just in front of the open window, puffing a cigarette.

"And there we have it," Red said.

"Have what?" Lawrence asked.

The seasoned vigilante ignored the question and motioned to Vail, who joined him at the window.

From behind them, the flat door creaked open. Everyone turned in that direction, except for Red who continued to puff smoke casually. Red's henchman stepped into the room.

"We've got this boss," Hannibal said as the shorter one nodded.

Red's forehead creased. "No room for error, boys." He stamped out his cigarette in a green glass ashtray before casually walking into the next room. In seconds, he reappeared with his weapon drawn. The two henchmen followed suit. The group collectively grew wide-eyed, and Cathy shrieked and shook her head vehemently. "No. No. This is out of control."

Red cut Lawrence a look.

"Cathy, don't worry. I'll handle everything. Just stick by my side," Lawrence said.

"What exactly is going on?" Tess asked.

"It looks like some of the Russians trailed you two." He eyed her and Vail. "Good news is they don't seem to know which building. So we have some time."

"Time for what?" Vail asked.

"Escape." Red spoke as if the answer should have been obvious.

Tess edged closer to the window, peering out cautiously. "This has gone too far. Guns, escape ...."

"Look, I don't make the rules here. But you're neck-deep in this, and from the looks of it, whether you want it or not, you're the cornerstone of this entire house of cards. I've seen people hunted down for much less. You hired me. Now you need to trust and listen to me."

Vail slipped his hand into hers. "I agree. We need to listen to Red. We're out of our element." He scanned the room. "Raise your hand if you've ever been in this situation before?"

No one moved a muscle.

"Good. It's settled then." Red began doling out weapons, giving short lessons on how to fire.

Hannibal called out from the window, "The Russians are leaving, for now."

"How much time?" Red asked.

"Probably a couple hours at the most before they come back with more."

"Before that happens, let's figure out how to move the group out of here." Red took a seat.

For the next fifteen minutes, the three men batted ideas around as the others listened in.

"Thank God the plan includes leaving for the United States," Lawrence whispered to Vail, who dipped his chin politely in agreement without diverting his focus from Red.

The conversation had moved from taking trains, crossing borders, flying from another country to beelining it to the private airfield where they'd landed, and leaving on the Ludwell jet.

"The jet gets my vote," Vail interjected.

"Mine too," Cathy said.

Roger and Tess nodded in unison.

"I'll call Mr. Ludwell," Vail offered.

Thankfully, he didn't spend much time on an explanation, only that his employees were in danger and needed to hit the air pronto. To everyone's relief, Ludwell took Vail at his word, and the jet was scheduled to be ready in exactly two hours.

Chatter ensued. "What about our luggage?" Lawrence asked over the din.

"Leave it. We'll deal with that." Red's answer sounded automatic like he'd been in this situation many times.

With staggered departures, the group eagerly fled for the refuge of the private airfield, luggage-less.

~76~

Just over two hours later, but what seemed like a lifetime, the engines roared and the wings of the airplane lifted the passengers into the safety of the sky. This time, Red and his men were aboard the Ludwell jet as well.

"All that's missing is Montague. What a shame," Roger said sarcastically, and after that, no one spoke for the first hour of the long flight home.

Eventually, Tess moved to sit in the seat facing Red.

"What happens now?" she asked, half-angry, half-defeated.

"Now, we wait. And one of my men sticks to you like glue."

"So, I just go back home and do what? Pretend everything is normal?"

"Unless you have somewhere else in mind. But my recommendation is to go home, yes. Go back to your routine—no. Predictability can be the kiss of death. Familiar surroundings on the other hand can be an ally."

"I can't believe this."

He observed her for a moment. Then, his face softened. "This isn't going to be what you want to hear. But, in these situations, it's more productive to go ahead and accept the reality. Deal with the denial phase later when it's all said and done. I'm sure that pushing away emotions ... well, it's probably taboo in your line of work, but in mine, it's a matter of life or death."

Taken aback, she marinated on his words. "You're not wrong. In my world, we usually have the luxury of dealing with things as they come. But I cannot deny that I'm not in my world anymore. I'm in someone else's, a hell custom-made for me by Norman Montague." Her lips twisted at the bitter taste of his name on her tongue.

Pressing his own lips together, he simply nodded.

Nearing the end of the flight, Red gathered the group to go over the new game plan, which meant sleeping with one eye open. Normalcy would be out of reach for a while.

Red looked at Lawrence. "You need to be extra vigilant."

"Why me?"

"The risk is low, but kidnapping isn't out of the question since you are the lead scientist."

Cathy gasped.

Lawrence cupped her hands in his own and smiled at her intently. "No way I'm leaving you alone. So either I stay with you, or you with me. Period."

Her nose crinkled as she blinked away tears. "My place. You have your cat, though—we have to go get him."

"It's decided, then. We will pick up Atom, and I'll pack what I need for a few days."

The frightened woman clutched Lawrence's hand.

77

FRIDAY, NOVEMBER 15

After a couple of nights sleeping in her own bed, the fog finally began to lift from Tess's psyche. She had checked in with Lawrence and Cathy probably too many times but felt better and better about their safety. She came to terms with them being back at work—doing the mundane lab stuff they loved to do. Plus, Lawrence had said they both needed to stay busy to stay sane.

Still, she worried.

"Penny for your thoughts." Vail said as he slid in next to her on the couch.

Blinking herself back into the present, she said, "Oh, it's probably nothing."

"The look on your face doesn't say *nothing* to me."

"It's just that we don't exactly know how much information Montague already gave the Russians. Roger has some idea, yes. There could be more. There is more. Probably on thumb drives or in files somewhere. And if we can't find him or the information, then how do we stop this completely?"

As their eyes met, she noticed how sullen his face had become over the past weeks. He seemed to be searching for the right words. "There's nothing we can do at this point, really. Just try to rest your mind."

She nodded and smiled.

"I'm going to grab a cup of that coffee." He walked into the kitchen.

Under her breath, she said, "Where are you, Norman Montague?"

A short time later, Vail left for his office. As she went about the day, prisoner in her own apartment, she couldn't get Montague off her mind.

Had the Russians killed him? As far as anyone knew, Montague had not returned from overseas.

Her phone buzzed.

"Hello."

"Thank God!" Todd huffed and puffed liked he'd just finished a race. This was the first time they'd had a chance to speak directly.

"I'm fine," she said with faux irritation as she tugged her thick sock over her yoga pants. Since she wasn't going to work or pretty much anywhere, she saw no reason not to dress comfortably.

"Listen. I can't get in touch with Red." He'd gone from sounding breathless to panicked in one sentence.

"Hmmm. One of his men is here—outside my door. I can—"

"Gemma just called me."

Her heart flipped. "She's in jail still, I hope."

"You knew!" His voice ricocheted through the phone.

"Of course, didn't you?"

"No. I thought she was at the bottom of the Hudson."

"What? Why? Weren't you there when they took her?" She gasped then added, "And you were okay with thinking that?"

"No. I wasn't. Not at all. It's just that I saw her leave with that guy Hannibal, and … well, I thought …"

"Yes, it's clear what you thought. Good grief. No. Red set her up—like she committed a robbery—and turned her in to the police. She confessed, so she was locked up right away. I guess he didn't tell you." She paused then added, "For some reason."

"I kind of told him not to tell me."

She huffed out a sigh. "I'm so confused."

"Me too. Let's just agree neither of us are okay with that, ah, other scenario. Anyway, she called me because some Russian guy came to see her at the jail. Asking questions about all of us. Saying they saw her that night coming out of my bar with Red's guys. And they offered to get her out if she talks."

"Why did she call you? And the bigger question—why didn't she just take the deal? I'm glad she didn't, but it is suspicious. Or just stupid."

"Look, I don't know, and to be honest, either of those descriptions could fit. She's a bit odd, to say the least."

Then a thought hit her. "Todd, are you at the bar now?

"Yeah. Why?"

"Maybe you should get out of there. If they went to her, then you could be next."

After a second of silence, he said, "I'll be fine. Remember where I grew up—this isn't all so new to me, which is probably why my mind went straight to the bottom of the river."

"Touché."

She heard a voice in the background. "Who's that?"

"It's Red's guy. I'll call you back."

78

Vail tossed the files onto the floor in a mad rush, calling out to his assistant, "Derek, can you help me out, please?"

Derek poked his head around the doorframe. "Sure thing. What can I do you for?"

Vail looked up from his squatting position amid the folders on the floor. "I need help sorting through these. Just look for anything that shows a money trail."

Without hesitation, Derek plopped down into a cross-legged position. They examined the contents of the folders, fanning through some, carefully eyeballing others. Eventually, Vail began to notice a pattern. "Interesting."

"Find something, Boss?"

"I think I may have. Take a look at these." He spread out a few pages on the floor, pointing to line after line of large monetary transactions.

"Clear as a bell now that you point it out. But what's that company? Is that German?"

"I'm guessing Russian."

Derek sprang to his feet. "May I?" He motioned to the laptop on Vail's desk.

"Be my guest."

He clicked a few keys, waited, then, "Yep. Russian holding company. Am I correct in thinking that's a bit weird?"

"You are not wrong, my friend."

Before long, Vail realized that if this money belonged to the Russians, then they weren't going to just let this whole thing go. "This is not over."

Derek stared and blinked, seemingly waiting for more information in order to offer up a reply. "Are you talking to me or yourself?" Derek shot him a cheesy grin.

"Sorry. I'm just working out something in my head."

"Don't hurt yourself," he teased.

"Funny." Vail then rose and grabbed a few files and his coat on the way out the door, leaving Derek standing in the midst of the disheveled pile of papers on the floor.

Vail dialed Tess as he headed to his car. "I've got some news. I'll be there soon," he told her.

79

Vail arrived at Tess's apartment, surprised to find Red already there.

He hugged her stiffly, but she wrapped her arms around him. His shoulders relaxed a bit. Tess gently tugged him into the living room. "You said you had news?"

Vail nodded and got right to the point, explaining the financial files.

Tess stayed quiet. He watched as she chewed her lip.

Then, Red took a deep breath and threw in his two cents. "They're going to want what they paid for."

Vail watched Tess go visibly pale as she said, "Do you think this has something to do with why Russians contacted Gemma."

"What? When did that happen?" Vail's mouth went dry as the tension ceased him again.

Red glanced at Tess. She nodded. He took a step closer and said, "It's looking like the Russians are going to make a go of this with or without Montague. We need to get ahead of them or ..." He looked at Tess again and then left his thought incomplete.

She dropped her eyes and twisted her hands.

"Or what?" Vail's throat fought to release the words.

Red continued, "Look, I know this stings. But I also know you're both the big picture type. Focus on that. On getting out of this."

Vail watched as Tess seemed to hold her breath and then let it out slowly "Are you sure there's not another way?"

Vail wondered what they'd discussed already.

Red shook his head. "Not one that's presenting itself right now."

"I just don't want to have to deal with her, not directly anyway."

Vail took her hand. It felt like ice. "Deal with whom?"

"Her."

Vail's brows knitted. Then he realized she must mean Gemma. "Can I do it, deal with her?"

Red cleared his throat. "That's gallant, and I get it's your job to save the day, Vail. But I'm going to need you to put your skills to work another way. Know anything about posting bail?" Not waiting for a response, he shifted his focus to Tess. "You're going to have to put your emotions aside. Take what I'm telling you to the bank. You are going to have to talk to her, plan with her, probably pay her too." He shifted in his seat. "You can put that in the *deal with later* file."

Confused at Red's words, Vail thought Tess on the other hand seemed to know exactly what he had meant.

He knew so in fact when she said, "That file is getting pretty big." Her shoulders dropped.

"Yep. That sounds about right in this business." With that, Red showed himself out of her apartment, popping the unlit cigarette into his mouth as the elevator doors shut.

~80~

SATURDAY, NOVEMBER 16

J ust twenty-four hours later, Red's plan was in motion. He dialed Roger.

"What's up, Red?"

"I told you not to use names."

"Yes. Sorry."

"We need another meetup—the whole group."

"On it. I'll let Todd know."

"Not at the bar. That place is compromised. Can you get us a conference room on Mr. Ludwell's private floor? Today?"

"I think I can. Bold move. Kind of like hiding in plain sight, huh?"

"Yep."

That afternoon, the group gathered, chatting in clusters around the conference room until the door opened to reveal a lanky, freckled woman with disheveled long hair. She was tall, almost matching Todd's six-foot frame, and carried herself awkwardly. The young woman's eyes surveyed the room from a face that looked intimidated and a head that hung slightly as if from shame.

Timidly, she sought refuge in a seat next to Todd and out of eyeshot of Tess.

"We have to get this right. There's no room for mistakes if we all want to come out of this with our lives intact. This, my friends, is the endgame. Here's how it's going to work."

Once the plan had been clearly laid out, everyone began to fidget with nervous energy, ready to get started. Roger, Cathy, and Lawrence left the room to get started on their assigned tasks. And Tess found herself face-to-face with the woman who had tried to dismantle her life for a few thousand dollars.

Tess's body stiffened. Vail mumbled, "Oh no."

The girl had to look down at Tess, but somehow, it seemed as if Tess were ten feet taller than everyone else. Gemma was biting into her lip, looking scared.

Red leaned toward Vail and whispered, "I don't know what's coming, but it looks like some pretty dark storm clouds to me."

Tess glared directly at the girl, and the girl shifted nervously, seeming unsure where to place her own gaze. Finally, she took a deep breath and made eye contract.

The three men left in the room shrunk back, moving quietly to a spot near the corner.

With a quivering lip, tears formed in Gemma's eyes.

"Don't. Don't try that sympathy ploy with me. Textbook defensive move." Tess's words cut like a blade.

Tears streamed anyway. "I'm so so sorry."

"I doubt that very much. Did you donate the money you earned off trying to destroy another woman's life to a charity that supports women in need?"

The girl looked confused but responded to the strange question with a shake of the head.

"Well, you kept the money, then? Maybe even spent some? New purse? Maybe on that lipstick you're wearing? Hmmm?"

Gemma wiped the back of her hand across her crimson lips.

"So, what that tells me is that you definitely aren't sorry for your dishonorable act against another woman, against me. You're sorry you got caught—that I believe. You do realize that what you did lowers all women? It splits us. Pits us against each other."

Gemma covered her face and sobbed.

But Tess didn't stop. "Your type, you profit from dishonesty, betrayal. You do know what betrayal feels like, right? The sting of it. How the pain never really leaves your soul, how it spans through generations. It's people like you who carry it like a virus, infecting the future."

Gemma looked up then, a shocked expression in her red-rimmed eyes.

Tess jabbed a finger at her. "Get. Your. Shit. Together."

Then she left the room.

~81~

A fter the meeting, Lawrence held Cathy's hand and carried a bag of Chinese food in the other as they walked up the steps to her front door. He thought how they'd become inseparable over the past few weeks, and how he wouldn't have it any other way—with or without the storm they were in at present.

"Poor Tess," Cathy said as they hung their coats next to the door.

"I know. I don't know how she's handling it all so well."

"Having to be in the same room with that woman, let alone having to work with her. I couldn't do it."

Taken aback and feeling suddenly protective of her in a way he hadn't before, he tugged her to a standstill and looked in her eyes. Then, he said, "That will never happen to you. Not with me."

She gazed up at him, wrapping her arms tightly around his waist. In that private moment, he realized making her happy had become the most important thing in his life.

"Hungry?" she asked as she pulled away from him, smiling.

"Hostage hungry."

She giggled.

Just as they finished off the last of the egg rolls, his phone buzzed.

"It's Red." Quickly wiping his fingers on the nearest napkin, he answered while still chewing his last bite.

"Remember that decoy we discussed?" Red said.

"Yes."

"It's time. Do what you do and provide Roger with enough fabricated data to point the Russians away from Tess's blood."

"I'm on it."

"Make sure it can pass the sniff test, though, with the Russian scientists," Red reminded him.

"I can manage that."

As he spoke, Cathy eyed him carefully.

"Good. We need it ASAP."

"Hey, should I use her name? Isn't it safer just to falsify a name?"

"No. Use Gemma's name. Gemma Stein."

Lawrence was floored. "You sure? I mean, doesn't it put her in grave danger like the rest of us in this mess?"

"That's the idea. Are you aware of what a decoy is, son?"

"Yes. Of course. I just don't understand. Why not use a fake person? Why put someone one else in danger?"

"Now listen, don't get me wrong. I appreciate your concern. You are a good guy, and I respect that, but you're going to need to trust me on this."

"It's just—"

"Listen, that's only step one. Step two is making all of Montague's research useless to the Russians. But first we have to move the target off Tess's back. And if you do this right, if we all do, then hopefully when we're done, the danger factor will be eliminated for all of us."

Lawrence swallowed hard. "But won't this get Montague killed, assuming he's still alive? He'll be in worse danger than before. And—" He stopped because his mouth went so dry that his tongue stuck to his lips for a moment. "Won't they blame me too? They might come after me. I mean it is my discovery after all."

He paused because Cathy started waving her hands and mouthing, "What?"

Then he said, "I'm starting to think I'm toast too. No matter what." The walls felt like they were closing in around him.

"This isn't easy for any of us. We are all taking risks. This is yours. I can promise you one thing—my team has your back. You will not be in this alone."

Despite the fear coursing through his veins, Lawrence heaved out, "Let's do this."

Cathy looked as if she'd explode if she didn't find out something from him soon.

He hung up the phone and stared at the floor. Cathy twisted her napkin impatiently beside him, practically bouncing in her seat. When he could find his voice, he said, "It's going to be a long night." Then he went to the door and put on his coat.

He turned to her. "You coming?"

Springing from her seat, abandoning the remnants of their meal, she followed him out the door to the lab.

MONDAY, NOVEMBER 17

With Montague still missing and no sign of activity on the man's phone or email, Roger assumed the worst had happened. "I bet the Russians killed him." He took a few swigs of soda. Just to be sure, he'd keep one screen on live monitoring for any pings on the old scoundrel's whereabouts. "Just a few more days." He popped a cheese puff into his mouth. Next, his fingers whizzed across the keyboard, creating a compressed file with the false data Lawrence had been sending all night long.

"This looks good. I mean I'm not a bio scientist, but I'd buy it."

An expected knock at the door drew him from his task. He glanced at the time, noting two hours had passed since he'd started coding. He spun in his chair toward the sound. With his hand on the lock, he checked the peephole before unlatching it, just to make sure. He stepped aside, holding the door open as a winded Vail barreled inside.

"You have the thumb drive?"

"Yep."

Vail plopped into his regular seat in what Tess had nicknamed "Roger's Matrix."

"You want a drink or something?"

"No, but thanks." Vail's attention was drawn to something on one of the monitors. "Hey, what's that?"

Roger turned around to face the flashing screen. "Well, I'll be ... That's Montague. The little cockroach did survive, and he's on the move." Then he second-guessed himself and said, "Or at least his cell phone is."

Vail telephoned Red. "We have a track on Montague's mobile."

"Can you confirm it's him?"

"Not yet. Roger's on it."

Roger spoke while typing, "There's one way to know for sure."

"What's that?" Vail asked.

"Call him."

The two men locked glances.

Red listened from the other end of the line and said, "Do it."

Vail nodded, giving Roger the green light.

And with that, they waited while Roger's skillfully blocked call rang in an otherworldly tone over the speaker.

"Hello," someone said in an American accent that sounded a lot like Montague.

"Mr. Montague." Roger spoke the name slowly.

"Yes, who is this?"

Roger's eyes went big as Vail motioned for him to say something else.

"Um, this is Stan DeMan, uh, from the office."

"Who? I don't know a Stan De ... de what?"

Roger gave Vail a look that said, *What do I say now?*

With a similar bugged-out expression, all Vail could offer was a shrug.

Roger said into the phone, "Stan from bookkeeping."

"Well, what is it?"

"I just need to confirm your employee badge number. The system crashed and has to be rebooted." Roger stretched out his mouth, showing his teeth, as he looked at Vail. "Yeah, so ... I'm just confirming our records before implementing the fix."

Clearly annoyed, Mr. Montague rattled off his number and a

complaint that Stan could have just asked Doris. To which Stan made an excuse about privacy policies.

Roger confirmed the number, giving Vail a thumbs-up.

"Is that all?" the old man grumbled.

"Will you be in the office today, sir?"

"No. Tomorrow."

"Thank you. That's all."

Montague grumbled something unintelligible and hung up.

"Stan DeMan?" Vail shook his head. "Really?"

"Okay. I'll admit it, I'm not great off the cuff. The bigger question is why he was so accommodating."

"Who knows? Probably in a rush. No theorizing." He pointed a finger. "Besides all we really need to focus on is that he's not dead and that he's coming back tomorrow."

Vail looked at his phone. His connection with Red had disconnected somewhere along the way. So he texted, *It's Montague. He'll be back tomorrow.*

We need that data in front of the Russians today, Red wrote back.

An hour and a half later, Vail sipped a glass of red wine as Tess opened the containers of Italian takeout he'd brought with him.

"I feel like I'm on house arrest." She placed the food on plates and tossed the container lids in the trash. "I haven't been to work in ages. The walls are closing in a bit. And poor Lawrence ... aren't we throwing him into the lion's den?"

"I know. I'm concerned too. But we should listen to Red. It's for the best."

"Couldn't we just do this in a less dangerous way? Maybe, I don't know, just turn in the shady financials to Mr. Ludwell or the authorities? Let Montague take the fall?" She pushed the steaming pasta around her plate.

"Don't forget about the fallout from the Russians." He put his fork down. "Just hear me out. For peace of mind's sake, let's think it through."

She relaxed a bit.

He indulged her idea. "We could turn the financials in, but that would most definitely take the company down as well. Do you want that? And that wouldn't stop the Russians. They'd come for you for sure. That's why we don't have a choice. See? The only way is to remove your value to the whole plan."

Chewing on a bite, she hesitated and then said, "No. The company shouldn't go down with Montague's ship. I guess that's not the best way out of this. Besides, that'd be hundreds of jobs and loads of valuable data from other studies that actually could be used for good, all down the drain. And then, yes, there is the issue of the Russians." She looked past him toward the large wall of windows. "I just want this to end," she paused, "well."

"Then that's what we will do. End this the right way. Once and for all."

Just after midnight, the trap had been set. Lawrence dropped a sleepy Cathy at home and fought one tormenting yawn after another the whole drive over to Roger's place. Once there, Lawrence found a comfortable seat. Roger handed him a burner phone and stood next to Red, watching as the sleep-deprived Lawrence dialed the Russian scientist's number. His finger shook, and just before he pressed send, Red stopped him and said, "Now, son, I just want to remind you of your mission here. You need to look like you've flipped sides, like the idea of groundbreaking science and personal profit have their grip on you. You want to work with the Russians. Tell them that Tess was a red herring, that you kept the real donor in your back pocket because you never trusted Montague."

Swallowing hard, his jaw set, "I got it. I'm ready. I can do this." He straightened his shoulders in a show of confidence before taking the jump. With a steady finger this time, he pressed call. His stomach flipped as he spoke to the Russian scientist, but he played the guise of greed well—like a seasoned actor. In just a few minutes, he'd confirmed the scientist was back at the Lineage off-site lab. Then, he set a time, place, and date to meet to undercut Montague and to introduce the new candidate: Gemma Stein.

After the call ended, Lawrence guzzled half a bottle of water before asking, "Do you think he bought it?" His glassy eyes met Red's steady gaze.

"You hit it outta the park, kid." He patted Lawrence on the back.

"We have eighteen hours to get this show on the road," Red said as Roger set a large timer on one of the screens for all to see.

Lawrence fell back into the armchair and, within minutes, nodded off, his long legs hanging off the edge of the ottoman, exaggerating his tall proportions.

Roger took one look and mumbled, "He's gonna be stiff as a board sleeping like that."

Red chuckled.

83

TUESDAY, NOVEMBER 18

Morning came fast and the tired team assembled at Roger's place, including Tess. Cathy doled out coffee and pastries.

"Thank you. You're a godsend," Tess said, taking a donut just as her stomach growled.

The lack of chatter remained disguised for the moment as individuals sipped and nibbled on their breakfasts. However, the collective somberness couldn't be denied indefinitely. They all stood keenly aware that in only a few hours, Lawrence and Gemma would be heading into a potential war zone. The meetup had been set at the location provided by the Russians, which proved not ideal in terms of safety, but Red had expected that caveat under the circumstances. The saving grace seemed to be that Lawrence had already been there before, so Red's team had some reconnaissance of the building.

Running on coffee and no sleep, Roger somehow kept the necessary pace. He expertly fitted both Gemma and Lawrence with trackers and even cleverly hid listening devices in buttons on their clothing.

"Upgrade, huh?" Lawrence said.

Red jumped in. "Only the best."

Lawrence grimaced. "Yeah, I guess earpieces are a bit obvious after what happened in Paris."

The atmosphere of the room became heavy with silence.

"Roger, can I top you off?" Cathy's cheerful voice cut through the gloom as she held the warm carafe of coffee.

"Sure. Thanks."

"How are you? Lawrence told me you've been up all night." She gave Roger a concerned look.

"I'm good. Being a former gamer and a current hacker, sleep often eludes me. Occupational hazard." He chuckled. "I'll make up for it when this is all over. Trust me."

Time seemed to fly by, and Red and his men left to established lookout points.

Lawrence and Gemma awaited the signal to follow.

Roger sat upright. "Red sent the signal. It's time."

Cathy bear-hugged Lawrence through tears.

"I'll be fine."

"You better be." She issued a faux smack to his bicep.

"We'll be popping champagne and slicing into a steak dinner tomorrow this time." He smiled and leaned down, giving her a quick peck before leaving.

The group offered wishes of good luck and shows of support to Lawrence. Finally, it was Tess's turn to say goodbye.

Peering up at him, the gentle giant, she said, "You are brilliant, selfless, a true hero. I can never repay you for this brave act."

Lawrence blushed. "Thank you."

Next, she approached Gemma. The others had already collectively wished her the best and thanked her, in guarded but genuine ways. Tess held her head high, knowing the right thing to do, even though she wanted to tell the woman to shove it. But Gemma wasn't really the reason behind all this calamity. The real culprit could not be denied—Norman Montague. Tess reached deep inside herself and said, "Thank you for doing this."

Gemma twisted the tip of her shoe into the floor and shook her head with an apologetic look. "I'm sorry. Really. I want to fix this. For you, for me."

Tess squeezed her hand and softened her gaze. "From the looks of it, you already have."

84

Lawrence gritted his teeth as he drove. He breathed deep, assuring himself that Red knew what he was doing. He did, right? He and his men would be watching the whole time, just outside.

"Red's a pro. He's got this," he said as his fingers turned splotchy white around the steering wheel.

Gemma eyed him from the passenger seat.

Parking on the street, he unlatched his seatbelt and gripped the door handle. "We're here."

"Wait." Her voice sounded desperate.

"What?"

"I don't know if I can actually do this." Her hands shook.

He agreed, but someone had to keep this train moving. So, he dug deep and turned to her, cupping her face in his hands, "I'll be there the whole time. We can do this. You are strong—I can tell."

She squeezed her eyes shut briefly as a faint tear streaked her cheek.

"On the count of three ... one, two, three. Let's go."

The two car doors opened in unison, and they stepped out into the quiet street.

Surveying the area, he remembered the building. It was burned into his memory, as was the day he'd met the Russians for the first time with Montague. He shuddered a bit as he faced the reality that he once again would pass through the threshold into that dark world. He looked at Gemma; her chalky face resembled that of someone who'd seen a ghost. He secretly hoped with everything inside him that they'd make it through this unscathed.

He knocked on the door.

Before he could lower his arm, a big man—hairy, wearing a silk shirt unbuttoned halfway down his chest, revealing a heavy gold medallion dangling from a chain—flung the door open.

"Names?" the man barked with a Russian accent.

They gave him their names.

Seeming satisfied with their answers, he relinquished them to another similarly dressed man who led the duo down the hallway to the same room Lawrence had visited weeks ago.

An almost inaudible groan escaped Lawrence's mouth as soon as he entered the room.

Gemma grabbed his hand and whispered, "Hey, you gonna make it?"

He nodded, but right there in front of him, scattered in chairs around the table, sat the Russians from the meeting in Paris—including Mr. Borin, who didn't look to have cooled down from their last encounter. Suddenly, he felt as if all the air had disappeared in the space, and he chastised himself for walking into this willingly.

"Welcome. Please sit." Mr. Borin glared like a cat with a canary.

"Thank you." Lawrence noticed his voice sounded small. He cleared his throat hoping next time he spoke he'd exude more fortitude. Trying to appear poised, he slowly pulled out a chair for Gemma. However, the spindly legs made the most ungodly screech against the floor. Defeated, they both sat.

The conversation got off to a quick start, Ivan once again managing the agenda. Finally, Borin seemed convinced of Lawrence's flip. He reported that the Russian scientist had taken a glance at the data presented on Gemma and given it the *a-okay*. When Borin stopped talking, a quiet fell upon the room, allowing Lawrence to detect the smallest creaking noise. Spinning his head, he observed a door on the far side of the room slowly opening. With a sense of dread, he observed as a familiar figure with short, gray hair and unkempt eyebrows emerged into the space.

Gemma gasped.

Lawrence groaned.

Norman Montague stomped toward them with a glint in his eye and a sinister grin on his lips. Veins bulged in his hands that gripped a sealed bag with a syringe.

Lawrence's heart sank. He knew Montague would call their bluff, and it didn't take much to guess what would happen next. Undoubtedly, the Russians wanted their own sample from the new subject, Gemma. He tried to find at least a bit of comfort in the knowledge that the kits weren't instant, so they'd have a couple days before the results revealed the damning truth, exposing this charade. He gritted his teeth, knowing the only goal now was to get out of there alive.

"Let's get to it." Montague tossed the kit to the Russian scientist and made a booming single clap that resonated through Lawrence's skin, right into his soul. Then he gave Lawrence a sinister, wicked, horrible smirk. In that moment, Lawrence truly wanted to kill someone for the first time in his life.

Gemma whimpered as the Russian scientist moved toward her with the syringe, the needle seeming to sparkle even in the dull lighting. She waved her arms in protest like a toddler.

Lawrence needed to think on his feet. An idea struck him. "You know what? If you don't trust us, then I'm sure someone else will. Come on." He tugged Gemma's arm. "We are leaving."

Borin scoffed and spoke in Russian. Ivan translated at lightning speed. "We call the shots. We will trust the science, not you. Now, tell her to cooperate, or we will do it the hard way." When Ivan finished, Borin's wicked laugh poisoned the air.

Lawrence aggressively kicked his chair, causing it to wobble and then fall to one side. "To hell with that!" He grabbed Gemma's arm again. She rose without protest, and he proceeded to pull her toward the door.

One of Borin's goons blocked their path.

"No one crashing in to save you this time, huh?" Borin laughed.

"No. We told you, we aren't working with them anymore. Isn't that evidence enough?"

To Lawrence's surprise, his words seemed to hit home as Borin's expression then shifted into ... well, Lawrence wasn't sure exactly what it was. Evil delight?

Lawrence looked at Montague, who must have noticed the change in Borin's demeanor as well, because he suddenly began rambling a list of reasons to get the sample done right then and there. Taking a bold chance, Lawrence maintained eye contact with Mr. Borin throughout Montague's desperate dissertation. Then, he took the bluff a step further, feigning confidence by letting go of Gemma and slowly approaching the skeptical man.

"I only see one thing standing in the way of our partnership." Lawrence spoke with authority as he cut a glance at Montague.

Borin listened like a dog with his head cocked to the side.

Ivan must have taken this as a sign of confusion because he repeated Lawrence's words with a finger-point, which fell short of the original performance and tone.

Soon, however, it became crystal clear Lawrence had done a bang-up job bluffing because Borin squinted his eyes and pointed at Montague while snarling at the goons, "Cease him."

Following orders, they barreled toward Montague, restraining his arms as the little man twisted and protested.

"This is preposterous," he whined, then pointed at Lawrence. "He's lying. You're making a huge mistake trusting him over me."

Lawrence didn't know how, but he managed to maintain his calm throughout the scuffle. He reached out a hand to Borin and said, "You can trust me."

The man shook his hand. "We will see."

"Why would I be here if I didn't have the anomaly? Why on earth would she be here? If I had nothing, you'd never see me again after what happened in Paris."

Borin tilted his head again. "Hmm. I think you make sense."

Lawrence managed to contain the sigh of relief that he really wanted to release. "Good. Now that's that. So, let's get on with it and decide on a deal first, then we'll confirm the variant as many times as it takes to satisfy your scientist."

"I'm starting to like you." The staunch Russian waved the goons away. "Yes. Let's make a new deal. I like that."

Lawrence flushed with an anxious heat because he saw his out, at least from this room. So he took the biggest risk yet and said, "Let's meet again once the deal is on paper." Unfortunately, he'd misjudged, pushed too far.

Borin's expression showed suspicion, then turned angry. Rattled, he edged toward Gemma and the unguarded door. "The girl stays." The words felt like an iron chain yanking them back into the room.

"No way," Lawrence protested and grabbed her hand.

"That is the only way. I need collateral."

"The data I just gave you is collateral enough, don't you think?" He squeezed Gemma's hand, secretly hoping she'd get his covert message to be ready to run.

But the Russian had a long history, experience in these underhanded dealings, and so he motioned again to the goons. One man pushed Montague into a chair, threatening his very life if he moved.

Fear took hold of Lawrence as reality set in—this may not end well for any of them.

The other angry thug took strides toward Gemma. She cried out, darting behind Lawrence as if he could shield her from him.

In a whirlwind of screams and violent shoves, one of the ruffians got a strong grip on Gemma's arms from behind. Her hair whipped about and tears streaked her face as she struggled. Her shrieking only halted after he whispered something in her ear, the effect of which was so strong that it caused her to stop in her tracks. The other thug jammed the cold end of what felt like a gun straight into Lawrence's back, forcing him out of the room and then out the front door of the building.

Stumbling down the front steps into the street, Lawrence turned in shock, looking up at the building as he found himself eerily alone in the damp street. He wondered where Red was.

At Roger's place, Tess rushed to a spot in front of the array of computer screens after hearing what had just happened at the meeting. "Let me go. It's me they want. I'll talk to them. I'm not going to let an innocent person get hurt or worse, not over this. Besides, Gemma isn't capable of handling this alone. We can't leave her as a prisoner. That's out of the question."

Vail shook his head, adamant. "Absolutely not. You will stay right here. Red will handle this."

"Stand down. Hannibal, I mean it." Red spoke over the transmitter linked to Roger's place.

Roger pointed to the first dot inside the building, "That's Gemma," then to the second dot outside of the building, "That's Lawrence."

All heads turned in response to a loud stomp on the floor. Tess stood with her hands on her hips and growled, "I know what is right. And so do all of you. Me hiding here while someone else is led to the slaughter is not okay." She stared at each man in turn.

"I'm not backing down on this. You are staying here," Vail said, unfazed by her show of force.

At that moment, Roger's phone rang. "It's Lawrence." Roger put the call on speaker. Lawrence said, "They've got Gemma."

"Yes. Red's on it."

"There's more. Montague. He's in there. He's in trouble too." Lawrence continued to fill them in, apparently not realizing they'd been listening all along. "I'm standing in the street in front of the building. Gemma's still in there. But ... something's not right. It's too quiet."

Vail looked at Roger and said, "Tell him to get out of there."

"Lawrence, you need to leave right now. Where's your car?"

"It's, uh, just a little ways down the street."

"Go, go, go. Now." For the first time, Roger raised his voice.

Cathy gasped. Tess moved to comfort her.

In the middle of the empty street, Lawrence's feet began to move, faster and faster as one foot slammed the pavement in front of the other, gaining momentum as he fled from the building for no other reason than a feeling of immense dread. He was almost to his car. He kept pushing.

A loud blast rang out, lifting his body from the ground and propelling him forward, crashing hard onto the pavement.

Pain reverberated everywhere—even his bones ached—and he tasted blood. The piercing ringing in his ears nearly caused him to weep. Thick dust swirled in the air to the point that he could hardly breathe or see.

Dazed from the blast, he pressed against the hard pavement, attempting to stand, but as he did so, his left ankle gave out on him. Desperate to leave, he tried again, managed to get to his knees, then his feet. He took a first step, then another. He reached an alleyway and turned into it, gulping in the somewhat cleaner air.

Sirens whirred in the distance. He leaned against the cool brick wall, listening and waiting for a sense of reality to come back. After a moment, he patted his pockets, looking for his phone. It was gone; he must have dropped it somewhere along the way.

Then, he looked toward the small sliver of sky between the buildings and said, "Oh, Cathy."

———————

Cathy screamed and fell to her knees, sobbing, talking incoherently.

Tess screamed at the same time, her whole body shaking as she ran toward the door. She flew past Vail who tried to stop her. She pushed him away.

Roger spun on his seat, dumbfounded at what they all had just heard over the phone and transmitter from Lawrence.

Vail started after Tess.

She turned and with a stone-cold face said only, "Don't."

He held up his hands. "I won't stop you, but I'm going with you."

"Fine."

———————

Standing in the street where they had last heard Lawrence's voice, Tess pushed through the crowd that had gathered, calling his name. An officer moved in front of her, "Miss, you can't be here."

From the crowd, Red appeared and said something to the officer that convinced him to allow her to pass. Vail and Red stayed close at her side. Tess spun slowly in the middle of the street among the rubble, hair blowing, and a hollow look emanating from her green eyes. She lifted her hand above her brow, as if trying to shield her vision from the fine dust in the air. Her focus landed on a man limping out of the gap between two buildings. Dust blanketed his clothes and masked his face.

"Lawrence, is it you?" Running like a mother to a child, she took off in his direction. She stopped just short of a collision and gently put a hand on his arm, repeating words of reassurance as they trudged away from the destruction.

"Gemma didn't make it out." His voice cracked.

"We don't know that for sure." She motioned to Vail and Red to come closer to help balance the limping friend.

Lawrence added, "Montague didn't either." At that moment, a paramedic pushed through and, after a quick assessment, swept Lawrence into an ambulance.

From the back of the rig, he looked at Tess and said, "Please tell Cathy I'm okay."

"I will. I will. Don't you worry about anything. Just get checked out. We'll be there to meet you soon." With that, the three friends watched the spinning red lights fade into the blur of traffic ahead.

~86~

Tess spread butter and jam on her toast and sipped her coffee. For her the days since the explosion had flitted by like fireflies on a summer evening, one after another, the previous indistinguishable from the next. Today, she expected no different.

The elevator dinged, and she could hear the sound of Vail greeting Red. Then some hushed mumblings.

Finally, the two men joined her in the kitchen.

"With cream for you, black for you." Handing over steaming cups, she smiled, expecting the same in return, but this morning both looked like deer in headlights.

"Okay. Out with it." She knew something was up. Maybe today wouldn't be like the rest, after all.

"The authorities determined that the explosion was due to a faulty gas line in the basement," Vail said.

Red shook his head.

"What?" Tess narrowed her eyes.

"The only thing faulty about that gas line was the hole Hannibal tore in it. If he'd been smart enough to make it out of there, I'd ..." Red's jaw tightened.

Tess bit her lip.

Vail started to speak, but Red's phone buzzed. He answered, and when he hung up, he explained that his contact at the morgue had an unofficial body count from the blast. "Four unidentified men and a young woman's body."

Tess gasped. Her heart felt like it stopped for a beat. "Gemma." She whispered as her legs gave out and she plopped onto a stool at the kitchen counter.

"But that's only four men." Vail pointed out the obvious. "From Lawrence's account, there should have been at least seven men, right?"

"Yep, between Ivan, two scientists, Mr. Borin, Mr. Montague, and one or two heavies near the entrance to the building, that's about right." Red added.

"So four does not guarantee that we're completely out of this." Vail said, rubbing his forehead.

Red shook his head. "But the one thing to remember is that in a blast of that magnitude, victims aren't always recovered."

"So, what do we do in the meantime?" Vail asked.

"We stay alert, keep watch, go about our daily lives."

"And Roger is keeping watch for any online activity in the unlikely case that Montague or the Russians are still out there," Vail interjected.

Red nodded, sipped his coffee.

"Well, how long is long enough to determine that we're free of them, of this?" Vail asked, obviously frustrated.

"There's not a hard and fast rule. But I'd say six months, and at that point, we can take a breath, start to put it behind us."

"Six months," Vail repeated, shaking his head.

"What about Gemma?" Tess put her hand on Vail's arm. His body slumped in defeat.

"I don't know. I don't think there's anything we can do. Except maybe keep moving forward."

"He's right." Red said. "You didn't start this fire. Remember that."

His words landed flat. She felt responsible on some level. She couldn't shake that.

"I'll keep an eye on things for now, just to be careful." Red set his cup in the sink.

They followed him to the foyer. Tess smiled at Red. "Thank you."

Red waved her off and stepped into the elevator. "Ain't nothing but a thing. I kind of owe you on this. It was my guy. My mistake."

When the doors closed, Tess said, "Let's get some air."

"It's freezing out."

"Come on. Let's live dangerously." She gave a playful tug on his shirt and headed to the elevator door. "I'm hanging by a thread here. I need to get out." She flashed a serious glance.

He forced a smile and put on his jacket.

As they strolled along hand in hand to the café, he said, "I just don't understand why Hannibal would blow up the building."

"I don't know. I should have made Red get rid of him after the dogs. I just don't know." She swallowed a lump in her throat.

"Hey. It's not your fault. And besides, we aren't going to figure it out now." His voice was soft, comforting.

They strolled a bit farther.

"I don't understand why the Russians let Lawrence go either," he said, almost as if his thoughts had escaped through his lips of their own accord.

She shrugged. "I don't think we'll ever know why. But I am thankful every moment of every day since that they did."

A few blocks later, they reached a coffee shop. Her feet and fingers had gone numb. It was freezing out.

She shivered. "Let's go in."

"*More* coffee?" he chided.

"They have tea."

Vail ordered, and Tess waited for him at a cozy table near the faux fireplace. Through the café window, the city seemed so alive. A clerk in the store across the street began hanging Christmas garland strung with lights.

"Decorating gets earlier and earlier every year." *Tsk, tsk* … and for a moment, she felt normal, hopeful. Then, she caught a glimpse of Red standing on the sidewalk, smoking, watching. Her heart sank a bit knowing that things hadn't been neatly tied up, not yet. "Almost," she said under her breath, not wanting to lose her good cheer.

Her phone buzzed and she pulled it out of her pocket, checked the screen, and answered.

"Hello, Lawrence."

"Can we talk later? I'm ah, not doing too well. Just heard the news about bodies. And, well." His tone sounded morose. She knew he'd already been blaming himself for mishandling the discovery, trusting Montague. All of it unfounded, in her opinion. He never meant any harm.

"Uh, sure. How about two o'clock? My place?"

"Thanks. See you then."

After hanging up, she muttered, "Time ... please let it get better with time."

But she knew secrets were like viruses, immune to time, relentlessly hiding and surviving deep inside, all the while boldly spreading from one soul to the next.

A shiver went down her spine. Oh how she hoped she was wrong."

~87~

Twenty minutes by car across the city, rock music blared at an unnatural volume in Roger's headphones as he worked diligently on erasing the group's digital footprints from the dealings with Montague and the Russians. Luckily, he hadn't found much to clean up—he'd been careful keeping house along the way.

Only one thing had him stumped. He shoved a few chips into his mouth. "What do I do with you?"

He fixated on the screen, the contents blaring at him, flashing the balance of a holding account in what he referred to as "digital limbo." The money hung between Lineage and the Russians—never actually making a hard landing. Did it belong to the Russians, Montague, Lineage, Ludwell? Considering the illegal nature of Montague's whole scheme, he couldn't be sure. So, he called Vail for legal advice.

"Let's meet in person to discuss this, please," was all Vail said.

And so they did about an hour later at Roger's place.

"Roger, how much is in the account?"

"That's the thing. It's, um, not a small amount." He paused, leaned in even though they were the only two in the room, "One hundred million clams."

"What?" Vail half-shouted, half-whispered.

Roger shrugged his shoulders.

"Well, we can't leave it there. And we can't steal it. What do we do?" Vail ran his fingers through his hair as he paced.

"It's gotta be your call. You know the legal mumbo jumbo. But we could get creative, maybe right some wrongs."

"I don't like the sound of this but lay it on me," Vail said, looking worse than when he'd arrived.

"For starters, I can maybe make an insurance payout to Gemma's mom, you know, from the explosion." His brows peaked as he cautiously awaited Vail's response.

"On second thought, I'm not sure I want to even know what you are thinking. This is going to have to wait." Vail patted Roger's shoulder. "You're a good guy, a little kooky, but all right." Then he left.

That was all it took. Roger felt a surge of energy. "This is my time to shine." He licked his lips confident that he'd read enough comic books in his life, seen enough superhero movies, hacked with the best in his college years. So he plopped on his headphones, chugged a can of soda, tossed a few chips in his mouth and got down to business. He'd make the money disappear in as stealth a manner as possible.

He knew that none of the group, including him, felt particularly entitled to the money, but in some alternate universe, he was sure that they'd all kind of earned a little piece of it and peace of mind. "Blood money." His lips mimed the words and it seemed to appease his conscience.

As he worked, Roger looked for every possible loophole. He found quite a few.

His fingers tapped and his thoughts slowly found order. He decided that in the end, each of them would have to decide how to justify it all, make peace with their souls, and most assuredly he knew that would prove very different for each of them. "We all have our own demons to face."

However, one thing remained the same for each and every one of them. Leaning back in his chair, he vowed, "None of it ever happened, and there won't be a trace when I'm through."

He worked relentlessly, deleting every loose end and telltale tidbit.

He even hacked into the Russian's data. Covering every angle, he prepared for the chance that the thumb drives of data still existed by creating decoy databases. If any data surfaced, the decoy data would show that the Russians manipulated the study for financial gain.

"No one will know what to believe." He chuckled.

In fact, only one thing stumped him. He couldn't erase human memories. He knew he'd meant it when he said his lips were sealed. He could only hope that the pact to never speak of any of it again would suffice for them all.

"I've done my part."

The only loose ends other than the Russians, in his opinion, were Lawrence and Cathy, who had sworn they never wanted to see any of the data again. They claimed that ship had not only sailed, but sunk deep beneath the waves, buried, never to resurface.

"It's too high a price," Lawrence had said. Cathy had agreed.

He thought of Tess's reaction to their words that day. He couldn't be sure, but she had looked haunted, burdened. Of course she was. It was her secret to bear. He shrugged.

"I believe them," Roger mumbled as his fingers hit the keyboard and his foot tapped with the drumming music.

~88~

A COUNTRYSIDE IN ENGLAND

Three months had passed, and a new year had begun, and things had mostly been quiet, except for Baby Face Roger's shenanigans. They'd all been a little miffed at the proverbial pots of gold he'd dropped into their laps, but what was done was done. They were all doing their best to move on—some better than others, apparently. Todd let out a breath. Mentally, he'd been checking off the days until today. He still didn't feel ready.

"I've got this." He straightened his shoulders and walked in alone. Today would be the first time since right after the explosion that everyone had gotten together. For him at least, tensions ran high. But he couldn't ignore that, for everyone else, so did a sense of hope.

The guests arrived, some alone, some in pairs, all the while fragrant wisteria cascaded from the indoor trellises blanketing the space with what resembled lavender raindrops frozen in midair.

Next to Todd, a lady in a lavender dress with a lacy shawl spoke to her husband in a British accent, "The house belongs to an American, a Mr. Ludwell. Isn't the conservatory grand? Truly a most magical backdrop."

Todd's heart sank as he took it all in. *This is happening. She's really going to marry him.*

Not feeling particularly at ease standing alone, fighting the sting of some pretty deep emotions, he retreated to an inconspicuous spot near the back of the large atrium, away from where the majority of guests had gathered. Positioned behind the cover of overflowing mounds of white hydrangeas, he sipped on a double pour of whiskey.

A familiar voice rang out from across the room. He caught a glimpse of the tuxedo-clad Vail making his way through the intimate crowd. Todd realized that with everything they'd been through, he didn't actually hate the man. No, Todd hated that he'd lost her to him. And being honest with himself, that blunder fell squarely on his own shoulders.

He polished off the rest of his drink, grabbed another as backup from the bar, and moseyed over to where the others mingled and chatted. As fate would have it, Vail looked his way. Todd didn't want to interact, but in his bones, he knew he had to be a gentleman about this. So he pivoted and strode straight toward the groom.

"Congratulations, man." He stuck out his free hand. Vail readily took it.

"Thanks. I appreciate it. Tess will be very touched that you're here." He paused then said, "I am too."

Todd quirked the corners of his mouth in a split-second smile. The two maintained eye contact for a second longer. The chips had fallen, and the best man had fairly won.

And so the heated competition between them evaporated in that moment.

Roger ambled up to them with a glass of white wine in one hand and a plate of shrimp in the other.

"How are you going to manage that?" Vail pointed, speaking with exaggerated doubt to the grinning man wearing a suit loudly accessorized by a Hawaiian print tie.

With jest, Roger delicately sipped the wine and then brought the small plate to his mouth, gobbling a shrimp right off the edge. After a few dramatic chews, he grinned and said, "Oh ye of little faith."

His antics served to bring a familiar chuckle from a few feet away.

"That's a pro move if I've ever seen one." Red's words floated ahead of his approach.

Before long, Lawrence and Cathy joined in the reunion of sorts. Out of the corner of his vision, Todd happened to catch a sparkle of light coming from Cathy's hand. He reached over, took her petite fingers in his, and in a playful tone not unlike that of a protective older brother, he asked, "What is this?" As he studied the beautiful diamond engagement ring she wore, the rest of the men looked to a shy Lawrence.

The men offered genuine congratulations and pats on the back to their blushing friend as Cathy giggled and beamed.

"Pardon my interruption," said a small lady wearing a fancy hat.

With that, Vail found himself being escorted to his place under the trellis with draping foliage at the front of the aisle.

"We should find our seats," Cathy said, and they did.

An elegant melody played. Everyone turned toward the start of the aisle. Todd gripped the back of a chair.

The sight of Tess in her wedding gown took his breath away.

The ceremony passed in a blur as he managed the breaking of his heart. And after it was all said and done, he searched for refuge from the ache in his soul. He stayed a bit longer, thinking he could mingle. He was wrong.

"It's time to go," he said as he quietly departed from the wedding and quite possibly her future.

The brisk English winter hit him like a brutal smack of freedom.

ACKNOWLEDGMENTS

A big *thank you* to my husband and children for the space and time in which to write, for their patience with too many takeout dinners, and for their relentless, yet amazing cheerleading. You are the reason for everything.

Also, I am grateful to my mom, dad, and brother for the unconditional praise—even before you've read the book. Every author should be so lucky.

From the bottom of my heart, I appreciate all of my family and friends whose fabulous conversations never fail to inspire and to remind me to believe in myself.

I humbly offer my eternal thanks to my editor and publisher Janet Fix, a true word whisperer. Thank you for sharing the art of storytelling and for showing me how to strive to create something worthy of reading, no matter how steep the hill may seem.

And last but in no way least, to all of my readers, thank you for giving my characters space in your imaginations—storytelling is life.

ABOUT THE AUTHOR

J. Leigh Jackson published her first suspense novel *Dark Wings* in 2020. Always an avid reader of mystery novels and literary classics, it proved only natural that in college she sought a bachelor's degree in English and a master's degree in communication. After several years of teaching others how to write, she decided the time had come for her to pick up the pen. Drawing inspiration from art, travel, and nature, Jackson savors snapshots of seemingly ordinary moments, trusting her imagination to fill in the pages with the rest.

Born in Virginia, she carries her Southern roots near to her heart, though she has traveled and lived in many towns across the United States. She currently resides in Southern California with her husband, their two children, and a mini Aussie with a not-so-mini personality.

If you want to learn more about what inspires J. Leigh Jackson, please visit her on Instagram @authorjleighjackson.

(Photo credit https://carollarsen.com/)

Made in the USA
Columbia, SC
21 December 2021